Praise for
Frank Peretti *and* Ted Dekker's novels

". . . Peretti is a bona fide publishing phenomenon."
—*BookPage* review of *The Visitation*

"Dekker delivers his signature exploration of good and evil in the context of a genuine thriller that could further enlarge his already sizable audience."
—*Publishers Weekly* review of *Showdown*

"In the world of Christian fiction, the hottest novels are those by Frank Peretti."
—*Newsweek* review of *Monster*

"Exciting, well written, and resonant with meaning, *Black, Red,* and now *White* have won over both critics and genre readers . . . An epic journey completed with grace."
—Editors, Barnes and Noble

". . . plenty of spine-chilling mayhem . . ."
—www.Amazon.com regarding *This Present Darkness*

"Ted Dekker is clearly one of the most gripping storytellers alive today. He creates plots that keep your heart pounding and palms sweating even after you've finished his books."
—Jeremy Reynalds, Syndicated Columnist

"Not only is Peretti the country's top selling Christian fiction author, but he has become, by any standard, one of current fiction's biggest stars."
—Chicago Tribune regarding *The Visitation*

Reading Group Guide Available at
www.westbowpress.com

HOUSE

OTHER BOOKS BY
FRANK PERETTI

Monster
The Visitation
The Oath
This Present Darkness
Piercing the Darkness

OTHER BOOKS BY
TED DEKKER

Showdown
The Martyr's Song
Obsessed
Black
Red
White
Three
Blink
When Heaven Weeps
Thunder of Heaven
Heaven's Wager

Coauthored with Bill Bright
Blessed Child
A Man Called Blessed

HOUSE

FRANK
PERETTI

TED
DEKKER

DOUBLEDAY LARGE PRINT HOME LIBRARY EDITION

WESTBOW
PRESS

A Division of Thomas Nelson Publishers
Since 1798

This Large Print Edition, prepared especially for Doubleday Large Print Home Library, contains the complete, unabridged text of the original Publisher's Edition.

Published in Nashville, Tennessee, by WestBow Press, a division of Thomas Nelson, Inc.

ISBN-10: 0-7394-6809-X
ISBN-13: 978-0-7394-6809-8

Printed in the United States of America

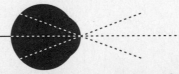

This Large Print Book carries the
Seal of Approval of N.A.V.H.

The light came into the darkness,
and the darkness did not understand it.

—~—

My heart holds all secrets; my heart tells no lies.

PROLOGUE

He stood motionless in the entryway, staring at his own shadow splayed before him like a stain upon the floor. He studied the patina of dust, sampled the stench of mold and rat urine, listened to a beam settling one more fraction of an inch toward the center of the earth.

This room bore so little evidence of the events that had led to the dawn. From this vantage point, it was just one more abandoned house. Interesting.

But the rest of the house told the truth.

Beneath his boots, the floorboards lay shoulder to shoulder like the buried dead, cupped with creeping moisture, edges buckling, obscured by gray dust and fallen flakes of white paint.

Across the foyer, at the base of a wall, the rose-printed wallpaper fluttered. Behind one of the roses, something scratched, pushed, gnawed, and clawed until a black, whiskered nose burst through. With a wad of shredded wallpaper in its jaws, the rat wriggled through the hole, then rested on its haunches and met his eyes. Neither found the other's presence alarming. The rat skittered along the baseboard and disappeared around a corner.

At the far end of the room, half a tattered curtain rustled and stirred before a broken window. A pitiful attempt at escape. Apart from the broken window, there was no sign that anyone had been here in years.

But when some curious passerby—or the police, should they be so fortunate as to stumble upon this place—wandered farther in, they'd find signs to the contrary in abundance. And those signs would lead them to the mysteries below.

Death lingered in the musty air, even up here. The walls were like shrouds, enfolding every space in exquisite darkness. It had been a perfect arena for a perfect game.

And already Barsidious White was looking forward to the next.

1

5:17 PM

"Jack, you're gonna kill us!"

His mind jerked out of a daydream and back to the lonely Alabama highway in front of the blue Mustang. The speedometer topped eighty. He cleared his mind and relaxed his right foot. "Sorry."

Stephanie went back to her singing, her voice clear if melancholy, her inflection classic country. *"My heart holds all secrets; my heart tells no lies . . ."*

That one again. She wrote it, so he never

criticized it, but those awful lyrics, especially today—

"Jack!"

The speedometer was inching toward eighty again.

"Sorry." He forced his foot to relax.

"What's the matter with you?"

"What's the matter—" *Easy now, Jack. No fuel on the fire.* "A little tense, okay?"

She smiled at him. "You should try singing."

His grip tightened on the steering wheel. "Yeah, that's your answer for everything, isn't it?"

"Excuse me?"

He sighed. He had to quit taking her bait. "Sorry." Always apologizing. He looked her way and forced a smile, hoping she would believe it.

She smiled back in a way that said she didn't.

She was beautiful, enough to capture the next man just as she'd captured him—blond, youthful, a real credit to those jeans—everything the guys in the lounges and bars could want in a country singer. No doubt those blue eyes could still sparkle, but not for him anymore. Right now they were hiding behind fashion-statement sunglasses, and she was craning to see out the back. "I think there's a cop behind us."

He checked the rearview mirror. The highway, which had narrowed to two lanes, curved lazily through late-spring forest and farmland, rose and fell over dips and rises, hiding and revealing, hiding and revealing a single car. It was gaining on them, near enough now for Jack to recognize the light bar atop the roof. He checked his speed. Sixty-five. That should be legal.

The police car kept coming.

"Better slow down."

"I'm doing the speed limit."

"You sure?"

"I can read the signs, Steph."

A few seconds more and the cruiser filled Jack's mirror as if he were towing it. He could see the cop's iron-jawed countenance behind the wheel, reflective black sunglasses obscuring the eyes.

Highway patrol.

Jack double-checked the speedometer, then slowed to sixty, hoping the cop wouldn't rear-end them.

The sedan inched closer.

He was going to rear-end them!

Jack smashed the gas pedal to the floor, and the Mustang shot ahead.

"What are you doing?" Stephanie cried.

"He was gonna hit us!"

The car fell back ten yards. Its red and blue lights flashed to life.

"Oh, great," she muttered, turning and flopping back against her seat. He could hear the blame in her voice. Always the blame. *But you're the one who walked away, Steph.*

The cruiser veered into the oncoming lane and pulled up beside them. The uniformed officer turned his face to Jack. Met his eyes. Or so Jack imagined. Black glasses. No expression. Jack forced his eyes back to the road.

The two cars were side by side, locked in formation at sixty miles an hour.

"What are you doing, Jack? Pull over."

He would if he could. Jack strained to see an opportunity. The forest, a thick tangle of maple, oak, and birch draped with kudzu, encroached like an advancing wall. "I can't. There's no shoulder. I can't just . . ."

He slowed. There had to be a turnout somewhere. Forty miles per hour. Thirty. The cruiser matched his speed.

Jack saw a break in the foliage, a sliver of

a shoulder, just enough room. He began to veer off.

The cruiser surged and left them behind, lights blazing in silence. Fifteen seconds later it was a dot on the road between the towering trees, and then it was gone.

"What was that about?" Jack asked, checking his mirrors, rubbernecking, and easing back onto the highway. He wiped a sweaty palm on his jeans.

"You were speeding." She fixed her gaze on the highway, fumbled with a map, avoided his eyes.

"He didn't pull us over. Why was he so close? You see how close he was?"

"That's Alabama, Jack. You don't do things their way, they let you know."

"Yeah, but you don't ram someone in the tail for speeding."

She slapped her lap, a release of frustration. "Jack, will you please just get us there, legally, in one piece? Please?"

He chose silence over a comeback and concentrated on the road. *Save it for the counseling session, Jack.* He wondered what she'd been saving up, what new claims she'd unload tonight.

She shook out her shoulders, put on a smile, and started humming.

You really think it will work, don't you, Jack? You really think you can save something you just don't have anymore?

If smiling and singing could bring back those days, he would laugh like a fool and even sing Stephanie's lyrics, but he was fresh out of illusions. All he had were the memories that stole his mind away even as his eyes remained on the road: her arms about his shoulders and the excitement in her eyes; the inner dawn he felt whenever she entered the room; the secrets they shared with a glance, a smile, a wink; all the things he thought life and love should be—

The accident changed everything.

He imagined himself sitting in the counselor's office, being honest about his feelings. *I'm feeling . . . like I've been had all my life. Life is pointless. If there is a God, he's the devil, and . . . What was that? Oh, you mean Stephanie? No, I've lost her too. She's gone. I mean, she's here, but she's checked out . . .*

He couldn't put away the idea that this whole trip was only a formality, another nail in the coffin of their marriage. Steph would sing her way to Montgomery and back and still get the divorce she wanted, go on her merry way.

"Jack, you're lost."

I sure am.

"Jack."

With a start, he returned his attention to driving. The Mustang purred along at sixty-five, gobbling up the highway. The forest was breaking up now, giving way to crude homesteads and stump-filled pastureland.

She was scanning the map, studying all those little red and black lines. Did she say *he* was lost? Right. *She* was holding the map, but *he* was lost.

He caught the sarcasm before it escaped. Hurtful words came so easily these days. "What do you mean?"

"Didn't you see that highway marker? It said 5."

He glanced at the mirror, then twisted to see the back of the receding sign. "5?"

She studied the map, tracing a route with her finger. "We're supposed to be on Highway 82."

He leaned and tried to read the map. The car swerved. He shot his eyes forward again, corrected the wheel.

"We're going to be late," she said.

Not necessarily. "You see Highway 5 on there? Where does it lead?"

She dragged her finger over the map and stopped about three inches out of Montgomery. "Not to Montgomery, unless you have a week to sightsee. How could you possibly have gotten off 82?"

Dare he defend himself? "I was a little distracted by a cop eating up my bumper."

She pulled her cell phone out of a cupholder and checked the display clock. "There's no way we'll make it."

Was that hope in her voice? He checked his watch. If they turned around now, maybe—

"I canceled a gig to go to this appointment with you." Stephanie hunched in the seat, arms folded.

There it is again. My fault. She started humming. *There it is again.*

Red and blue lights flashed up ahead.

"Oh, great," Stephanie said. "We *really* don't need this."

Jack slowed as they approached the patrol car parked just beyond a turnoff. Orange cones and a sign blocked the road ahead. "Repaving Operation. Highway Closed to

Through Traffic," Jack read. "Well, we have to turn around anyway." Jack pulled onto the gravel shoulder but had a second thought. "Let's ask. Maybe there's a faster way."

Jack eased the blue Mustang forward, up to the turnoff, and stopped a few feet behind the patrol car. The cruiser's door swung open and an officer—the officer—stepped out, aviator sunglasses still hiding his eyes.

2

The patrolman rolled his head to crack his neck, then kept his face pointed at them as he donned a broad-brimmed smoky-colored hat. He wore a short-sleeved gray shirt, and pants with a black stripe running down the outside of the legs. A breast badge flashed in the late-afternoon sun. His large leather holster hung on his right hip, his baton on his left.

The man touched his hat as if by habit and walked toward them, confident. Cocky. The man's pants looked a tad tight.

"Good night," Stephanie said.

Jack rolled the window down. A hot breeze blew into the Mustang, chased by the sound of crickets. The officer's black leather boots were silent on the pavement.

The patrolman stopped by their window, hand on the butt of his gun. He leaned over and gave them a close-up view of his black lenses. Morton Lawdale, the badge said.

"You mind showing me your license and registration?"

"We—"

"License and registration. Now."

Jack leaned over to the glove box, dug out the papers, and handed them through the window.

The cop took them with a gloved hand and straightened, scanning them at his leisure. "You mind stepping out of the car?"

Jack wasn't sure what to make of the request. "Why?"

"Why? Because I want to show you something, how's that for why?"

"Did I do something wrong?"

"Are all you Alabama boys so dense? An officer tells you to step from your vehicle, you argue as if you're the king of the hill. I have something you need to see. Get your butt out of the car."

Jack exchanged a glance with Stephanie, opened the door, and swung his legs out.

"There, was that so hard?"

"We took a wrong turn," Jack said, looking up. He was at least a head shorter than the patrolman. "We were headed to Montgomery on 82."

Lawdale pulled out his billy club and waved Jack to the back. "Come 'ere."

A chill slipped down Jack's back. How'd he end up here, out in the middle of nowhere with this character, a trigger-happy, blow-'em-away-and-ask-questions-later kind?

He hesitated.

"You gonna make me say everything twice?" The cop slapped his palm with the stick.

"No." Jack walked toward the trunk.

He stopped by the fender, facing the cop who stood with feet spread, staring directly at him. As far as Jack could tell.

Lawdale swung his black stick down to indicate the left rear brake light. "Were you aware of the fact that your brake light is out?"

Jack breathed. "It is? No."

"It is. I nearly crawled up your backside. I oughta know."

"Oh."

"Oh," the patrolman mimicked. Sweat stained the man's shirt around his collar and under his arms. "And I'd suggest you start driving your car the way it was designed to be driven."

The passenger door opened and Stephanie stepped out, smiling like a ray of sunshine. "Is everything okay?"

"My taillight's out," Jack said.

Stephanie tilted her head playfully. "We'll get it fixed in Montgomery. Right, Jack?"

"Of course. As soon as we get there."

The patrolman tipped his hat at Steph and evaluated her low-rise jeans and silky blue tank top. "And who might you be?"

"Stephanie Singleton."

The man's eyes dropped to her ringless hand. Her taking that off last month had cut Jack more than anything else she'd done. "Siblings? Cousins?"

"Husband and wife," Jack said.

The cop looked at Stephanie. "You let this maniac drive?"

"Maniac?" Jack asked.

The cop dipped his head, pulled down his

shades, and stared at Jack over the silver frames.

Blue eyes.

"Are you trying to be smart, boy? No, you're not, are you? You're just a bit thick."

It occurred to Jack how much rudeness one must stand and take when the other person is wearing a uniform.

The patrolman removed his sunglasses and gave Jack a stony blue glare. "Not only *like* a maniac, but a maniac who doesn't *know* he's driving like a maniac, which would make you an idiot. But I'm going to pretend I'm wrong. I'm going to pretend you're not an idiot and can understand what a maniac does. How would that suit you?"

Lawdale expected an answer. Jack could think of several but limited himself to "Fine."

"Fine. Then I'll tell you what a maniac does around here." The cop tapped Jack on the head with a pointed finger, hard enough to hurt. "A maniac doesn't watch his speed, and he doesn't use his mirrors. Use your mirrors, Jack. I was following you for five minutes before you saw I was on your tail. A truck could squash you flat and you'd be dead . . ."

The cop snatched his revolver from its

holster, fanned the hammer, and fired into the nearby field like a gunslinger. *Blam!* Both Jack and Stephanie jerked.

". . . just like that." Lawdale blew the smoke from the end of the barrel and slipped the gun into its holster with a precise little spin. "Making a point, my friend. These are dangerous roads out here." He jabbed Jack in the temple again. "Watch your speed and use your mirrors."

All things considered, Jack thought it best to answer succinctly. "I will."

"Good." The patrolman returned Jack's license and registration, then pointed down the road. "Now we got a little detour here. Next three miles of highway is all torn up. Where'd you say you were headed?"

Jack's heart sank as he answered, "Montgomery."

"Montgomery." The cop almost smiled, obviously amused. "Can't you read a map?"

"We missed a turn."

The officer snorted, his way of snickering, Jack supposed, then pointed. "I'd take the detour. It's maybe one hour faster than backtracking to 82—if you know where to go. It's not marked too well, and you don't want to get caught out in the dark."

"Could you show us?" Jack asked.

The man walked back. "You do have a map, don't you?"

Stephanie held out their map, which he unfolded on the trunk of the Mustang and studied briefly. "Old map." He refolded it with a grunt. "Okay. You follow me clearly, you hear? You think *I'm* a bit pickled? Trust me, couple city folk like you don't want to be caught waltzing through the backwoods asking directions from the inbreds. You never know who you'll run into. Now you start here—"

"Inbreds?" Stephanie's smile contradicted her tone.

The cop dismissed the word with a wave. "Backwoods rednecks. Idiots like Jack was trying to be a moment ago. No understanding of any law but their own. Evil folk. Type who haven't discovered the toothbrush, much less the law."

He pointed down the turnoff. "Now you go south on this road until it comes to a *T*. Go left, that'll take you past the flats, back into the forest a ways. You'll be on a dirt road for a good forty miles but don't worry, it'll dump you out on 82. Should take about an hour."

Jack looked at the gravel road headed

south. It disappeared into tree-covered hills topped with heavy clouds. "You sure?"

"Do I look unsure?"

Not again. Jack grinned. "No sir."

Lawdale acknowledged with a slight nod. "Now we're beginning to understand. That's the road I take home every morning. If you break down, just stay on the shoulder. One of us will find you."

"You say that like it's happened before," Jack said.

"It has."

Stephanie followed their eyes, her smile faltering. "Jack, maybe we should just get on back home."

"No need for that," Lawdale said. "If you go now, while there's plenty of light, you'll get through without missing another beat. You all be careful now."

The officer touched the rim of his smoky hat and walked back to his cruiser.

Jack climbed behind the Mustang's wheel and slammed his door shut. "You ever wonder what kind of man patrols the back-woods?"

Stephanie dropped in beside him. "Not really."

"Now you know."

"I'm sure he's pulled plenty of your kind from the ditch. I say we turn around."

Jack checked his watch. Quarter till six. They could still make it. He eased the car forward.

Stephanie pressed it. "The appointment can't possibly be worth this much trouble."

Jack turned onto the gravel detour.

"Jack."

He picked up as much speed as he dared. "We've come this far, right? I'd like to try to get there."

3

7:46 PM

"Slow down, Jack."

Jack wasn't going that fast, not a shade over forty . . . well, sometimes fifty. The washboard road and potholes made it seem a lot faster. He remembered to use his mirrors but never saw more than a billowing trail of dust behind them. "He said it would take us an hour, but we're going on two." He ventured a sideways glance. "How far did he say it was to 82?"

"I think he said forty miles after the T."

Jack checked the odometer as he had

several times already. "We've gone sixty at least. Are there any towns around here, any landmarks?"

She sat with her arms crossed, looking out the window. The crazy winding road had taken them back into dense forest. With the exception of a tiny roadside sign a half mile back, they hadn't seen so much as a mailbox. "Wayside Inn," the sign read. "Rest for the Weary Soul, 3 Miles." The sign was painted in cheery yellows, pinks, and blues, with a pink arrow pointing in the same direction they'd been headed for so long.

"This road isn't on the map, Jack. We only know what he told us."

He gripped the wheel and leaned into his driving. He was eating crow—and it was going down sideways. "Would you call and tell them we're running late?"

Steph picked up her phone. "No coverage out here. You may as well relax. We've missed the appointment."

He'd already run some time and mileage figures in his head and knew she was right. Figured.

"Well, apparently there's an inn up here somewhere," Jack said. "Maybe we can at least get off the road for the night." He met her eyes and looked for longing there, the meaningful glances she used to give him before their trouble. Nothing. He turned forward and tried to find words—

What was that? His foot went for the brake—

Bam! Something metallic thudded under the tires and screeched against the floorboards. The car lurched, shuddered, and wobbled, sliding on loose gravel.

Stephanie screamed as Jack struggled with the wheel. The car slid broadside, tires roaring over the rocks and raking the powdery surface into a wall of dust. Sounded like they were riding on rims. The wheel edges dug into the surface, and the car tipped to the passenger side. It teetered, then came down on all four wheels with a crunch of metal and shattering glass, the dust swarming over it.

Silence. Stillness. They were alive.

"You all right?" Jack asked.

Stephanie's voice trembled. "What . . . what happened?"

The left side of his head throbbed. Jack touched his hair and brought his hand away bloody. He must have hit the door.

"There was . . . something in the road."

He unbuckled his seat belt and let it slip into its retractor as he opened his door. Dust drifted in, settling on his clothes and coating his nostrils. He stepped out, unsteady on his feet, and noticed the car was lower to the ground.

All four tires were flat. The skid had nearly torn the shredded rubber from the wheels.

He looked back, squinting through the haze of dust and dusk, and saw a vicious contraption lying in the gravel like roadkill, flopped and twisted from the impact. It was a thick rubber mat, long enough to span the road and bristling with steel spikes.

His guts wrenched. He looked up and down the road, probed the thick forest and creeping kudzu on either side with his eyes. No sounds. No movement. "Steph . . ."

She emerged from the car and gasped at the damage. He pointed up the road at the monstrosity lying in the dust. "It was a trap, or a trick, or . . . I don't know."

She scanned the thick woods on either side of the road. "What do we do?"

His eyes were on the trees, both sides, back and forth. It seemed someone would have made a move by now, would have pounced, ambushed, fired a weapon, *something*.

"Well, whoever did this, they're bound to come back and see what they caught. We'd better get out of here."

"What about the car?"

"It's not going anywhere. Grab your purse. We'll head for the inn."

She ducked inside the car and pulled out the handbag, then plunked her cell phone in it, her eyes darting everywhere, afraid. Jack could see she was weighing the same possibilities: Inbreds. Weird, backwoods people. No regard for the law. Lawdale had warned them about being out here after dark.

"Come on." Jack reached for her hand across the hood of the car, urging her around.

She came to him. He clamped his hand on hers. They started out together, hurrying, looking back at their stricken car for as long as it was in sight.

They settled into a walk-run for nearly two miles. The sunlight continued to fade. They rounded a bend and saw a small sign at the top of a long gravel drive.

WAYSIDE INN

Jack let go of Stephanie's hand and turned up the narrow road. "All right. We'll use their telephone."

The house was nothing Stephanie expected, not out here in the remote Alabama backwoods. When she and Jack reached the gated stone wall and looked up the flagstone walk, her fear of the gathering darkness and threatening weather dropped away; her sore feet and the grit in her sandals became bearable; even their wrecked car and meaningless road trip were not the end of the world. She felt so relieved that tears blurred her eyes.

They could have been looking back in time. Somehow, while vast plantations gave way to open fields and shady lanes decayed into potholed strips of red dust and gravel, this grand old lady stubbornly remained in a more genteel era. She was not quite a mansion, but her imposing white walls, dormer windows, and tall, glowing lights invited thoughts of hoopskirted southern belles and drawling, frock-coated gentlemen.

"Oh," was all she could say as relief gave way to joy, and joy gave way to amazement.

"What's a nice house like that doing in a place like this?" Jack wondered aloud.

He opened the gate and started up the walk, looked back, and then waited, which surprised her. She hurried to join him and they walked together, but *not* hand in hand, entering another world.

Miniature lamps cast a warm glow on the flagstones every few yards. The hedges on either side of the walkway were neat and precisely cornered; even in the dim light, the flower beds were hilarious with color. Beyond the beds, ancient oaks stood at ease on a parade ground of manicured green.

"Wish I had my suitcase," she said. "I want to stay here."

"We'll telephone for some help, then maybe go fetch our stuff," he replied. "Officer Lawdale might be around somewhere."

She winced at that. He was probably joking, but it wasn't funny.

They crossed the veranda and found a note on the door: *Welcome, weary traveler. Sign in at the front desk.*

Jack put his hand on the knob as she spotted her reflection in the door's ornate stained glass. That flushed, dust-streaked face and windblown hair would never do in a place like this. "Wait." She groped in her purse for a brush.

He opened the door, swinging her mirror away. "Steph, we have enough trouble right now."

She followed her moving reflection, pulling the brush through her hair. He never saw things her way. Her own disgusted face looked back at her. "I'm so sweaty."

Jack went inside without her, and it stung. *Sure, just keep walking, buddy.*

She stowed her brush, worked up a sweet smile, and turned into the foyer, closing the door behind her.

Now she felt all the more dusty, dirty, wrinkled, and out of place. The room was open to a high ceiling, and a fancy chandelier hovered over their heads. The spotless hardwood floor reflected a wide, carpeted staircase. Flower-filled vases perched on tables, in wall niches, and small stands in corners. The living room to their left boasted a yawning fireplace with a carved mantel. She should be dressed for a party, but here she was looking like—

"You don't look like *you* own this place," a man's voice boomed from above.

A man and a woman came down the stairs. He was tall and well built, in crisp jeans and a celery-green sport shirt—the

neck was open to show off a color-coordinated T-shirt. She was tall, brunette—not
beautiful by Stephanie's estimation, but chic
in her stylish white slacks and sleeveless
red tunic. Silk, probably. Silver drop-shaped
earrings. She descended with a professional
grace she must have learned somewhere,
and one quick, sizing-up glance from those
green eyes made Stephanie's face flush.

"We need a phone," Stephanie said.

If Jack was conscious of his own dusty
condition, he didn't show it. The novelist in
him never put much stock in physical appearances, to her aggravation. Right now
he was dressed as always, casual if not
sloppy in baggy chinos and an untucked
denim button-down, open over a white
T-shirt. His reddish hair could use a comb,
but other than that, he was a fine-looking
man—yes, even finer than Mr. GQ now taking the stairs like a catalog model. Unfortunately, she needed more than *fine* these
days. Her career was about to take off, but
Jack was so stuck in the past that he would
hold her back, no doubt.

"Run into trouble?" the man asked.

Jack answered, "We had some car trouble
a couple miles down the road."

The man's eyes narrowed, and he shared a knowing look with the woman. "So did we."

Now he had Stephanie's wide-eyed, unwavering attention. "Our tires were slashed."

The man's right eyebrow arched. "So were ours."

The revelation alarmed her. "You too? How . . . how's that possible?"

"In these backwoods? Anything is possible," the man said with a coy smile.

"But that can't be a coincidence. Both cars?"

"Settle down, honey. Just some hillbillies laughing their guts out in a tree about now. It'll be just fine. Where you come from?"

"We were coming from the north, from Tuscaloosa," Jack said.

"We were coming from the south, from Montgomery."

"Did you turn off 82?"

"That's right."

"We had to walk for miles," Stephanie reminded him out loud.

"So did we," said the woman, not looking one bit like it.

The man jutted out his hand. "Randy Messarue."

Jack gripped his hand. "Jack Singleton. This is Stephanie, my, uh . . ." He deferred to her.

"I'm his loving wife," she said.

The woman was taller than Stephanie, which helped her look down when she said, "Charmed." She turned away and offered her hand to Jack. Stephanie bristled. "I'm Leslie Taylor. Randy and I are longtime associates."

"Looks like you hit your head," Randy said. "You okay otherwise?"

Jack touched his head again. The blood was mostly dry now. "Tired, but okay. Have you called the police?"

Randy sneered. "Got a cell phone with service?"

Stephanie pulled her cell phone from her purse. She checked once more, but, "No, no service. Isn't there a land line here?"

"Good luck finding it."

Stephanie's subdued fear raised its head.

"We've checked the main floor and some of the rooms upstairs. If they have one, it's locked away."

"We can ask the owners when they get here," said Leslie.

"Yeah, when they get here," said Randy.

"Don't know what kind of a business they think they're running, but you don't just leave a note on the door and leave the customers to fend for themselves."

Leslie smiled, cocked her head. "Randy runs a chain of hotels."

Jack's eyebrows went up. "Wow. That's something."

"And a chain of restaurants, but that's beside the point," said Randy.

Stephanie offered, "Jack's a writer. He's got several novels published."

"Oh," said Randy. "Bring any luggage with you?"

"No," Stephanie answered quickly, giving Jack an appropriate eye stab. *My husband doesn't consider such details.*

But he wasn't looking at her. "It's still back in the car. We were pretty nervous. You know, we figured . . ."

"We thought it was a robbery," Stephanie explained, feeling silly about it now. She forced a giggle. "I left my suitcase, and he left his, and we had a garment bag . . ."

Randy shook his head and sniffed. "It's a robbery *now*."

"I'd sure love to change out of these dirty clothes."

"Don't worry," Jack said. "We'll figure something out." He pointed at a small table in the corner of the foyer with an open registry and a pen on a chain. "I'll get us signed in."

"And you may as well pick out a room," said Randy. "The keys are in that cabinet."

"Randy, we don't own the place," said Leslie.

Randy ignored her. "I'd recommend room 4, across the hall from us. It has a great view of the gardens in back." Leslie shot him a reproving glare.

Stephanie caught Jack's eye and held up two fingers. As at home, she'd take her own room here, thank you very much. Jack sighed and went to the desk.

Leslie turned her nose down toward Stephanie. "And what do you do?"

"I'm a singer," Stephanie replied. She hummed a bar of her favorite song, an upbeat ditty she'd written called "Always All Right."

"Oh. Creative types."

Jack returned, discretely bringing two keys. He slipped Stephanie the key to room 4, and she concealed it in her purse. He pocketed another key. Leslie raised an eye-

brow in Stephanie's direction but then pretended not to notice. The witch.

"Looks like we're the only ones signed in
for tonight," Jack said.

"I don't think they're expecting anyone,"
said Randy.

"Are you sure?" said Leslie. "The house
looks ready for visitors. The lights are all on,
the sign was on the front door . . ."

"So where are the owners?"

Stephanie turned on one heel to take in
the first level. "The dinner table's set for
four."

They all looked through an archway into
the dining room opposite the living room.

The room was not lavish, but lovely. A
fringed brocade cloth and runner covered
the table; the four place settings also included bread plates, salad forks, and
dessert spoons. A pitcher of iced tea stood
at the near end of the table, beaded with
condensation.

Randy went to the table and picked up the
pitcher of iced tea. "Anybody thirsty?"

Leslie stepped up. "Randy, that isn't for
us." He shot her a look, then filled a glass
from one of the place settings. "Randy!" He
sipped from the glass, keeping his eyes on

her. Stephanie raised an eyebrow in Leslie's direction and then pretended not to notice. So there. Apparently these two had issues of their own.

"So . . . they're expecting four people," said Stephanie.

"Right about now," said Randy.

"Well, they aren't expecting us," said Jack.

"Nope," said Randy, enjoying the tea. "But we're going to be their guests tonight, whether they—" The lights flickered. "Oh, now what?"

The house went black.

Stephanie involuntarily reached out for Jack. "Oh, my Lord."

"Now it's getting fun," she heard Randy say.

———

Just like this whole trip, one disaster after another, Jack thought. He looked out the window, now a black rectangle framing a world of bottomless shadows and indistinct shapes. "The yard lights are out too."

"Hold still till we get used to the dark," Leslie said.

"Anybody got a lighter?" Randy asked.

"Stephanie," Jack said. He knew she kept a lighter on hand to offer her smoking friends. He always thought it was weird, since she swore cigarettes were death to the vocal cords, but apparently it was her way of schmoozing. He heard her fumble through her purse, then felt her press the cheap plastic gadget into his hand. He flicked it. Light from the small yellow flame dimly lit the room.

"There you go," said Randy. "At least *she's* prepared. Come on." He headed into the foyer then crossed into the living room. Jack went with him, lighting their way. Randy went to the fireplace and took a decorative oil lamp from the mantel.

"Randy, that's not ours," Leslie called.

Randy took a wooden match from a box on the hearth. The match flared with one scratch on the bricks, and the lamp lit easily. "Now. We can take a look around for candles, matches, a flashlight, anything to take care of this situation—since the owners aren't here to take care of things themselves."

Jack heard a sound he couldn't place.

Something resonant. A high note. "Wait a minute!" said Jack, pocketing the lighter.

"What?"

"Shh."

They all listened. Jack thought—

"Cool," said Randy, returning to the foyer, taking the oil lamp with him. "Just like a haunted house, right? Nobody here, then the lights go out, then . . . *OOOOOO*." He wiggled the fingers of his free hand as the oil lamp cast eerie shadows on his face. "Creaks, and groans, and footsteps in the dark."

Leslie wagged her head in good humor.

"Don't do that," said Stephanie, setting her purse down behind the sofa.

There it was again. "I did hear something," Jack said.

From somewhere in the dark expanse of the old house, timbers groaned under their load and then were silent.

"It's just house noise—," Randy started to say, but Leslie shushed him.

Now, somewhere, floorboards creaked.

"Somebody's here," Stephanie whispered.

Jack put up his hand for silence, cocked his head to hear, listened.

A voice. A song. A child.

He met the eyes of the others, but saw no awareness there. "You hear that?" Randy started to smirk as if Jack was playing around. "I'm not kidding. I hear somebody singing. Sounds like a little girl."

They all listened again, and this time awareness, if not a shade of fear, crossed their faces one by one. They heard it too.

"So the owners have a daughter," Randy said.

Leslie gave a little shrug.

Stephanie only looked at Jack, clearly unnerved.

Two more seconds, and then Randy broke the silence with a commanding voice. "Okay, that's enough Halloween. The kitchen's this way. Let's light this place up."

He led, holding the lamp high. They followed. As a tight band of four, they moved into the dining room, then traveled through an archway, down a short hall, and into a large, well-equipped kitchen.

Randy pointed. "Let's check these cupboards, that pantry over there. Jack, look out on that porch. We're looking for a flashlight, a breaker panel or a fuse box, candles, anything." Then he shouted so loudly Jack flinched. "Hello! Anybody here? You've got company!"

Leslie started going through the cupboards, top and bottom, opening, closing, opening, closing.

Jack opened the back door and used his lighter to probe around the enclosed porch. He found an old icebox and some canned goods on shelves, but nothing they needed at the moment.

— —

Stephanie was angry with herself for trembling and hoped the others didn't notice. She'd learned to be brave and independent over the past year—she'd had to. But it was so dark in here; they'd already been through a car wreck and an almost, maybe robbery; and now they were wandering through a big, empty house—

She put her hand to her forehead and tried to get a grip. *Be brave, girl. It's only as bad as you make it. Keep smiling. That's how we get through, remember?*

She tried humming a tune, couldn't think of one, hummed aimlessly anyway.

"How about that pantry?" Randy asked.

Boy, he's bossy. Almost as bossy as Jack.

She found the handle to the closet, but it was hard to see anything inside. Randy had the only light and wouldn't set it down. First she could see into the pantry; then she couldn't. It was deep . . . it was dark . . . her fingers found shelves along the walls . . . it was dark . . . that may have been a mop or something . . . it was dark—

The lights came on. A single bulb dangling on a wire from the center of the ceiling. Stephanie grunted, shielded her eyes. For a second she couldn't see.

"What you doin' in my pantry?"

4

Jack heard Stephanie's scream and was at the pantry door in an instant—so were Randy and Leslie. The three collided, then stood staring.

"Screaming like that we save for the outdoors," said a broad-faced woman standing in the pantry, covering her ears. When the screaming stopped, she dropped her hands and took a large jar of applesauce from the shelf.

"I'm sorry," Stephanie gasped. "You startled me."

"Well, it works both ways. I almost thought you were *him*."

Stephanie looked at the others. "Who?"

The woman frowned and handed her the jar. "Here. Pour that in a serving bowl and put a spoon in it." Then she walked into the kitchen, bumping through everyone, went straight to the oven, and peeked inside. For the first time, Jack caught the aroma of a roast. He realized how hungry he was. "Meat's almost ready. Better get the food on the table."

She was big-boned and strong-backed, wearing a housedress with a cheerful flowered pattern. Her graying hair was gathered into a comb behind her head. She turned from the oven. "Well? Am I talking to myself or are you all standing there?"

Jack was first to come out of the stupor. "Uh, we're, uh, your guests for the night, I think. I'm Jack—" He held out his hand.

"Looking for a bowl?" the woman asked Stephanie. Jack lowered his arm.

Stephanie wasn't but said, "Sure."

Randy stepped forward. "Ma'am, are you the owner of this place?"

"I am. And you're the fellow who helped

himself to room 3." She looked past him at Leslie. "Or was that you?"

Leslie put on a disarming smile. "It's both of us. I hope you don't mind—"

"Are you paying for it?"

"Of course."

"Then enjoy it but keep the noise down." She opened a cupboard and brought down a serving bowl, handing it to Stephanie. "Here, sweetie."

Randy put himself between the middle-aged woman and Stephanie. "We had no idea you were here. It caught us off guard."

She looked at him then at the lamp in his hand. "The lights are back on."

Randy extinguished the oil lamp and set it on a butcher-block island. "Do you have power failures like this very often?"

She shuffled to the other side of the kitchen. "Only when we have guests." Betty turned to Leslie, "Looking for something to do? Check those peas on the stove and put 'em in a dish." She pulled open a drawer and extracted a dish for that purpose. Leslie set to work. Betty looked at Jack, "Now, what's your problem?"

"Well, actually, we had some . . . car trouble."

"Spikes in the road," said Randy.

"Do you have a phone anywhere—"

The woman came in close, inches from Jack's nose. "Car trouble? That's why you got two rooms? *Car* trouble?" The woman turned to Stephanie. "Is he mad at you or something?"

"Um . . ."

"Can he carry chairs?" The lady turned back to Jack. "Can you carry chairs?"

He nodded. He would have to take mental notes. Use this character in a story sometime.

"Then we're gonna need three more."

"Oh," said Leslie, now apologetic. "You *are* expecting someone else."

"Nope." She pulled plates and saucers from the cupboard and asked Randy, "Know how to set a table?"

"Of course I do. And by the way, my name is Randy Messarue. And this is Les—"

She pushed the plates into his stomach. "Three more place settings."

He nodded in Leslie's direction. "That's Leslie. And you are?"

"Betty. Silverware's in that drawer."

Jack's bewilderment gave way to irritation. "We could really use a phone."

"Don't have none."

"So what do you do when the power goes out?" Randy asked.

"Wait for the guests to leave." Betty waved Jack toward the hallway with the backs of her fingers. "Chairs! I've got three more in the closet."

He went into the hallway between the kitchen and dining room with no idea where the closet was. There were two doors on his right. He tried the first one—

"Not that one!" Jack jerked his hand away from the knob as if it had burned him. "That's the basement! Nobody goes in the basement! Nobody!"

Oh, for crying out loud. He took a calming breath. "Then why don't you tell me where the closet is?"

She wagged her head and rolled her eyes as if she were dealing with an idiot. "The other door. Try the other door." She turned back into the kitchen, waving him off like unwanted trouble.

Jack opened the next door and found a closet. Inside, three folding chairs leaned against one another, but Jack took his time pulling them out. He needed to breathe a moment, just separate himself from that woman long enough to recover his balance. In one short evening he'd gone from disappointment to anger to fear to exhaustion to frustration, and now, to top it all off, his stomach was growling and the cook was crazy. He heard Stephanie begin to hum in the kitchen.

He wagged his head. Why should he be surprised?

Come on, Jack. After all, it was your decision to turn down that dirt road. You do have to take responsibility for your part . . .

He carried the chairs into the dining room and squeezed them in around the small table as Randy laid out the extra place settings.

"Silverware doesn't match," Randy muttered.

Jack couldn't manage pretending to care.

They headed back to the kitchen, passing Leslie on her way out.

꘎

Leslie took the bowl of peas into the dining room, having to nudge a few plates and glasses aside to make room for it. With three more chairs and place settings, a floral centerpiece, a bowl of applesauce, a pickle dish, a pitcher of iced tea, a bowl of potatoes, condiments, and a soon-to-arrive platter of roast beef, the dining table quickly shifted from close and intimate to packed and crowded. And now the glasses didn't match.

"Coming up behind you." It was Randy with a basket of rolls. She turned.

"We're running out of room."

"We're eating, and we've got a place to spend the night. Don't complain."

She kept her voice down. "Doesn't she strike you as odd?"

"You're the shrink and you're asking me?" He handed her the basket then lowered his own voice. "If I had her people skills, I'd probably have to put spikes on the road to bring in business."

He left her to think about it.

Leslie turned back to the table—

She gasped, fumbled the basket. The rolls tumbled onto the table, dancing on the plates, bouncing off the glasses. One landed in a water glass with a splash.

A man sat there, watching her with obvious fascination, a napkin tucked down the front of his brown bib overalls.

She had never felt so embarrassed—in recent times, at least. "I am so sorry. I didn't see you come in."

"You're pretty," he said, not taking his eyes off her. His boldness gave her pause. She guessed him somewhere in his twenties, a gorilla of a man with biceps the size of his neck and short-cropped blond hair. He wore a soiled T-shirt under the overalls. His stubbled face was dirty and shiny with sweat, and she could smell him.

"Um, my name is Leslie."

He eyed her as if she were naked.

"And you are?" she prodded.

"Better clean up your mess before Mama finds out."

Leslie hastened to gather up the fallen rolls, plucking one from the center of the table, another from a dinner plate. She leaned to grab another from the plate next to his.

He looked down her blouse without the slightest shame.

She straightened, incredulous. He smiled as if she'd done him a favor.

Professional detachment. Emotional distance from the subject. Don't let his issues become yours.

She knew she was glowering, but he'd

caught her off guard and vulnerable, two things she'd sworn never to be again. She swallowed, willing herself to be professional, clinical. She softened her expression. "Now," she said in a nurse's bedside tone, "we don't do that."

He wouldn't take his eyes off her. They were childish eyes, vacant and unblinking. What was she dealing with? Mild retardation, apparently. Social ineptitude for certain.

His eyes finally went elsewhere—to her hand, still holding a roll. He pointed.

She rotated her hand and saw a small trickle of blood near the knuckle. "Now, how did I do that?" It must have happened when he startled her. She put the roll with the others, then pulled a small hanky from her pocket to cover the wound. She checked the table and basket for any sharp points or edges. Nothing obvious here.

He reached into a glass, pulled out the sodden roll, and held it out to her, heavy and dripping.

She took it from him and their fingers touched.

Leslie tasted bile.

"All right," Betty hollered from the kitchen, "everybody wash up."

Of course, thought Randy. *Perfect. Everybody handle the food and dishes and then wash up.* He gave Jack and Stephanie a once-over. All that road dust.

The others went up to their rooms to wash. Randy spotted a bathroom opposite the closet in the hallway and thought that more efficient.

The bathroom was clean, with white fixtures, pink towels, a pink bath mat, and a soap dish with red soaps in the shape of roses. The faucet provided hot water in an instant.

Randy soaped up. *Such a contrast. How can anyone so inept at hospitality maintain such a lovely facility? And where are the personnel, or do they always put their guests to work?* Right now he'd give the service in this place a one-star rating.

He felt some tension ease out of his spine as the water massaged his hands. He put in the stopper, then cupped his hands and brought a splash to his face. He allowed the sensation to block out the Wayside Inn for a moment.

"You done yet?" The rumbling voice was followed by the smell of sweat and machine oil, the touch of another body crowding him. Randy opened his eyes.

He saw a reflection in the mirror—a big man looming over him looking none too happy.

Randy reached for the towel by the sink. "Well, good evening to you too. I'm washing up for dinner."

The man snatched the towel away and looked about to slap him with it. "Don't you have a bathroom of your own?" The man was built like a bull without an ounce of fat, big brown eyes, and a long filthy face with a hawk nose. Bald head with three long scars above his left ear.

From somewhere long ago, a deep terror flashed through Randy's body. He slapped it down with a cold, controlled temper he'd honed through years of such encounters. He faced the man, his muscles steeling and ready for whatever might come. "Right now it's this one." He held out his hand. "Towel."

Clearly, the man was not expecting that kind of answer. He held onto the towel, then stuck a dirty finger in Randy's face, his eyes red and bulging. "Guess you don't know whose house you're in."

"They're going to hear about you, bud. Count on it."

Randy snatched the towel back and dried his face, careful never to cover his eyes. Then, when he was good and ready, he tossed the towel back. "Try making yourself presentable. You have guests."

He walked out, keeping an eye on the brute. The big man bent over the sink and splashed in the water Randy had left in the sink. "You like the water, don't you?" He gave Randy a sly smile, a leering gaze.

The deep terror returned. Randy felt himself tip and reached out to touch the wall.

He hurried past the dining room into the foyer, walked a few slow circles to calm himself, check the rage, force a smile. He went back to the dining room still trying to relax his clenched fists.

5

Betty was just a little frazzled as she herded everyone into the dining room. "Hey! You like your food cold? Come on, come on!"

"If you don't get it, the hogs will." Stephanie giggled.

Betty failed to see the humor in that.

Jack took the chair to Betty's left, which put him next to the big guy in the brown overalls. The fellow didn't seem too talkative. From his gawky expression, Jack surmised he may have had too much lead in his water. Stephanie took the chair to Betty's right.

Randy came in from the foyer, his smile saying one thing, his body saying another. He paused for an awkward moment, sizing up where Jack and Stephanie were seated; then he selected the chair next to Stephanie. "May I?"

"You may," she said with a bright smile.

He sat next to her, and Leslie sat next to him.

That left one empty chair.

"Stoo-wart!" Betty bellowed. "You stuck on that commode or did you fall in?"

Jack caught the others exchanging careful little looks, sitting quietly, waiting, acting like polite adults.

Now that they were sitting, maybe he could finally get some answers. He turned to Betty. "Anyway, we've all had some car trouble, and if we could get a telephone or you could tell us where we might find one—"

Her eyes were on the archway leading toward the kitchen. "Stewart!"

A toilet flushed. Heavy footfalls came down the hall.

Randy joined ranks with Jack. "Betty, are you listening? We have a problem here and we need—"

A big man came through the archway, a

wide leather belt draped over his hand. The buckle jingled like a horse's bridle. He sent a knife-eyed glare Randy's way.

Randy caught it, cooked up a glare of his own, and shot it back.

Apparently these two had already met.

"Siddown, Stewart," Betty said. "We're always waiting on you."

Stewart fed the belt through the first loop on his trousers, then the second, then the third, as if making a show of it, his eyes always on Randy. When the belt made it all the way around, he cinched up the buckle and sat.

"So you're Stewart," Jack said, just to see if this guy talked.

"Who are you?" the man replied, not smiling.

"Jack Singleton. I'm a writer, live up near Tuscaloosa."

"What about your wife?" asked Betty. Jack didn't understand.

"I live in Tuscaloosa too," Stephanie replied. "When I'm not on the road. We're getting a divorce."

Jack focused on the bowl of peas. *Well, let's just tell the world. And for the record, we haven't agreed to that. Yet.*

"Help yourself to the peas and pass 'em on," Betty said. Looking at Stephanie, Betty said, "So he'd just as soon not talk about you, is that it?"

Was she baiting him, trying to stir something up? He didn't bite; he just took a spoonful of peas. Stephanie kept smiling and dished up her potatoes without comment.

Leslie speared a slice of roast beef while Randy held the platter. "It's a lovely place you have here, just like the old South." Jack was grateful for her intervention. He tried to thank her with his eyes.

"Not as lovely as you," said Stewart.

Leslie smiled. Randy didn't. "Randall and I are from Montgomery. I'm a professor of psychology at Alabama State University, and he's CEO of Home Suite Home—you know the hotel chain?"

"Are you married?" Pete asked, his first words at the table.

"Pete here would like to get himself hitched," Betty said, patting his hand like a mother would.

Leslie kept her eyes on the roast beef as she served Randy. "We thought we'd take a little road trip, spend a few days in the Talladega National Forest. We weren't planning on dropping in on you like this."

"Are you married?" Pete asked again.

She finally looked at him. "No, but we're very close."

"They're shacking up," said Betty. She cackled. "Probably gonna violate each other up in room 3."

Leslie's mouth fell open slightly, but Randy managed a wry smile and said, "Probably."

"You can be my wife," said Pete.

Leslie spoke down to him like a teacher addressing a kindergartner. "Well, thank you. I'm flattered, but I'm afraid I'm spoken for."

"Eh, she'd be quite a catch, now, wouldn't she, Pete?" said Stewart, seeming to contemplate the prospect.

Jack stole a quick, discrete glance at Leslie to understand what Pete and Stewart saw that he didn't. If beauty was the determining factor here, why weren't they all over Stephanie? His eyes went to his wife, checking her out by way of comparison . . .

Her pursed lips sent him a signal that she didn't care for such comparisons.

He tried the potatoes. A little mealy.

"Stewart, don't encourage him," said Betty, a wad of food in her mouth.

Pete pointed at Leslie. "I want her."

Randy cut in, eyeing Stewart. "Speaking of catches, where do you suppose those spikes in the road came from?"

Stewart sniffed.

"Jack," said Betty, "why don't you tell us about your wife? Leslie told us about Randall."

Jack jumped at the chance for a little damage control. "I'd be delighted to talk about her." Stephanie rolled her eyes. "She's a singer and a songwriter. Country, mostly. She has a great band, sings in clubs and lounges around Tuscaloosa, sometimes Birmingham. Got a good job in Atlanta once."

"And aren't you glad?"

About what? "I think she's done very well—"

Betty asked Stephanie, "You having fun, sweetie?"

Stephanie smiled at Betty and at Jack. "Yes, as a matter of fact. I'm having a lot of fun."

"I s'pose you're on the radio."

Jack said no and then wished he hadn't.

Stephanie's eyes turned down toward her napkin. "But someday," she said.

"Have some iced tea." Betty poured her some. "Want more ice?"

"No thanks."

"You sure?"

"Uh-huh."

"I can get you some more."

"No, thanks; I'm fine."

Randy asked, "So you do listen to the radio?"

"Don't have one," Stewart replied.

"No radio. No telephone either?"

Stewart met Randy's eyes as if challenged. "We have what we want. We don't need what we don't want."

Jack said, "Well, we could sure stand to talk to somebody in the outside world. We've both had our cars damaged—"

"—by spikes someone left in the road," said Randy. "You did hear me mention that, didn't you?"

"*He* did it," said Betty.

"Who?"

Betty just chewed.

"Um, maybe you have some neighbors nearby who might have a phone?" asked Jack.

Betty swallowed and stood. "Let me get you some ice, sweetie."

"No, thank you," said Stephanie. "Really, you don't have to; I'm fine."

But Betty headed for the kitchen.

Pete pointed at Leslie again. "I want her to be my wife."

Leslie sighed.

"Yeah," said Stewart, "she probably wouldn't mind too much, considering where she's been."

Leslie paled just a shade. "I'm taken," she said.

"Makes me wonder how many times she's been a 'wife' before."

"She's taken," said Randy a little louder, and Jack could see the veins and muscles in Randy's neck restraining curses.

"Taken once, taken again."

"Stewart." Randy leaned toward Stewart, gesturing with his fork as if it were a dart. "I'd like you to make it clear to your son Pete that Leslie is not interested in being his wife, and we would both appreciate it if you and he would drop this subject—and while you're at it, try looking at something else."

"Randy, it's oka—"

"And just whose table are you sitting at, young man?" Stewart bristled.

Stephanie said, "Pete, I can sing a song for you."

Jack and Pete looked at Stephanie. *Uh-oh.*

"That's a very good question," Randy said, rising now. "Just what kind of innkeepers don't use matching silverware and glasses, aren't even here when their guests arrive, don't have a telephone . . ."

Stephanie started singing. "Hold my hand, walk me through the darkness . . ."

Jack hated that song too.

"Randy." Leslie put her hand over his.

He brushed off her cautionary touch. ". . . and then put the guests to work. What kind of low-overhead excuse for an inn are you running here?"

". . . we can make it, dear, if we make it together . . ."

"As long as your feet are under this table," Stewart growled, "you will watch that mouth of yours or *button* it!"

"And let's talk about the cars!" Randy demanded. "Pretty strange for both our cars to be spiked not far from your establishment, don't you think?"

". . . we can make it through the night . . ."

Oh, Stephanie, just stop.

The tendons on Randy's neck were showing. "And stranger still that you and Betty won't say a word about it."

Leslie winced and touched her left cheek. Jack noticed a spot of blood. She examined the tines of her fork.

Pete looked curiously—then hungrily—at Leslie.

"And you think you can just help yourself to anything in this place anytime you want?" Stewart said, dropping clenched fists on the table. "Take our rooms, take our lamps, drink our tea, use our bathroom . . ."

"Am I a guest here, or aren't I?" Randy shouted. "Who do you think the rooms and lamps and tea are for? And as far as that bathroom goes—"

Jack was in no mood to referee, but he was getting a bad taste in his mouth. He set down his silverware. "Hey, listen, everybody, look at the bright side here—" Stephanie stopped singing. "Stewart and Betty, you have guests, and that's business, and that's what you want. Now, we've all fumbled a bit, we've had a rocky start, sure, but we can make this work—"

"Now there's a line I've heard before," Stephanie muttered under her breath.

Jack heard her but pretended not to. "We

have a wonderful place to spend the night, dinner's on, the food's great—"

The bite that just dropped to his stomach wasn't that great.

Randy noticed Leslie's cut. "What happened?"

She was irritated, dabbing her cheek with her napkin. "I stuck myself again."

"I can kiss it and make it better," said Pete.

Betty strode in with a bucket of ice. "Herrrrre we are." One of her fingernails was blackened. Jack hadn't noticed that before.

"I don't need any more ice," Stephanie insisted, taking a bite of roast. She gagged and spit it out, pushed back from the table.

"Problem?" Randy asked, obviously hoping for one.

Jack looked at the meat on his plate.

It was moving.

Leslie squealed, her hand over her mouth, her eyes on her plate.

Stewart stabbed a slab of meat and crammed the whole thing into his mouth. Pete did the same, filling one cheek.

Jack looked closely at the roast beef on his plate and felt sick.

Tiny white worms were squirming, writhing, tunneling through the meat.

"Sweetie," said Betty, "I brought you more ice."

Stephanie watched her drop a cube into the tea.

Jack's peas were sagging; putrid juice puddled under them. "Looks like we took too long to eat," he said. He thought he'd better add a little chuckle to soften things.

Leslie threw down her fork and almost shouted at Pete, "Will you *please* stop staring at me?"

"Can you blame him?" Stewart asked.

"That's it," Randy said, taking hold of Leslie's arm and lifting her to her feet. "If you'll excuse us."

"Sit down," Stewart said.

"Leslie, come on." They stepped around their chairs.

"SIT DOWN!" Stewart yelled, half rising.

Randy swore, but Stewart laughed in his face. "Kid, you're nothin'."

Leslie tugged at Randy's arm until he left with her.

Betty grinned her gap-toothed grin at Stephanie. "Don't tell me you don't like ice, dear." She lifted a cube from the bucket and shoved it under Stephanie's nose. "You think about it all the time, don't you?"

Stephanie shied back. "No. Please, I don't."

Jack leaned across the table. "Whoa, whoa, wait a minute now!"

Betty followed Stephanie with the ice cube, wiggling it in her face. "I don't hear you singing."

What was it with these people? "Betty, she doesn't want any ice, and she doesn't want to sing. Now put that down!"

Stephanie's voice trembled. *"We can make it through the night . . ."*

Enough. More than enough. Jack went to Stephanie's side. "It's been fun."

Betty cackled again. "You can't rescue that one, boy. Nope, she don't want to be rescued."

Stephanie ran from the room.

Jack ran after her and caught up in the foyer.

She smiled through tears. "Isn't this the strangest place you've ever been? It's just so . . . so . . ." She started a laugh; it became a sob. "I can't stay here."

He held her to keep her from bolting. "Steph, I understand. But we have to think this through."

"Think *what* through?"

"Reality," said Randy. He and Leslie were near the stairs. Leslie steadied herself with one hand on the railing; with the other she held a hanky to her cheek. She was breathing slow, rhythmic breaths with her eyes closed. "Such as where to go in the middle of the night in the Alabama backwoods without wheels."

"What about Lawdale?" Jack wondered aloud. "He said he drives that road every morning. He'll see our wrecked cars."

"Lawdale?" Randy asked.

"Highway patrol," Jack said.

Stephanie peered over Jack's shoulder, and her eyes filled with dismay.

Jack looked.

Betty, Stewart, and Pete were coming their way, walking shoulder to shoulder with Stewart in the middle. Betty looked hurt. "Always running. What are you always running for?"

Stewart was about ready to take that belt to somebody. "The food was fine till you came in here."

Randy stepped out, hand extended in a clear warning. "Keep your distance, please."

Stephanie bolted for the front door, flung it

open, and dashed out onto the veranda. Jack ran after her.

She pulled up at the top step, her hands over her mouth.

"Steph, take it easy now. You—"

She was trembling. She took a step backward. Another step. She was peering down the flagstone walkway.

Jack approached and touched the small of her back—and then he saw it too.

Halfway between the house and the gate loomed the immense shape of a man, a shadowy silhouette veiled by a light rain. A duster draped the body to midcalf, and the face was obscured by the shadow of a wide-brimmed, drooping hat. The man held a shotgun, the barrel glinting in the lights lining the path.

Behind them, Betty sucked in a rasping breath and hissed, "Get inside."

They lingered, unsure.

She lunged and took hold of them. "Get inside! It's *him*!"

The figure started walking their way, the duster billowing, the boot heels clacking on the stones. The barrel of the shotgun swung forward.

6

Jack and Stephanie were already back-pedaling toward the door when they tore their eyes away from the apparition, turned, and dashed inside.

Jack slammed the door shut and locked it. He snatched a chair from the foyer and wedged it under the knob, momentarily uncertain if they were any safer inside. Well, their hosts were crazy, but they didn't sport a shotgun.

Randy rushed from the stairs, demanding, "What is it? What's going on?"

"Get away from the door!" Betty hissed, flicking off the foyer lights.

"What are you doing?" Randy said.

"You don't want him to see you."

They fell silent, motionless, and heard the sharp, staccato clicks of boot heels on the veranda. A shadow rose upon the door's stained glass, a hulking shape topped by a broad-brimmed hat.

The barrel of the shotgun came up against the glass. *Tap, tap, tap.*

Jack and Stephanie pressed themselves against the wall to the side of the door, watching.

Tap, tap, tap.

Leslie whispered, "Who is it?"

Stephanie shook her head, then mouthed and pantomimed, *He has a gun.*

Leslie drew herself up and asked in a calm and quiet voice, "Well, maybe he's a law officer. Why don't we ask him who he is and what he wants?"

Stephanie shook her head.

"He's no law officer," Jack whispered. He grabbed a vase off a stand and took the stand for a weapon, holding it high and ready. "Remember the spikes in the road?" He caught Randy's eye and jerked his head toward the door. "I don't think he's from AAA."

Randy stole close to the wall, taking hold of a chair. "He knows we're in here. That was the whole idea."

"What are we gonna do?" Stephanie squeaked. "Oh, dear God, help us."

Where is the loony crew? Jack did a quick check and saw the three peeking through the dining room's archway. *Best not to expect any help from those three.* Betty disappeared from view. *Click.* Dining room lights went out. Stepping out of the prismatic light coming through the stained glass, Jack tightened his grip on the vase stand. He'd never assaulted anyone with a piece of furniture before.

Randy braced himself against the wall near the lock, the chair ready in his hands. He called, "Who are you?"

The lock began to creak and jiggle.

Jack could feel Stephanie's trembling body next to him.

"Not a chance, pal," Jack shouted, making Stephanie flinch. "The door's locked, you're outnumbered, and we're armed."

Leslie ducked behind the registration table and peered over the top of it.

There was a *clank* like a dead bolt sliding home.

Randy raised the chair above his head.

The shadow remained for a moment, then retreated from the glass. The boot heels clicked across the boards, down the steps, dropped to the flagstones, and went away.

There were audible sighs of relief in the room, but Jack felt no safer, not yet, and he did not part with the vase stand. He asked Betty, "Who was that?"

"It was him," Betty said.

"Who's *him*?" Randy demanded.

"The devil himself."

Leslie stood up behind the desk, her voice professionally calm. "Betty, it's all right. Just tell us who he is and what he wants."

"You'd better start prayin' that lawman friend of yours shows up, is all I can say."

Randy checked the lock.

The knob broke off in his hand.

He cursed. "He did something to the door." He stuck his fingers through the resulting hole, jiggled the latch. The door held fast. Randy banged on the door, kicked it, banged it again. It would not open.

Jack set the stand down and tried to find

any crack he could pry into with his fingers. No good.

"You have *got* to get us out of here, Jack," Stephanie cried.

Randy and Jack looked at each other, speaking the same thought—"The back door!"—at the same time, the screen door to the enclosed back porch squeaked.

The men ran through the house, through the dark, groping, skidding at the corner, through the dining room, through the hall, into the light of the kitchen, and across to the back door.

The lock was creaking when they got there.

Jack slammed against the door, grabbed the knob, and tried to twist it.

A stronger hand on the other side torqued the knob against him.

Randy's hand wrapped around his, and together they tried to turn the knob, tried to pull the door open.

Through the pane, Jack saw the drooping hat and, just under the brim where a face should be, a plate of steel with ice-cold eyes watching him through two jagged holes.

There was a *clank* like a dead bolt sliding home.

The knob broke off in their hands, throwing them off balance.

They recovered in time to see the figure crossing the back porch and going out the tattered screen door, the shotgun slung over his shoulder.

Randy exploded in a stream of profanity and grabbed up a broom, ready to dash the handle through the glass. Jack stopped him. "Easy now, easy. Don't lose it."

Randy stood down, got a grip, and threw the broom aside.

The lights in the kitchen flickered, dimmed, and went out.

Another stream of expletives.

Jack stood still and remained quiet, trying to think. *What would happen next? What did this creep have in mind?*

Clumsy footsteps clattered and galloped into the kitchen, and he could see the others as dark shapes against the cabinets.

"Jack?" Stephanie cried.

"Over here," he answered.

She made her way toward him, and he took hold of her hand. She pried it loose but stayed close.

Leslie asked, "Did you see who it was?"

"He was wearing a mask," Jack said, "some tin contraption."

Stephanie groaned and slid down a cabinet to the floor.

Randy pushed himself away from the wall and strode up to Betty and Stewart. "Now you are going to tell us exactly what's going on. Who is this guy?"

"I think he's here to kill us," Betty answered.

The stunned silence lasted only a moment.

"Are you in on this?" Randy got in Stewart's face. "Did you rig the locks to break off?"

Stewart's eyes locked on him like a tiger on its prey. Jack touched Randy's arm but spoke to Betty, "How do you know?"

"Is he connected to the spikes in the road?" Randy demanded.

"You think you're better off stumbling around in the dark?" Betty asked.

Stumbling around . . . ? "Better off than what?" Jack asked.

"Help me find that lamp," Randy ordered no one in particular. "Get me some matches."

Jack, Randy, and Leslie groped about the

counter in the dim light until Randy found the lamp he had brought in before dinner. Betty produced a box of matches from a drawer. Soon they all stood in the orange glow, the flame casting eerie, dancing shadows across their faces.

Jack looked toward the windows. He saw faint orange reflections from the room, but outside there was only blackness. "We'd better make sure the house is secure. Just make sure we're safe for the time being, and then we can—"

"Secure the house!" Randy said. "Check the doors, check the windows, and let's get some lights back on."

"Do you have a gun in the house?" Jack asked the strange family.

"Got my shotgun," Stewart replied. "And buckshot."

"Then let's get it—"

Something bumped and creaked above their heads.

They froze in the glow of the lamp, eyes turned upward, listening.

A thump. Another creak. A succession of thumps—like footsteps.

"He's on the roof," Betty whispered.

Randy kicked a cupboard door and

started pacing in a show of some bravado, but Jack noticed the sheen of sweat on his forehead. "He's trying for an upstairs window."

Betty looked toward the kitchen windows. "What's wrong with these?"

Randy grabbed the lamp. Jack and Stewart followed him as he took off down the hall toward the stairway, leaving the women in the dark.

⌒ ⌒

"Jack!" Stephanie shouted. "Jack! Don't you leave us here!" *Gone again. If you make me cope alone one more time, I'll . . . I'll . . .* She covered her face.

"Stephanie, come on now, it's time to be brave," Leslie said. "There's a time for feelings, and there's a time for strength. This is a time for strength. You have to find it."

Stephanie had no more country-girl smiles left in her tonight. "Don't you talk down to me, Dr. Shrink. I am not your patient."

"Stephanie—"

"And I'm no helpless little bimbo either, if that's what you're thinking, and just for the record, Jack and I are still married." Leslie touched her shoulder, but Stephanie jerked away. "Don't touch me!"

They could hear the running, frantic footfalls of the men upstairs going from room to room, apparently checking all the windows.

"The men are still between us and . . . whoever he is," Leslie offered.

"Humph," grunted Betty, only a shadow in the dark kitchen. "If he wanted in, he'd be in."

Stephanie clung to her anger. She called up her mental catalog of Jack's offenses toward her and started thumbing through them. *You are so insensitive to me, always leaving me alone . . .*

"Can't we get the lights back on?" she heard Leslie say.

. . . and you have never understood what I really need.

"Nope," Betty replied.

Stephanie recalled the anniversary of Melissa's birthday . . .

"There was another oil lamp on the mantel," Leslie said.

. . . when Jack completely broke down. Abandoned her again. I want to move on, but you just can't, Jack.

"Come on," Betty said.

You loved Melissa more than you ever loved me. It wasn't my fault.

"Stephanie."

It wasn't my fault.

"*Stephanie.*" Leslie's voice jerked her out of her mental tirade. Leslie and Betty were leaving the kitchen. Stephanie followed, placing her hands on the walls to guide her as she moved into the hall.

"Wait a minute," Leslie said. "Where's Pete?"

Betty kept moving, leading them into the foyer, which now felt like a subterranean cavern—limitless, unknowable, so dark. Stephanie not only felt the wall, she was sure it felt her. Her fingertips tingled.

Leslie asked again, insistent this time, "Betty, where is Pete?"

"He likes to hide," Betty said.

"Hide?" Stephanie saw Leslie look back over her shoulder and stumble.

"Oh, are we having *feelings*, Doctor?" Stephanie said.

"Not at all!"

Stephanie found her ruffled tone quite satisfying. Dr. Shrink had a chink in her armor. *Ha. Dr. Shrink has a chink.* That was something to sing about.

Betty rounded the corner into the living room and threaded her way through the furniture while Leslie and Stephanie followed with the cautiousness of unfamiliarity. Stephanie could barely discern the huge fireplace, but Betty had no trouble finding and grabbing a second oil lamp from the mantel.

The flare of the match was blinding. Stephanie squinted while Betty lit the lamp and placed it on the hearth. The room appeared in the soft yellow light.

Stephanie and Leslie scanned the sofa, the chairs, the coffee table, and the bookshelves, looking for anything out of place. Stephanie didn't see any shapes or shadows that could be Pete, but this room offered an abundance of places to hide.

A dancing, swinging light shone into the foyer from above, casting elongated shadows of the stair railing and three men on the walls and floor. The guys were coming down the stairs.

"We think he's off the roof," Randy reported. "He didn't get in."

"Considering the locks, I'm beginning to wonder if he wants to keep *us* in," Jack said.

Stephanie asked, "Did you find the gun?"

Leslie leaned close and predicted, "Randy will have it."

Randy led the trio into the living room, carrying the shotgun, loading cartridges. Jack carried the lamp. Stewart brought up the rear, as grim as a thundercloud, boots clomping down the stairs. "He may have left, but we can never be sure," Randy barked. "The upstairs is secure for now."

"None of the windows will open," Jack reported grimly.

"There are seven of us and only one of him," Randy said. "Isn't that right, Stewart?"

Stewart didn't answer, maybe just to spite him.

Betty dug through a stack of newspapers in a basket on the hearth and pulled out a section. She crouched, then flattened it open next to the lamp. "So you want to know who he is?"

She tapped a news article on the front page and stepped aside.

COUPLE FOUND DEAD

Stephanie crowded in with the others, skimming the key phrases: ". . . man and wife, found dead in abandoned house . . . possible suicide, but authorities have not ruled out homicide . . . similarities to other

deaths . . . dead for almost two weeks before they were found . . ."

Oh, dear God.

"Seems like it's been going on forever,"
Betty whispered, her eyes glistening in the
lamplight. "People going into old houses
and never coming out, and when somebody
finds 'em, they been dead so long it's hard
to tell how. But me and Stewart, we know
it's him."

*No, it's not him, right? It can't be him. Not
here, not now.*

"Who is he?" asked Randy.

"The cops are still trying to find out. We
call him White, after the first family he took
down. He's been busy in these parts. We
were wondering when he'd get around to
us."

"Well, nobody's going to die in this
house," Randy said. "We'll assign guard
posts and hold him off until someone finds
our cars—"

*Right. Nobody's going to die. Everything's
going to be all right. Always all right . . .*

A distant thumping. Some creaking. All
eyes went toward the ceiling.

"He's still up there," Leslie said with a side
look at Randy. "He's still on the roof."

Randy pumped the shotgun once.

"Why the roof?" Jack asked. "Why the roof when any window on the main floor would be easy enough to break through? This guy has to be following a plan."

Then came a sound: a weird, tinny rattling like a soda can falling down a narrow well, careening, pinging, and clinking off the sides. It was close, maybe in the room. Stephanie ducked and swiveled, her hands raised to protect her head. Randy swept the room with the shotgun, making Jack and Stewart duck.

"Pete?" Leslie said, her voice tight with alarm.

"No," Betty said.

Poof. Something landed in the fireplace, sending up a little cloud of ash. It bounced onto the hearth, rolled forward with a gritty, metallic sound, and came to rest inches from the edge.

Jack brought his lamp closer. Betty approached it.

"Don't touch it," Stephanie said.

Betty leaned in for a closer look. "You're right, writer boy. He doesn't want in."

Jack reached down and picked it up.

It was an old soup can, the label faded

and half-gone, the print now obscured by a bold message scrawled in black marker. Jack sat on the hearth, set down the lamp, and rotated the can as he read aloud:

Welcome to my house.
House rules:
1. God came to my house and I killed him.
2. I will kill anyone who comes to my house as I killed God.
3. Give me one dead body, and I might let rule two slide.
Game over at dawn.

He passed the can to Randy, who read the message to himself. Stephanie began to shake. Leslie touched her arm and this time, Stephanie took her hand.

Above them, the sound of boot heels crossed the roof, descended the back side, and then stepped off.

Silence.

7

10:27 PM

Stephanie was the last one to hold the can, rotating it back and forth as she read the message several times over. Jack could hear her quick breaths. "Does he mean . . . ?"

"It means he's one sick character," Randy said, scanning the room like a sentry.

"It's psychological," Leslie said. "He's playing a mind game."

"Except for the dead people," Randy replied, nodding toward the newspaper on the hearth.

"But that's impossible." Leslie looked at

Randy, then Jack, then Stephanie. "He doesn't actually expect us to kill each other."

"Not each other." Randy snatched the can from Stephanie and read it one more time. "Just one."

Jack favored Leslie's theory. "I think he wants to divide us, get us at each other's throats."

Betty cackled low.

"Something funny?" Randy asked.

"That'll be easy enough," she said.

Randy leaned toward her. "You're speaking for yourself, of course?"

"We'll find out, won't we?"

"What *is* it with you?"

Jack extended his hand, not touching either of them, just enough to slip in a word. "Hey, come on. We don't have to play his game. We can choose."

"Hoooo!" Betty hooted, twisting her neck to look up at him. "Listen to *you*."

Leslie brought her wristwatch closer to the lamp. "Ten thirty. Dawn's at six. That gives us seven and a half hours."

"Six seventeen, to be precise." Everyone looked at Stewart. He shrugged. "I have an interest in these things."

Randy snorted. "I won't need that long.

I'm ending this right now." He grabbed the lamp off the hearth and strode toward the foyer, shotgun in hand.

Betty took a seat on one of the chairs, mildly interested. Stewart sank onto the couch, a comfortable spectator.

Jack went after him. "Randy."

"Stay back. This'll only take a second."

Leslie followed as far as the archway, then turned back to the living room and said, "Take cover. He's really going to do it."

Before Jack could stop him, Randy had reached the front door, set the lamp on the floor, and taken aim.

Jack wasn't concerned about the door, just Randy and all human bystanders. "Randy, be sure you know—"

Boom! The shotgun spit white fire, and the percussion rattled the house. The lead shot shattered the stained glass.

To Jack, the hole looked large enough to squeeze through. "That should do it. Why don't you put the gun down—"

Randy pumped and fired again, peppering the door, the jamb, the bolt. In the living room, Stephanie screamed. The door quivered as chips of wood flew into the room. The foyer filled with blue smoke.

—~—

Randy grunted as he chambered a third cartridge. He leveled the shotgun at his hip and centered the barrel on the lock. Fire, lead, and smoke exploded from the barrel; the recoil bruised him. The doorjamb shattered. The dead bolt fell free.

He knew even as he pulled the trigger that his crazy display was asinine given their predicament, but he couldn't stop himself. His own fear had taken over. The realization only steeped his anger.

Try to mess with my mind . . .

One more round rattled the windows, and the door's hinges creaked. He pumped the action, ready to go again—

The chamber was empty. He patted his pockets, then hollered over his shoulder at Jack, "Give me more shells."

Jack just stood there, almost hidden behind the lamp-lit smoke. Randy knew he had more rounds in his pockets, but he wasn't digging after them. "Randy," he said, "the door's open. Give it a rest."

"You bet your life the door's open! Give

me some shells before that creep crawls in here!"

Jack still didn't move.

—~—

Jack knew Randy's point was valid; they were vulnerable now to danger from outside. But that didn't mean things weren't dangerous inside too. *Give me one dead body . . .* "Why don't you let me take the gun for a while?"

Randy put his face within an inch of Jack's. "Gimme those shells! That creep's still out there!"

"Randy. Just take a short break. Let me have the gun."

Randy wrapped both hands around the weapon. "*I've* got the gun!" He shouted toward the women, "Come on! Let's move, let's get out of here! The shells, Jack! Let's have 'em!"

Leslie spoke from the shadows, "Randy, just let Jack hold the gun until—"

"Shut up! I'm in charge here!"

Jack heard an engine rev. Through the open front door he could see headlights playing about the front yard.

"All right," Leslie conceded, her voice controlled. "You're in charge, Randy." She and Stephanie stepped into the foyer. Leslie went to Randy and put an arm around him. "You're in charge." She stroked his shoulders. "You're the one, Randy. Good job." It seemed to settle him, at least make him reasonable.

Stephanie stood alone in the haze, clutching herself in fear. Her eyes were on those headlights sweeping around out front—

With a lurch, a rattle, and the growl of a half-muffled engine, the headlights lumbered over a flower bed, through a hedge, and onto the flagstone walk. From the fenders and the roundish cab stark against the stone wall, Jack realized it was an old pickup truck. It turned toward the house, disappearing behind the blinding headlights, backlighting a curtain of pouring rain. The light beams blasted through the front door, cutting a rectangular tunnel of brilliance through the smoke.

Jack found himself in that rectangle, his shadow extending behind him as he stood mesmerized, wondering, guessing—but only for an instant.

Whoever was driving that old heap opened

the throttle. The vehicle lurched forward, accelerating up the flagstone walk.

Right for the front door.

"Look out! Look out!"

They scattered to the left and right, running for cover, knocking things over, tripping in the shadows and smoke.

Jack was close to the dining room and fled in that direction, the headlights burning against his back, his frantic shadow running in front of him.

The engine's roar, the smashing and splintering of lumber, the screech of metal, the shattering of glass, the crunching of wallboard, trim, and fixtures, all melded into one bone-jarring, earsplitting *crash* as the truck climbed the steps, leaped over the veranda, and punched its way through the front wall of the house. Jack heard screams as he dived and hit the table as bits of wallboard, shards of vases, and a spray of rotten food rained down on him from a roiling cloud of plaster dust.

The skewed lights from the truck flickered, then died.

"Stephanie!" he yelled.

He pulled his feet under him and stood, unsteady, unsure which direction the foyer was. Turning, squinting, searching through the dark and dust, he sighted a fuzzy center of orange light bouncing and swinging in the haze. He followed it, stumbling on debris.

"Leslie!" Randy called, the light moving about in the murk as Randy searched. "Leslie!"

"Over here," came Leslie's voice.

The light zipped across Jack's vision, across the foyer into the dining room.

"You're bleeding," Randy cried.

"Stephanie!" Jack called. "Are you all right?"

"I'm okay," she answered, and then he saw her emerge as out of a fog, meeting him in the middle of the foyer. He held her and, under the circumstances, she let him.

The oil lamp returned to the foyer, floating in the cloud, held high in Randy's hand. Randy was helping Leslie along with his other arm. She held a hanky to her forehead. A trickle of blood stained her right cheek, a mirror twin to the cut she'd sustained during dinner.

"I'm all right," she kept insisting, as if trying to convince herself. "I'm all right. It's just a scratch."

Randy turned his lamp toward the damage. The front doorway was gone—no frame, no door, no lintel. Shards of glass, splintered molding, broken pottery, and dashed house-plants lay everywhere; puzzle pieces of wall-board dangled from shreds of wallpaper. In place of the door was the battered, crumpled nose of a brown truck, its windshield cracked like a collage of spiderwebs, the roof col-lapsed, the fenders folded back, the head-lights broken and walleyed. Steam hissed from the radiator as water trickled onto the hardwood.

Randy let go of Leslie. "Where's the shot-gun?"

Nobody saw it.

Randy spun, casting the lamplight in all di-rections. The dust was still thick in the air. "Where's the shotgun?"

He held the lamp high, letting the light penetrate the crack-webbed windshield and the collapsed cab.

No sign of the driver.

For several long seconds they stood in the gritty air with the taste of dust in their mouths and the pricking particles in their eyes—star-ing, disbelieving, and then realizing that the front wall had sagged and closed around the hulk of the truck, sealing off the exit.

Jack could read in their silence what he was feeling himself: the game had not ended. If anything, it was just beginning. "I think we should try to find that shotgun."

"Find the shotgun," Randy said, starting to search again.

"Looking for this?" came a rumbling voice out of the haze.

The other lamp came their way from the living room, illuminating two ghostly, fur- rowed faces. Betty was holding the light. Stewart was holding the shotgun, loading cartridges.

"You dropped it," Stewart said, unhappy about it. "Is this how you treat other peo- ple's property?"

Randy rolled his eyes and moved forward, shining the lamp in Stewart's face. "We don't have time for complaints, Stewart."

Stewart brushed past him and perused the damage to the house, in no particular hurry. "Now look what you've done." Outside, the rain intensified, pummeling the roof and ping- ing off the protruding bed of the truck. A strong gust blew in under the crumpled carriage and extinguished the flame in Randy's lamp. He swore and set it down.

Randy pressed into Stewart's space, reaching for the weapon. "He means business, Stewart. We can't wait around—"

Stewart pumped the action and raised the barrel, pointing it at Randy's chest.

Horrified, Randy bobbed, first down, then sideways. "Hey! What are you doing?"

Stewart kept the barrel aimed at his head. "One dead body, huh? Maybe it should be yours."

Randy ducked again and ended up on the floor crawling, rolling, backing away while Stewart followed his every move, chuckling with wicked amusement.

"Yeah," Stewart rumbled. "Crawl on the floor. *Squirm.* It's right where you belong!"

Jack ticked off his options. Randy was on the floor between him and Stewart, which put Jack—and Stephanie, still clinging to him—only inches from Stewart's line of fire. "Stewart, easy now . . . just take it easy."

Stewart didn't take his eyes or his shotgun off the cowering Randy. "Don't worry. This punk's not bothering me one bit." Stewart turned to Randy, "*Are* you?"

Leslie sidled close to Betty and whispered, "Betty, can you talk to him?"

Betty just held the lamp high, seemingly mesmerized.

"Are you?" Stewart growled.

"No, no," Randy said, his voice trembling.

"Betty," Leslie whispered. "Do something."

Betty looked at Leslie, then said to Stewart, "Stewart, don't you make a big mess now."

Leslie fell back, stunned. Jack searched the woman's half-crazy eyes but could not read them.

"Up against the wall, all of you," Stewart growled, swinging the barrel in an arc toward them.

"Wh-what?" Jack felt the same consternation he saw in the others' faces. He raised his hands, not yet believing. "Stewart. What gives?"

"Against the wall!"

Leslie helped Randy off the floor. Jack guided Stephanie to the wall that separated the foyer from the dining room, putting himself between her and Stewart's line of fire. They fell into place like four deserters before a firing squad.

"Stewart, I don't want you ruining the plaster either," Betty protested.

"Shut up!"

She took her place beside him and remained silent.

Stewart eyed them one by one with murder in his eyes. "You are the sorriest bunch of sinners I ever seen. Come in here acting like you own the place, all well-to-do like we can't tell what lies you're hiding. Filthy atheists! But you're guilty! Guilty as sin!"

Leslie turned on her most soothing, professional tone. "Stewart, perhaps we owe you an apology—"

With a blinding flash and a deafening explosion that mingled with Leslie's scream, Stewart ruined the plaster above Leslie's head. She cowered, hands raised in pleading surrender. Randy grabbed her to keep her from falling. Stephanie collapsed against Jack's legs, almost knocking him over.

"Oh, now you've done it," Betty whined.

Stewart pumped the action again. "Stand up."

Jack helped Stephanie to her feet but didn't let go of her. Her hands quivered in his. His heart was pumping so furiously he could hear it in his skull.

Stewart waved the barrel back and forth, the very picture of murdering madness. He jerked his head at the crumpled wreck embedded in the entry. "We know all about this killer, more than you ever will, so we know it's you that's brought us the trouble. You brought it in here like a dog carrying fleas."

"But we're more than happy to leave," said Jack. "Just let us go and—"

"*Go?* You think he's gonna let anyone out of here? You ain't goin' anywhere till Mr. White gets what he wants."

"But don't you see? This *is* what he wants, for us to harm each other."

"So what's wrong with that?"

Randy looked to Betty. "Betty. You understand what's going on, don't you?" He nodded toward Stewart. "Tell him."

She looked at the mangled truck and what was left of the front entry. "Tell him what?"

"Betty. Are you too stupid to—"

That got her attention. Her icy glare clipped his sentence like a pair of scissors. "What do you want me to say, smart boy? That we do what we have to do?" She eyed Jack. "That life's just a big joke?"

"No . . . ," Stephanie cried, her hand over her mouth.

Betty reached out and tucked a stray strand of blond hair behind Stephanie's ear. "Or maybe we should just sing a song and make the trouble go away." Stephanie let go of Jack, doubled over, and retched.

"Betty," Leslie said, her voice barely audible, "we're all human beings here. We can be reasonable."

"Human beings?" Betty looked injured. "Sweetheart, this is what human beings do."

Stewart grabbed a fistful of Betty's dress and yanked her back. "That's enough talking. We got ourselves to think about."

"As if I could think of anything else," Betty murmured, sidling up to him.

"But you don't all need to worry," Stewart said. "Just one of you."

8

Jack concentrated on Stewart's eyes, trying to detect the slightest hint of a bluff, a ruse, even a joke. The eyes were glassy, the red vessels distended, and behind them lay a darkness that was eerily familiar, like the hellish depths he'd seen through the window of the back door, through eyeholes cut in a metal mask.

This was no bluff.

Stewart wiggled the barrel toward the hall. "Get moving. Into the kitchen."

Betty moved into the hallway, holding the

lamp high, showing the dim way while casting long shadows. Jack exchanged a
glance with the others, then followed, hands
raised to indicate surrender, to prevent a
haphazard shooting. They followed Betty in
single file, first Jack, then Stephanie, Leslie,
and Randy, all with hands raised. Stewart
lumbered behind them, shotgun level.

Jack made a conscious effort to walk
slowly, hoping the others were searching
the hallway, the doorways, anywhere, just
as he was, for any ideas on how to escape.
There were plenty of places to flee from this
hallway—the kitchen, the dining room, the
stairs, the living room. Stewart couldn't
possibly contain all four of them if they
bolted, and the darkness would hide them.

But Stewart could kill one for certain, two
if he could pump another round in time,
maybe three or even all four if they could
find no other way out of the house.

Jack kept walking, looking, hoping, waiting for *the* moment.

They entered the kitchen, Stewart prod-
ding them from behind.

"Betty," Stewart rumbled, "open up the
meat locker."

Stephanie gasped then started bawling. "No. No . . ."

Stewart jabbed her with the shotgun and kept her moving.

Betty said nothing. She only scowled at them—and Stewart—as she went to the far end of the kitchen, raised the latch on a thick wooden door, and heaved the door open. Wisps of chilling fog poured into the kitchen and snaked along the floor.

"Nooo!" Stephanie tried to bolt, but Stewart grabbed a fistful of her long hair and yanked her back. She screamed, stumbling. Jack took hold of her, put her in front of him and out of Stewart's reach, and stepped into the locker. The others followed, crowding and stumbling in the dark. Betty stepped in last, closing the door with a *thud* as the orange glow from the lamp filled the room.

The meat locker was much larger than Jack would have expected, made of sawn timber with bins and shelves for holding produce and slabs of meat. There was a huge ax hammer leaning against the far corner, the kind with one blunt end for knocking out cows and one sharp end for cutting their heads off. A bloodstained workbench featured an assortment of butcher knives and meat cleavers; meat hooks dangled from the ceiling.

Jack could see his breath. He rubbed his hands together for warmth.

We can't run from here. We shouldn't have let them take us this far. We should have tried something.

"Turn around, hands on the wall," Stewart ordered, and the four faced the wall, hands raised and flat against the rough boards. They were frosty and bloodstained.

"What are you going to do?" Randy asked, his voice high and shaking.

"Can't you read?" Stewart said. "What do you *think* we're gonna do?"

Leslie began, "But we don't deserve—" Stewart pressed the gun barrel against her neck, and she went no further.

"Another lie. Ain't found a sinner yet who thought he deserved it, but they get it every time, now don't they? You all deserve it."

Jack peered over the women's heads and met Randy's eyes. They were frantic, vacant, like a trapped animal's. *Randy, come on. I need you to work the problem with me. We're after an idea, any idea.*

"But we can make this fair," Stewart said. "The killer only wants one, so we'll only take

one." He paced behind them, down to
Randy, back up to Jack. "And we'll even let
you decide which one it's gonna be."

They glanced at one another. Stephanie
was weeping now, her tears dripping onto
the floor.

*How could we possibly make that kind of
decision? But this is life, right? Just one
cruel absurdity after another,* Jack thought.
"You know we can't do that."

Stewart's voice dropped an octave. "You
don't fool me. I know what you can and
can't do. I know what you are."

Betty piped up, "No sense talking to him.
He thinks it's all a bad joke."

"I don't—"

"How about you, country star?" Stewart
moved sideways, touching the barrel to the
back of Stephanie's neck, making her flinch.
Her crying intensified. "You think there's nobody here you wouldn't trade for your own
life? Know what I think we oughta do with
you? Leave you right here to freeze to
death, long and slow."

"Please help me . . ."

"Now wouldn't that be justice?"

"But it wasn't my fault!" she screamed.

And then she looked at Jack.

Jack's very soul froze at Stewart's words, Stephanie's cutting gaze, his own memories: he'd had such thoughts about her. He'd told himself such things over and over. He never said them; he only thought them. *Justice. I don't know. But if the accident wasn't her fault, the breakup of our marriage sure was.*

"That's more like it, boy," Stewart murmured.

Randy spoke up. "Stewart, listen, this whole situation could work out really well for you. You have the advantage; I have money. We can work out an arrangement. You could be a rich man."

"Ohhhh, yeah." Stewart stood behind Randy, the barrel of the shotgun just under Randy's ear. "Just how did you come by all that money, anyway? By making choices just like this one, am I right?"

It took Randy a moment to formulate an answer. "Good businessmen weigh the alternatives."

"Well, here's an alternative for you: Pick somebody to die, or I will." He clutched a fistful of Randy's hair and slammed his head against the wall. "And I'm liking you for the part more and more, so you won't get off easy. No going quick. I'm gonna *drown* you, just like an old cat I wanna be rid of. You think about that!"

He poked Leslie, who stood silent, eyes closed, resolutely bearing up. "As for you, little Miss Taken, we'll wait till Pete's through with you, and then we'll decide."

Leslie maintained her stony expression, but her jaw began to quiver.

"I've chosen!" Jack shouted. He had no idea what his next move would be, but he tried to catch Randy's eye.

He caught everyone's eyes. Now what?

"Well, I'll be. Maybe writer boy really does care," Betty said.

"No," Jack said, meeting Betty's eyes with a boldness that surprised even him. "You were right the first time. I don't care. Life is a big joke."

Stewart bored into him with those hateful dark eyes. "This boy's got quite a philosophy."

Jack turned and faced Stewart, his hands raised. "If life made any sense at all, we wouldn't be here having to make this ridiculous choice, and that sadistic killer wouldn't be outside waiting for a body." He allowed himself a short chuckle and caught Randy's gaze. Randy was paying attention at least. "Listen, I've tried to understand why things like this happen to people, and I've given up." But Randy didn't appear to be with him yet. Jack engaged Stewart's eyes. "There's no point to life, and if that's the case, you're right, Stewart, what's so wrong about us harming each other? Why not?"

Randy, Leslie, and Stephanie were staring at him, hands still against the wall. Their eyes were full of questions.

The muzzle of the shotgun filled his vision as Stewart said, "All right. Who's it gonna be?"

Jack shot a nervous glance toward Randy. "Uh, who do you think? I mean, it's obvious."

Come on, Randy. Work with me.

Stephanie's voice was weak. "Jack, you can't possibly mean what you're saying!"

Thanks, Steph. Why don't we have another marital spat right here while Stewart's trying to kill us?

"Don't tell me what I mean!" he shouted at her, trying to stay in character as he moved out from the wall a few inches. "Look around you, Steph. Do you see anything good happening in this room? Do you see any point to any of this? And where's God, huh?" He inched sideways, looking down the barrel of the shotgun that never strayed from his face. "If God cared about us at all, he'd do something about this fix we're in, but guess what? No God, no help, no rescue, no point." He looked at Stewart, even leaned toward him just a little, and said, "And no guilt either. There's no guilt because there's no right or wrong, no sin— there's only that shotgun."

Stewart shoved the barrel at him. "So maybe it oughta be your brains all over the wall."

Betty slapped the back of Stewart's head. "Stewart! Do it outside or you clean up the mess."

Stewart's closing in gave Jack an excuse to back up, moving along the wall, away from the others. The gun followed Jack.

"Hey," Jack protested, trying to catch Randy's eye over Stewart's shoulder. "You said you were going to be fair, you were going to let us choose which one. Well . . ."

Just a few more inches. Jack didn't have to act scared—he really was—as he continued backing away, drawing Stewart's attention. In his worst nightmares he couldn't have dreamed up a story like this. "Okay. I choose me."

"You? You can't choose you."

Stewart turned his back on the other three.

Jack had to keep his attention. "Why not? Betty's right. I've lost the dearest thing in life to me, and my wife just wants to run off and be a country singer. I don't care if I live anymore." Stephanie looked away. There. A light went on in Randy's eyes. His hands came off the wall. "So in the grand scheme of things, I'm not losing anything and you get your body."

Stewart seemed a bit rattled. "You're supposed to pick somebody else."

Jack looked at Betty, who stood against the workbench to his right. "Betty, talk to him. Doesn't it make sense?"

Betty glowered at him, but mostly at Stewart. "Maybe he ain't the right one. He doesn't seem to mind."

"Shut up," Stewart said, his eyes still on Jack, pushing that barrel in Jack's face.

"Or maybe he is. Drowning the other guy'd take too long."

Stewart looked her way. "I said *shut* up." *Now!*

Jack brought both arms down and grabbed the barrel, sweeping it aside.

Boom! The gun discharged, blowing a hole in the floorboards. Stephanie screamed.

Randy, where are you?

After an eternity, Randy pounced on Stewart, riding his back, trying to bring him down, arms groping. "Get the gun, get the gun!"

All three men had a death grip on the shotgun as the barrel swept the room. Leslie and Stephanie dropped to the floor. Jack kept his hand locked on the shotgun's pump action to keep Stewart from chambering another round. Stewart spun, smashing Randy's body against the wall. Jack tripped over Stewart's leg and fell, still clinging to the shotgun even as Stewart's boot came down on his rib cage.

"Run!" he screamed to Stephanie and Leslie. "Get out of here!"

"STOOO-WART!" Betty screamed.

— —

Leslie jumped across the room and took hold of Betty's right arm just as Betty's fist closed around the handle of a meat cleaver.

The woman possessed surreal strength, bucking, twirling, and pummeling Leslie's head and face with bony knuckles like little hammers. Leslie, with both hands clamped around Betty's right arm, could only duck, wrestle, and use a knee when she got the chance.

"STOOO-WART!"

— —

Stephanie leaped for the door and threw her weight against the latch plate. The plate depressed, releasing the latch outside. The big door creaked open, and she stumbled into the kitchen, slipping on the fog-dampened floor. Before any thought arose in her mind, she was crossing the kitchen for the hallway, running into deepening shadow. *Get away, girl; get away! Run!* Betty's screams, Stewart's roar, and the sound of blows and struggle chased her up the hallway. *Faster!*

— —

Stewart kicked Jack in the gut hard enough to separate Jack's will from his hands. His grip on the shotgun fell away. Stewart gave a mighty backward thrust with the shotgun butt and sent Randy backward, doubled up in pain. Jack heard the pump action chamber another round.

— —

Leslie clung by sheer force of will to the tireless, whirling machine that kept screaming and swinging a meat cleaver. Much more of Betty's bony fist in her face, or just one more violent body slam against the rough planks, and Leslie's strength would fail. A blur that was Randy's body collided with the wall behind her and doubled over. Jack was still on the floor, trying to get his feet under him while—

Stewart aimed the shotgun at Jack's head.

Leslie couldn't end Betty's violent struggling, but perhaps she could redirect it. She planted a foot, extended her other leg to trip Betty, and let both of them tumble headlong into Stewart, slamming him against the wall.

Boom! Splinters of wood flew up from the floor.

A tangle of bodies, kicking legs, groping

arms. Leslie lost her grip on Betty's arm. She looked around—

The meat cleaver thudded into the floorboards inches from her shoulder.

Stewart lurched from a kick to his midsection. Jack was still alive.

Betty bent over Leslie, trying to wrest the meat cleaver from the floor. Leslie brought both legs up and kicked Betty's stomach with enough force to throw her against the opposite wall.

———

Stephanie skidded to a halt in the blackness, then turned and realized she was alone. No one had escaped with her.

Worse yet, she was unsure of where she was. *Was* she in the hallway? A flash of lightning painted momentary streaks on the floor and walls, disguising corners, distorting angles, changing features.

"Jack!"

The sound of the struggle had dropped to a distant rumble, as if behind a wall. She set out to find it, arms extended, feeling her way. She contacted a wall and followed it to a corner. She made the turn, followed farther, and came to another corner. Wasn't there a door somewhere? How had she gotten here?

"Jack." She could hardly whisper.

An outside corner led her into a space that seemed larger, but there was no light to show her the smallest patch of surface. She moved along the wall, groping for a piece of furniture, any object she might recognize. As far as she might reach, she felt nothing. Fear began turning her guts, making her tremble. She felt faint.

She stopped breathing and listened.

Nothing.

No sound. No light.

She was lost.

9

Randy was sure he would need surgery to repair his bowels, stomach, and liver, but first he would put Stewart down. Jack was still wrestling with the man for possession of the shotgun, slamming against the shelves, careening off the walls. Randy maneuvered, waiting for Stewart's head to pop out of a shadow—

Betty blindsided him, bit him on the hand, took hold of the ax hammer. He screamed in pain.

Leslie came up behind Betty and dashed

the back of her skull with a sizable chunk of ice. The ice shattered in all directions and the woman's jaws relaxed, allowing Randy to twist free. "Get her out of here."

Betty went limp as Leslie pulled, wrestled, and dragged the heavy woman toward the locker door. It was a vital mission. With Betty out of the picture, Jack and Randy could deal with Stewart two-on-one. If Leslie could remove Betty permanently, she could return to help, making the match three-on-one. Divide and conquer.

Just inside the locker door, Leslie felt Betty's body go from sack-of-potatoes cooperative to wild-tiger deadly. Screaming like a great cat, Betty lurched, spun, and flung Leslie through the door as if she weighed nothing. Leslie floated through space for an instant, no up, no down—

Her body—head, hips, elbows—hit the floor, and she tumbled over the tile. Her head was spinning when she came to rest, dizzy in the dark. She oriented herself to the dim light of the oil lamp that still burned, righted herself. She was in the kitchen.

She heard the big door shut, slamming with a wooden thud and the clank of the latch falling into place.

Darkness.

Breathing.

"Betty?"

The breathing was through a large windpipe. Not Betty. She heard phlegm rattling, then a low, wheezing chuckle. Three slow footsteps shuffled toward her, and then a flash of lightning through the small window over the sink illuminated a face that seemed to float without a body.

Pete.

"You can't hide from me," the man's thick voice yelled.

Leslie pushed herself to her feet. Another flash of lightning illuminated the archway out of the kitchen and into the hall. She dashed that direction as the light vanished, running madly into the dark unknown.

He shuffled after her.

—◦—

Jack was losing. He could feel his hands slipping from the shotgun. His ribs screamed in pain with every breath. He tried kicking Stewart—again. He missed—again.

Betty had thrown Leslie out, locked her out. She came rushing to Stewart.

Clunk! Stewart's head jerked sideways, struck by the ax hammer in Randy's hands. The man staggered. Jack lost his grip on the shotgun and let him fall—

Just in time for Jack to see a wild-haired, bulb-eyed wraith charging into the lamplight.

"Randy!"

Randy was still holding the ax hammer at shoulder height. Betty's own momentum brought her forehead dead center with the blunt end, and she bounced off it.

Without having to consult, Jack and Randy half ran, half limped to the door. Randy slammed the latch plate with his palm, they shoved with their full weight, and the big door eased open in no hurry at all. Betty and Stewart were on their feet again. Stewart was loading another cartridge.

Jack bellowed as he and Randy tumbled around the door and pushed it shut.

Almost.

The two bodies on the inside collided with the door, punching it open. Jack and Randy leaned into it, forcing it shut again, but they couldn't hold it forever.

"We've got to jam this latch," Jack said.

Randy checked his hands, only now discovering they were empty. He'd dropped the ax hammer inside.

Ka-thud! The door jerked again, sending a brief flash of orange light into the kitchen, enough to reveal a mop against the wall a few feet away. Randy reached for it.

Boom! Jack could feel the shock of the shotgun blast on the other side of the door. It jerked.

Randy had the mop. "Push!" Jack and Randy gave the door their shoulders and all that remained of their strength. The latch fell into place, and Randy jammed the mop under the latch handle.

The locking mechanism banged and rattled as Stewart and Betty tried to operate it, but the handle was jammed solid.

"Good work," Jack said.

A *boom-boom-boom!* carried right through the door and into Jack's skull.

The ax hammer.

They began to shout. "Leslie! Stephanie!"

There was no answer from either.

Crack!

They noticed the change in the sound of the blows. Namely, ax instead of hammer.

"They'll be through that door soon enough," Randy said. "Let's find the girls and get out of here."

"Pete went after Leslie," Jack said.

Randy didn't respond.

Jack dug in his pocket for Stephanie's lighter and flicked it. The tiny yellow flame was just enough to guide them through the kitchen and toward the hallway. Randy spotted a rack of kitchen knives near the butcher block and helped himself to an eight-incher, tucking it in his belt. "Bring it on," he muttered.

"Steph!"

"Leslie!"

Still no answer.

———

"Jack!" Stephanie called into the darkness, but only silence answered. "Jack, I'm in here! *Jack!*"

He didn't answer.

"Jack!"

She flopped against an unseen wall as little thoughts buzzed in her mind: she didn't need him anyway. Jack had died with their daughter. Why *should* he answer? Maybe he was being quiet because he *did* hear her.

She started humming, trying to make the thoughts go away. *"My heart holds all secrets; my heart tells no lies . . ."* She couldn't remember the next line. She sang the one she remembered twice, then hummed the melody until the fear eased up and she could think. She'd been on her own since Melissa's death. She could manage this. *Get yourself out, girl. Jack isn't going to do it for you.* Everything would work out okay in the end.

She had no idea where she was. There was still no light. She'd gone through a door into what felt and sounded like a hall, but it wasn't *the* hallway she was hoping to find. She'd encountered a table and some chairs, and then a painting on the wall, but these were entirely unfamiliar. When she tried to backtrack and find the door she came through, her hands found nothing but blank wall.

Jack! So help me . . .

Now she heard commotion and voices, some footsteps far away and muffled. She followed the sound.

Crack! Jack and Randy could hear it from the hallway between the kitchen and dining room. Stewart was making quick work of the barricaded locker.

Jack's lighter illuminated a door that stood half-open. The one Betty had scolded him about.

"The basement," Jack said.

They paused at the threshold. Dirty shiplap walls and wooden stairs descended into a black void beyond.

"What do you think?" Randy asked.

Bam! Crack! Not much time for conversation.

"*Somebody* went down there."

"It wasn't the girls. They got out. They had to."

"Got out to where?"

Bam! Bam!

Randy took off toward the dark foyer, his shoes wandering on the hardwood, stumbling on the debris. "Leslie!" Jack heard bodies collide. A woman screamed. Randy screamed then cursed.

Jack leaped back into the hallway and

squinted. Stephanie. She was flailing and pounding Randy, who was only trying to help her. "Steph!"

She stilled, swept the hair off her face. "Where have you been? Didn't you hear me calling you?"

"Not so loud," Jack cautioned.

Stephanie marched at Jack, anger in her steps. "Maybe you don't think I'm worth keeping, but I'm still a human being with feelings, and I'm still your wife!"

"Where is Leslie?" Randy asked.

"I don't know. Jack, can we please get out of here?"

"Was Leslie with you?"

"*No!* Can we go now?"

Jack looked down the basement stairs again. The light caught a sparkle on the first step. He bent and picked up a silver drop-shaped earring, held it up for them to see. "She went down there. She's in the basement."

"That doesn't prove anything," Randy said.

Stephanie paced. "I'm not going down there, Jack. We have to get out."

Boom! The shotgun put another spray of lead into the meat-locker door.

Jack raised his lighter high and turned in place, starving for an idea, a lead, a course of action. He spotted the other door, the closet. He ran to it, jerked it open. Without the extra chairs, there was plenty of room. Coats, enough to conceal someone, hung from a rod.

He motioned to Stephanie. "Steph. Inside."

Her feet were planted. "Are you crazy? I'm not going in there!"

He took firm hold of her arm and got her moving. "We can fight about it later. Right now I need you where I can find you."

She stumbled backward into the black cavity under his firm guidance. "What are you going to do?"

"Find Leslie."

"Oh, so *she's* worth looking for, is that it?"

"Not now, Steph." Everything was all about her, wasn't it? Her selfishness was wearing thin. "Stay put till we come back. I'll make it quick."

"What about—" He put his hand over her mouth. She pried it off and whispered, "What about Stewart and Betty?"

"They'll be chasing me and Randy. Stay put."

"But you can't leave—"

He closed the closet and went to the basement door. The silence, the darkness down there, was hiding something. He could feel it. "Randy?"

Randy started to argue, "We don't know for sure she's down there—"

Crash! Wood splintered in the kitchen.

Jack stepped into the stairwell.

10

10:55 PM

Barsidious White stood at the top of the brick stairwell that led into the basement, arms crossed, waiting. Waiting . . . waiting. So much of life was waiting. All good things came to those who waited, as the saying went.

He lifted his face to the pouring rain and focused on the pelting of his skin. Lightning flashed. This storm was the kind that brought flash floods. Good thing to know.

He knew a few things none of those inside knew, naturally. More than a few things. The game was being so perfectly executed that he wondered if his luck would run out before he had a chance to introduce the real stakes.

Or show his true power, for that matter.

If all good things came to those who waited, and he was waiting for evil to work its magic, did that make evil good? If he was waiting for the hour of the killing, did that make killing good?

Killing one person makes you a murderer. Killing a million people makes you a king. Killing them all makes you God.

In the end he would be God, because the game being played behind these dirty white walls wasn't unlike the game all people played everywhere, every day, every last dirty one of them.

In the end they all killed; they all died; they all would rot in hell.

But in this house they would play his game, which boasted enough drama and delight to bring a smile to the blackest of souls. Assuming he won. But he would win. He was born to win, born to rip their filthy heads off their scrawny necks in a way that made it all at least interesting.

White took a deep breath. After weeks of waiting, each second now delivered enough reward to justify it all.

He unfolded his arms and walked to the edge of the stairwell. The sounds of an ax or a hammer slamming into a door resounded with each blow. If he was right, if he'd judged correctly, the players would soon be in the basement, and the real game could begin.

Of course, the real game was already in full swing, but they didn't understand this. By dawn he'd bring everything into clear focus.

Driving the truck into the front door had been a nice touch. Put the fear of God into their hearts. And that would be him because, as he'd just established, he was God.

"Welcome to my house, Jack." He let out an amused grunt. "Jack in the box."

White descended. Packed leaves and dirt had long ago covered the concrete, raising the landing several inches so that when the door opened, decaying leaves tended to spill into the basement. But there was more than a little decay waiting to enter this world tonight.

He put his hand on the keyless door latch and pressed it down. Locked. As it should be. He would wait.

White walked back up into the night. The methodic thumping of the ax inside morphed into a muffled sound of splintering wood. A loud crash. Pounding feet.

White's right hand began to quiver. He made no attempt to stop it. Deep in the backwoods of Alabama where no one was watching and the darkness had swallowed all light, he was allowed to enjoy life a little, wasn't he?

———

Jack's lighter flickered above the old wooden stairs. Jack paused halfway down, straining for a glimpse of something. A repulsive odor—rotten eggs or sulfur—filled his nose. He tried to breathe shallow.

He wasn't sure what he was looking for, other than Leslie. The floor below was gray concrete and the walls were red brick, he could see that much. Nothing more.

He leaned forward and shouted. "Leslie!"

"What are you doing?" Randy whispered from behind. "They'll hear you!"

"I *want* her to hear me; isn't that the point?"

"*Her*, not the whole house. They'll know we went after her."

"They're in the meat locker making themselves deaf—no way they heard me."

Stephanie's muffled voice called from the closet. "Jack!"

He ignored her and continued four steps before realizing that Randy wasn't following. The man still stood at the top of the stairs.

"You coming?"

"You sure this is a good idea?"

What made him think he could waltz into this dungeon of theirs, find Leslie, deliver her from the brute, and skip off into the woods without catching a blast from their guns? Or from White's. That's the likelihood that awaited them outside.

"We don't have a choice." A few more blows and Stewart would be through. Then he added for Randy's sake, "They have to have more guns down here."

Right. Guns. He turned back down the stairs and descended quickly, now eager to follow his own advice. Gun first, Leslie second, because it was clear that without a gun, they were dead men. Whatever this house was, it wasn't a quaint little inn inhabited by ordinary proprietors filled with goodwill toward weary travelers.

The sickness here was palpable. Death hunted them all, and the only way to survive might very well be to kill.

Jack blinked at the boldness of his own thoughts and stepped onto the concrete floor. Randy clumped slowly down the steps behind.

The basement opened up before Jack. One low-wattage bulb hung from the ceiling. He let the lighter die. A wide concrete-and-brick hall with three corroded steel doors on each side ended in a solid redbrick wall. The corridor looked like something out of an old prison movie.

Water trickled down the right wall in a couple of wet trails, then ran along the floor into a grate.

"What's that smell?" Randy asked. "What is this place?"

"The basement."

"Looks more like a . . . sewer."

"Let's go."

"That smell . . ."

Jack tried to ignore the sickly stench. He walked up the hall, now faced with an unexpected dilemma. The thought of opening one of the doors, any of the doors, struck him as foolish. But short of going back upstairs, there was no other option.

Jack hurried to the first one on his right. Put his hand on the rusted handle. He hesitated.

Crack!

The muffled sound of Stewart's progress on the heavy meat-locker door reminded him of the terror close behind. He turned the knob. Pushed the door.

The room that opened up to them was dimly lit by another bare low-wattage bulb. No immediate threat, no gun in the face, no booby trap, no spring-loaded arrow aimed for their hearts. Just a room.

No, not just a room.

Jack and Randy gazed about. Four burgundy sofas, two quite new, two very old with torn upholstery. Lots of throw pillows. A tan-and-black woven rug covered most of the concrete. Paintings. At least a dozen paintings hung on brick walls. Almost homey in an eccentric sort of way. A strange blend of the old and the new, grungy and clean.

Jack walked in. "Look for a gun, a gun cabinet. Hurry."

There was an old potbellied stove at one end of the room, shined clean as if it had never been used. A thick cobweb peppered with mummified bugs stretched from the top of the stovepipe to the adjacent wall. Why would they clean the stove and leave the web?

Other interesting pieces of furniture were

set about—a loom, a coatrack, an antique rocker . . . a rusted washing machine?

The room added a whole new dimension to Jack's understanding of Betty and Stewart. The problem was, the dimension wasn't clear.

And then Jack saw something that cleared things up a bit. There was a pentagram painted in red on the wall to his left. A threat scrawled in black ran through it. *The wages of sin is death.*

Stewart's accusations filled his ears: *Guilty as sin.* Below the pentagram sat a sofa table, and on that table stood a ring of black candles. Looked like the hosts were a religious lot.

Somewhere deep in the house a door slammed.

"What was that?" Randy asked.

"Check that closet," Jack said, pointing to a door beside the pentagram. He ran across the room to a second closet door. "Keep looking!"

The closet he tried was filled with junk. Candles. Rags. A broom. Nothing that looked like a gun or anything he could imagine using to incapacitate Pete, which he thought it might come down to.

"Uh, Jack?"

When he turned back he saw that Randy's door opened into another room.

"What is it?" He hurried across the room.

"Another room."

"I can see that. What . . ."

He poked his head into the room. Gray concrete, all sides. Heavy cobwebs in all the corners and along the walls. A single writing desk in the middle of the room. No other furniture. Looked like a huge study. Sort of.

Jack stepped in. Long red drapes framed a huge mirror on the left wall. Another pentagram with the same words appeared on opposite wall. *The wages of sin is death.* That was it. Just the desk, the mirror, the graffiti.

And three more doors, one of which looked like it led back out to the main hall. The other two stood straight ahead in the opposite wall. They led deeper into the basement, maybe.

"You think that door leads back out to the hall?" Randy asked. "This isn't good. I don't like it. We have to find the storage room, or wherever they'd keep guns."

He hurried toward one of the doors directly ahead. "Tell me what kind of a freaking place this is . . . ?" *He's beginning to melt down,* Jack thought.

  Weren't they all?

  Randy reached for the knob, pulled up short. He was staring at the mirror. Why, Jack wasn't going to spend precious time finding out.

  "Okay, we have to split up. Just go, run." Jack ran toward the door that he guessed opened back into the main hall. "Cover every room and meet back in the hall."

  Jack threw open the door and bolted into darkness. Dripping water. Smelled musty, sweet next to the rotten-egg odor that permeated the room behind him.

  Randy was still blinking at the mirror, waving at it now.

  "Snap out of it, Randy! Did you hear me? We have to move!"

  "I don't . . . Something's wrong with this mirror."

  "Who cares? Let's go!"

  "I don't have a reflection."

  The ridiculousness of Randy's claim ballooned in Jack's mind. He released the door and crossed to Randy, who was still staring, stupefied.

Jack stood next to him and looked into the mirror. No reflection.

Correction: no reflection of them. The desk behind them was in clear view. So was the far wall.

"We should leave," Randy said.

"It's a trick mirror or something. They make them like this." Maybe Betty and company had once been a part of some gypsy circus. It might explain a few things.

"No, this isn't some trick mirror. We're like vampires down here, man!"

"Don't be an idiot. Come on, we have to be reasonable about this. Cover the—"

"I'm not splitting up."

"Stop it! Leslie's out there!"

"We're going to die down here, Jack. All of us. We're all going to die."

"Yeah, if we don't move. Follow me."

He ran for the door he'd opened, Randy at his heels now.

"Find a switch." He slapped the wall on the right. Wet and cool. No switch. He raised his hands and started waving high.

A string hung low several yards in. He gave it a gentle tug, lighting a bulb mounted to the beams above. Now this was the kind of room Jack expected to find down here.

Wet, mildewed walls lined with wooden racks. Two more doors.

"Root cellar," he said.

"Where's the hall?"

"Must be through that door."

The fact was, based on what he'd seen down here so far, the basement wasn't laid out like any he'd ever seen. Jack crossed the cellar and pulled open the door. As expected, the main hall. He released the handle with a small measure of satisfaction.

Randy hurried past him.

"Try one of the other doors," Jack said.

The sound of running boots pounded over their heads.

Randy jerked his head up and stared at the labyrinth of pipes that crossed the ceiling. "They're coming!"

As if to emphasize the point, a muffled shotgun blast boomed above. Stephanie? No, she was still in the closet, and the sound had come from the kitchen area. Unless she'd given up after five minutes and made a break for the back door. Would they come directly downstairs or search the upper floors first?

The faint sound of humming came again, as it had upstairs. Jack whirled. "You hear that?"

"The singing . . ."

But neither could place it.

Jack wasn't waiting. He tried the door directly opposite the root cellar's. Locked. The footsteps pounded in the other direction. They couldn't risk it. Jack grabbed Randy's arm and tugged him back into the root cellar. Closed the door behind them.

"Where we going?"

"Anywhere but the hall. Keep it down."

They rushed through the cellar, ignoring a door on their left. Back into the study, past the freaky mirror.

"Where we going?" Randy asked again.

Jack pulled up. "Did we leave the door into the first room open?"

Randy stared at him with dawning horror. "They'll see it! They'll know . . ."

The humming again, from their right, very faint. Then silent.

Jack ran toward one of the doors they hadn't tried yet. He could now hear the sound of footsteps on the stairs.

"Don't say we didn't warn you!" Betty's voice echoed. "Not the basement, we said, but no, you wouldn't listen. Don't you dare say we didn't warn you!"

"Hurry!" Jack said.

He slid up against the door. If their hosts followed the trail of open doors . . .

He grabbed the door handle and pulled. The door moved an inch, then pulled free from his hands and slammed, as if sucked by a vacuum.

"Try the other door!"

Randy ran toward the only door they hadn't tried yet.

Jack pulled the door again. This time it opened six inches—wide enough for him to see the blackness beyond. A deep sucking sound filled the room.

"It's locked!" Randy cried.

Pushed by the threat of Stewart blasting into the room, Jack ignored the voice in his head that suggested forcing a door open against such a strong underground air current was not a good idea.

He pulled harder.

The door gaped wider. Where could such a strong draft come from? The study's one light dimmed. Something was very wrong with this room.

It became immediately clear to him that no matter what the threat behind them was, they could not, should not, enter the space beyond the door. Jack released the handle.

The sucking sound ceased. But instead of slamming shut, the door hung free, gaping where he'd released it.

Beyond, silence. No humming.

"Go!" Randy whispered. "Go!"

Wrong. Something was terribly wrong.

Jack reached out his hand. Before his fingers touched the handle, the door flew open of its own accord. Wide open.

For a brief moment Jack faced a doorway of inky darkness. No floor or walls that he could see.

He felt his body being pulled into the doorway before he became aware of any suction, any draft, any force that drew him.

It was quick and it was silent, like a magnetic force. One second he was staring at the blackness, the next he was flying into it.

Smack! With a bone-crunching jar he crashed into a wall no more than five feet in.

Boom! The door slammed shut.

11

Randy Messarue stared at the door that had slammed shut behind Jack, frozen by indecision. He wasn't sure which was worse: following Jack in, or making a run for it alone. Usually he could make choices in a snap. Must be the house. This stupid, stinking house. And its wacko proprietors. His mind had started to fray the minute Stewart had snuck up on him in the bathroom.

And when the man had turned against them, the erosion of Randy's confidence had become a crumbling of his psyche. He could feel himself coming unglued, disjointed. Weak. Not the stuff CEOs are made of.

He hated himself for it. Hated the way his gut was telling him to run. Hated the fact that he would probably save himself at Leslie's expense if it came right down to it. Hated the terror that had him squealing like a schoolgirl in his own mind.

He was sweating profusely despite the basement's cool air. His hands were trembling and his heart was pounding. *Don't be a wimp,* his dad used to say before taking the belt to him. He probably deserved a good whipping, and Stewart seemed all too eager to oblige.

Clack, clack. Shoes on the concrete, walking, not running. An image of Stewart's large leather boots striding across the floor flashed through his mind.

He leaped to the door and cranked the knob. It refused to budge.

"Don't you dare say we didn't warn you, you filthy atheists!"

Stewart was in the next room.

"Just go easy, Stew," Betty was saying, trying to keep the calm when they all knew there wasn't a bone of calm in that inbred husband of hers. "They got nowhere to hide. You just go easy. Nothing rash."

Randy was out of options. Two doors, locked. The root cellar exposed him to the hall. He spun, frantic for a way out. But there was no way out. *Hide. Hide, you pathetic little baby. Hide!*

He tore his feet from the ground and ran past the desk. Too small. To the curtain that framed the mirror. Behind the curtain.

But he could not still the curtain, and his lungs were wheezing like worn-out bellows. He pressed his back against the wall and willed his muscles to relax.

Clack, clack.

The boots stopped. They were in the doorway. Randy held his breath. For a moment the room fell silent.

"Where are you, you little rat?"

Randy tells Betty to shut the door.

The door shut. A lock engaged.

"That one too," he said.

The door to the cellar closed. Locked.

"They came this way, didn't they? I can smell the city stink."

"You think they made it to the tunnel?" Betty asked.

"Not unless they can walk through locked doors, they didn't."

"Then where?"

"Probably through the cellar. For all we know they're at the top of the stairs now, trying to figure out how to get back out."

"No way past that lock," Betty said. "The halls down here will drive them nuts. They'll never make it out."

Stewart had trapped them in the basement?

Stewart grunted. "I say we hunt them ourselves. We got them trapped like rats now."

"That wasn't the deal," Betty said. "You want to live through the night, we open that door for him."

"You open the door. He's not gonna let this slide. I swear he's gonna fillet us like fish. He's gonna slaughter everyone in this basement like he's done a hundred times before. You know how it works."

Pause.

"You think they'll find her?" Betty asked.

"Pete'll find—"

"Not her. The other one."

Stewart paused, breathing loudly through his nose. "Not before we do. And if they do,

no doubt she'll use 'em. She's a sneaky little piece of trash."

For a while neither spoke. Then Stewart
clacked toward the far corner and Betty followed. Keys rattled. A door squealed. The
door closed. They were gone.

Or were they? What if they had seen him
and faked their conversation and exit for his
benefit? He'd pull back the curtain and face
a loaded shotgun.

Randy waited until he couldn't bear not
knowing any longer. He inched his head
around the curtain, eyes peeled.

The room was empty.

He ran to each door, testing the knobs.
Locked. The one to the room with couches,
the one to the root cellar, the one Jack had
been sucked through. That left the door
Stewart and Betty had used, and he had no
intention of following them.

Randy put his ear against the door, heard
nothing, and tested the handle. Unlocked.
His intentions hardly mattered any longer.

He paced for ten seconds, nerves dicey. If
he waited here, they might sneak back and
shoot him like a rat in a cage. No options,
not a single one, other than going through
this door.

He put a trembling hand on the knob, twisted it slowly, and cracked the door. Dim light. No sound. He eased the door wider.

The hall on the other side of the door was made of wood beams supported by thick posts. Stone floor. A bulb in a beam scattered light to the far end where some steps met an old wooden door.

No sign of Betty or Stewart. They must have gone through one of three passages cutting into the hall's left wall.

Staring at the passage, Randy was struck by the scope of what he'd seen in the basement thus far. Clearly the house didn't sit on a square foundation, but on a maze of rooms and halls. Which meant chances were good the basement had another exit. If he was right, he was staring at one right now. That door at the end of the hall sat at the top of three steps. The bottom half was visible to Randy; the top half seemed to be set above ground.

You want to live through the night, we open that door for him, Betty had said.

Meaning what? That door was the door that would let *him* in.

White in.

Or Randy out.

He stepped into the passage and walked on his toes. The first of the three passages cut into the left wall ended at a door five feet in. But Randy wasn't interested in another door. He only wanted one thing now, and it lay at the end of the hall.

He could now see that a large padlock had been opened and the door's latch was sprung free.

His heart knocked in his chest. White could be on the other side of the door; he knew that; he did. Knew it and hated it.

If the killer had come in, he'd have locked the door behind him, right? Sure he would have. Of course he would have. Randy repeated that a dozen times as he eased over the stone floor toward the wooden door.

──

They'd unlocked the door and left, as White had requested. Demanded. A request and a demand were one and the same now, because now they were all playing his game.

When you played White's game, either you did it White's way or you did it the dead way. Everyone learned that sooner or later.

Of course that meant he had to follow the rules as well. His rules.

House rules.

The time had now come to enforce those rules. A little discipline to guide them down the crooked lanes.

He descended the stairs evenly. He straightened his trench coat, took a deep breath, and pushed the door open.

Then White, who was really black, stepped into his house.

━ ━

Randy was adjacent to the second passage when the door swung in and the boots stepped out of pouring rain, over the threshold, and onto the concrete landing.

There wasn't a shred of confusion in Randy's mind about the identity of this person. The shape of those black boots, the length of the trench coat—these were all emblazoned in Randy's memory with enough clarity to test a thousand hours of therapy. This was the killer they'd all seen on the path leading to the house.

Two things saved him in those first few moments. The first was that the killer didn't have a direct line of sight down the hall as he descended the steps on this side of the landing. The ceiling cut off his vision.

The second was that Randy reacted without thought, before he fully realized the danger that he was in. He jumped to his left. Into the passage.

Against a wall.

And there he froze. He could have tried to sneak farther in, through the door, away from the killer, but he froze.

And this, too, may have saved his life. He had no illusions that White was some ordinary lumberjack with a penchant for killing strangers. He struck Randy as a mastermind of sorts. The slightest sound would undoubtedly alert him.

Randy was breathing heavily again.

He clamped his hand over his mouth and strained to keep his lungs in check. His heart he couldn't control, but he doubted the man was that good.

White reengaged the latch and squeezed the padlock shut, making no attempt at stealth.

He stepped down to the stone floor, then stopped. Randy didn't need eyes to see what was happening. White was staring down the hall, thinking he'd heard something out of place. The patter of a heart. The rush of breath. The seeping of sweat.

For a long time, silence. Then White's boots moved, twelve or fifteen paces. They stopped again.

Water was trickling somewhere. In that moment, Randy felt his last reservoirs of strength fall away. He actually began to relax.

And when he did, a strange kind of resignation—no, peace—began to lap at his mind. A silent resolve not to care. No use fighting White. No use running. He didn't have the strength to run. Or resist at all, for that matter. A small corner of his mind wondered if it might be better to step out and cut a deal with White.

For seconds that stretched into an eternity, nothing happened. He couldn't hear White breathing, so maybe White couldn't hear him.

The boots headed toward the study. A door opened and closed.

Randy slid to the cold stone floor. Okay, so maybe he did care a little. He ground his molars and muttered under his breath, "Take that, you sick vampire."

He was shaking. But he was alive.

Leslie had vanished into these halls. At least, he was pretty sure of it. Was *she* alive? The thought surprised him, more because it was the first time he'd given the matter head-space than because he worried for her safety. Amazing how quickly a little stress can reorganize your priorities.

He hated himself. In reality, he always had. If he managed to survive this night, he might work on that.

The exit was now locked. The room he'd come from was locked.

Randy turned down the passage he was in and tried the door at the end. It led to a small utility room. There was a closet door on his right. Every room in the house seemed to have a closet. He scanned the walls. Shovels, buckets, a pitchfork, rakes. Several rakes.

A shotgun.

Randy blinked at the gun leaning in the corner, not sure his eyes were seeing correctly. Yet there it was, a single-barrel job that looked as old as the house. The question was, did it work? He cocked the barrel open at its hinge. Two rounds. He looked around. Rifled through jars of nails and lightbulb boxes on a shelf. Nothing that looked like ammo. Two would have to do.

A door slammed and footsteps sounded in the hall he'd just come from. *Clack, clack.*

Betty's *clack, clack*? Or Stewart's? Or White's?

Randy picked up the gun as quietly as possible and moved cat-like toward the closet. But even as he moved he realized he was no longer panicking.

"Stewart?" Betty called out.

He yanked the closet open, saw the floor inside was a foot or so lower than the one in the utility room, and stepped down.

Was he afraid? Sure. But he'd made it this far. He closed the door, thinking that he might not have entered a closet after all.

Randy turned around in the space. Not a closet. Not even close. He was in a shadowy concrete tunnel of some kind. It ran from the door to both right and left.

You think they made it to the tunnel? Maybe he should reconsider. A thin crack of light marked the utility-room door's outline. Then again, Betty was somewhere on the other side.

He faced the tunnel again. Maybe, just maybe, it had an exit. He'd seen the pouring rain when White came into the base-ment—if he found rainwater, he just might find a hatch or something.

He looked both ways, and seeing no rea-son why he should go either direction, he turned to his left and walked, shotgun in hand.

He had a gun; that was the main thing.

It hit him then that what faint light there was had come from the crack below the door. The tunnel was dark ahead. And be-hind.

He'd taken maybe twenty steps when a loud *clang* rang down the tunnel. Like a hatch opening. Back, way back. He turned. Too far back to see anything.

Something dropped into the tunnel. Some-thing heavy. And something that could run. *Thump, thump, thump, thump.* Headed right for him. A steady but heavy breathing chased the echoing footfalls.

Randy whirled and ran for his life.

12

There were two ways for Leslie to look at her predicament: she had escaped the beast, or she had simply taken a long and terrible dive over the lip of the frying pan and into the fire.

Or into hell. Honestly, she didn't know which.

In the terror of her escape from Pete, the open door to the basement had at first struck her as her only escape. The fact that they'd been told earlier not to enter barely registered. It was the odor that sharpened

her recollection of Betty's warning. The
smell of rotten eggs assaulted her the moment she landed on the concrete floor. But
by then, it was too late. She heard Pete's
grunts upstairs and knew that he was following. With a glance back, Leslie ran forward, down the hall, and past three doors
before veering into another hall on her left.
She tried to regulate her breathing.

She couldn't shake the feeling that she'd
entered far more than any ordinary basement. The rooms, for one thing—there were
far too many, and if these halls were any indication, the space reached way beyond
what she thought reasonable for the size of
house above her.

But at the moment, the compulsion to escape the man crashing down the stairs behind her pushed caution from her mind. It
hardly mattered that the concrete passageway she'd entered was dripping with water
and lit only by a naked bulb here and there;
it hardly computed that there were too
many doors. The suggestion that she was
already lost whispered through her mind
only once.

She sped forward on her tiptoes, around a
corner, through a doorway, into a smaller

hall, to the end, and confronted by a door on her left and another on her right, Leslie chose the one on the right.

Into the room without taking stock. She closed the door behind her and locked it, quite sure that the lock couldn't be disengaged from the other side. But she was too unnerved to open the door to make sure.

Leslie turned around and stared at the room she'd entered. Her breathing stopped almost immediately.

Not from fright.

Not from shock.

Not because her body was suffering a heart attack.

Then her heart began to race. She'd been here, she could swear it. This wasn't just any room. Déjà vu swarmed her, so strong that she couldn't separate it from reality.

She stood on a thick Turkish rug. Purple and orange were the first colors she saw, but they were quickly joined by a surprising array of improbable colors for a windowless room tucked away in the corner of some basement maze. Bright colors: green, blue, and red.

But it wasn't the colors that pulled her forward. There was a texture in this room that she found reassuring. Almost safe in its limited power to undo her. It was like facing a familiar monster and knowing that no matter what it did, you were better than it, and you would walk away alive. So really, you were safe. In control, even.

This room emboldened her. She'd been here before and walked away from whatever horror it contained to tell the story. This room was why she'd first decided to study psychology. Her fascination with the human mind began with her own need to understand how she could possibly suffer what she had suffered as a young girl and rise above it all, as so many millions of other women had.

A king-size bed with a tattered red-velvet canopy sat against the main wall. Drapes on either side. A thick lavender comforter with no fewer than a dozen holes chewed through by rats.

She walked forward and put her hand on the comforter, a patchwork of velvet and satin. No, this wasn't simply a figment of her imagination. She was here, in a room at the end of a maze of halls, confronted with a terror so great that it was causing her to hallucinate.

Swaths of red and purple and blue material had been hung from the ceiling to hide the mildewed concrete, which still showed in wide gaps. The room was lit by several strings of white Christmas-type lights behind the material—someone's attempt at ambient lighting.

There was a white dresser with a mirror, the kind with pink accents that might have been in a little girl's room once upon a time. Very similar to the dresser she had in her own room when she was nine, in fact.

The walls were cluttered with painted portraits, mirrors, china plates, candle sconces. Lots of sconces. Several dozen candles. A large pentagram was painted on the wall between two of the sconces. Didn't surprise her.

The one other feature that stood out to Leslie in her first examination of the room was the two pinball machines opposite the dresser. One was a Batman machine; the other was a Barbie machine. Beside them, mounted on the wall, was a huge round dartboard that spun on an axis. The kind that would be used in a knife-throwing act.

The sweet scent of roses mixed with vanilla commanded her attention. Leslie looked for the source, transfixed by the odd blend of terror and desire. Half of her mind screamed for her to run, to escape the house and its bizarre inhabitants.

But another half suggested that she breathe deep and let that aroma calm her frayed nerves. Her grandmother had kept the stuffed pillows in her old house scented with vanilla and potpourri, and the scent had always brought a cleansing calm to Leslie, even in the worst of times.

Like now.

There had to be an explanation for the eerie familiarity of this room. If she slowed down and applied her mind, she'd make sense of it all. She'd always told herself that, and it always worked.

Leslie walked to the dresser and bent for a whiff from a bowl of potpourri. The pungent odor of lavender and vanilla worked deep into her sinuses. No more roses. She closed her eyes and exhaled slowly. Emotion swelled, and for a moment she thought she might cry. She swallowed hard, melancholy. A slight quiver took to her chin, and she bit her lower lip.

Think, Leslie, think! You're letting emotion bend your mind.

She was here for a reason, wasn't she? No four travelers could possibly find their way into such a strange house without some elaborate scheme drawing them. Whoever this stalker-killer was, he wasn't the Jason-with-a-machete-variety. He was a deeper thinker, much deeper.

Another scent mixed with the vanilla, and Leslie opened her eyes. There was a bowl of cream next to a candle. Without thinking, she lit the candle using a book of matches to one side.

The cream beckoned her. She lifted the bowl and sniffed it. Not a chilled cream. Vanilla pudding laced with caramel.

Again without thinking, Leslie dipped one finger into the cream and put it to her lips. The sweet taste of caramel pudding was unmistakable. Impulsively now, she dipped four fingers into the bowl, scooped out some of the pudding, and shoved it into her mouth. A small glob plopped onto the breast of her red blouse. She dabbed it with her finger and ate that too.

For a brief moment the realization of what she'd just done horrified her. It was unfor-givably irrational. And of all people, why was she, who had such control, who rode the crests of reason and logic as a way to make sense of her world, now eating from a bowl in a stranger's bedroom?

She should be vomiting and searching for a way out.

Instead, she moaned, fingers stuck in her mouth like a child who snuck a treat from the refrigerator an hour before dinner when she knew good and well that it would be frowned upon by Mother.

Still, the smell of caramel pudding was so strong, and the forbidden taste so sweet, that rules such as these demanded to be compromised, particularly when the rest of your life was hell.

She froze, fingers in her mouth. The clarity of her predicament sliced through her foggy mind. She was a grown woman in her late twenties, not an adolescent sneaking pudding before dinner. Worse, she was a grown woman in a basement that belonged to Pete . . .

The closet door opened behind her. Leslie dropped the bowl on the dresser and spun, gasping.

Pete stood in the doorway, eyes fixed on her. She had pudding on her lips and on her fingers. Pete looked at her mouth, her fingers, the bowl behind her. But he didn't smile. Didn't flash a grin of wicked intent. Didn't approach her with force.

He just looked at her like a deer in the headlights.

Time seemed to stop.

"My room," Pete finally said, voice thick with pride. He released the closet door and stepped in.

Pete's room.

"Do you like my room?" Pete asked the question like an expectant child.

Leslie faced a critical decision. Did she play along or spit in his face?

She took a long look at the locked door to Pete's right. A long look at Pete, who waited for an answer. But she was alive. And her whole life she'd stayed alive by playing smart. By playing their games. Today was just another day in the game, though this particular game seemed to have unusually high stakes.

Mind over matter. Life was won and lost in the mind, end of story. So here she faced off a man who was her opponent more in mind than in body. And of the two, she had the stronger mind.

"Yes," she said. "Yes, Pete, I do like your room."

Pete lit up like the sun, rushed over to the bed and straightened the cover. Picked up a candle that had fallen to the floor and busily reinserted it in its holder, all the while keeping his eyes on her.

When he finished, he clasped his hands behind his back as if to say, *There, now it's perfect.*

"We have to be quiet," he said, eyes flitting to the door. "Mama will hear. She can't come here."

The candle he'd just put in the holder toppled over, rolled off the dresser, and fell to the floor. He didn't seem to notice. His eyes were singularly focused on her.

It occurred to her at that moment that she really didn't feel threatened by him. He was nothing more than an overgrown child.

Then she reminded herself where she was, and her fear returned, a new kind of fear motivated more by what lay outside this room than by Pete.

An image of Stewart slipped through her mind. He seemed bent on giving the killer a dead body. Betty might be their best hope for survival. Were the others even alive? Or bludgeoned in the meat locker?

She envisioned Jack blasting his way through the door with a shotgun. Jack? Yes, of course, Jack. Randy didn't possess enough backbone to save anyone, even he knew that. She used him just like he used her, but at a time like this, Randy was useless. Jack . . . she sensed Jack was a completely different animal.

The thought surprised her. Did she want him to rush in, put a slug in Pete's skull?

Yes, she thought. She did. A slug through that forehead, no matter what kind of victim Pete himself might be, seemed like the right kind of ending to this mind game she'd never wanted to play.

But short of that, she had to play smart. Play along. Millions of years of evolution had turned the human mind into an amazingly resourceful instrument of survival, capable of far more than ordinary life demanded of it. She'd read dozens of cases that demonstrated this fact, and now she would become one of those cases.

She smiled and clasped her hands behind her back to match his stance. "I like your room very, very much."

Pete blushed. He eased into a large stuffed recliner, leaned forward, and watched her as if he wasn't sure what to do with his catch.

Leslie made a show of interest by examining the room more closely—touching the candles, feeling the bedspread, smelling a few of the other potpourri-filled ceramic bowls.

She could feel his eyes on her, worshiping her. But not in a threatening way. She would have expected terror to fill her mind at a time like this, but it didn't. She was beyond that, she told herself. And being the object of such pure, perhaps even innocent, adoration struck her as interesting at least, even now in this black hellhole.

Perhaps particularly now, in this black hellhole, where the slightest reprieve from suffering would show like a bright beacon of hope.

The smell of sulfur seemed to have dissipated some. Maybe it was the potpourri.

"Where did you get the potpourri?" she asked.

An odd first question from a captive, but a smart question. She had to play smart. Distract him so that when the right opportunity presented itself, she would have the upper hand.

"The what?"

"This," she said, holding up the bowl. "It smells good."

His unblinking eyes remained on hers. "It's for you," he said.

Such sincerity, such innocence in his voice.

"Thank you. Where did you find it?"

"From the house," he said.

"You mean upstairs?"

"Sometimes. There's other houses. Do you like the pictures?"

She set the potpourri down and walked to her left, examining the portraits. "Yes. Do you know any of these people?"

"No. But I won't be lonely now."

Meaning he had her. She felt momentarily nauseated, but the feeling passed. She had to control the conversation, keep him on her track.

"I especially like the dresser. It reminds me of . . ." She stopped in front of the mirror.

She couldn't see herself. The mirror reflected the room but not her.

She turned around. "What's wrong with this mirror?"

"It don't work," he said.

"But . . ." She faced the mirror again. "But it shows other things. Why can't I see myself?"

"It's broken," he said.

Leslie shivered. She wrapped her hands around her bare arms. She'd never heard of such a thing. She reached out and touched the glass. Normal, as far as she could see.

Smart, Leslie, be smart. Don't lose your head.

"Can I ask you some questions, Pete?" She faced him.

"Yes, we can talk. I would like that." He stood, unhooked the bib portion of his overalls, and pulled off his T-shirt. He flexed his biceps, grinning from ear to ear.

"Do you think I'm strong?"

She was so taken aback by his display that she didn't answer him.

His smile faded.

She caught herself short of displaying disgust. "Yes. Yes, you are very strong."

"I can throw you," he said, encouraged again.

"Yes, I suppose you—"

"Look!" He ran to the closet, yanked open the door, and pulled out a huge purple bag of Purina Dog Chow. "Cereal. It makes you strong."

"I'm . . . I'm sure it does. How long have you lived here?"

"Do you want to be strong?"

"Maybe. But can we talk first?"

He carried the bag to her, still gazing into her eyes with boyish wonder, took her left hand, and placed it on his chest. Then he flexed.

There was no room for embarrassment. No need. She was playing his game, and that meant doing what he expected. To a point.

Leslie moved her fingers on his flesh, feeling the hard muscle beneath the skin. "Wow," she said, and a small part of her meant it. His chest was cool and smooth. Maybe he'd shaved it. White skin, nearly translucent, but it showed no veins. Soft skin like lily petals, softer than any of hers. But just below the skin, rocklike muscle.

She kneaded it and raised her hand to his shoulder, where the muscles parted like cords. What was she doing? She pulled her hand back, aghast at her momentary fascination.

But she immediately covered her rejection by smiling. "You are so strong."

"Thank you," he said. But he didn't move. His breath was stale.

Leslie averted her eyes, eager to step beyond this moment and redirect him. "So, how long have you lived here?"

"Do you want to be strong like—"

"If you want me to be your wife, then I have to know more about you, don't I?"

Her challenge caught him off guard.

"Please," she said. "I just want to know more about you."

He stepped back, unsure. "A long time."

"Where did you come from?"

He frowned as if trying to remember. "The circus. We were gypsies and did fun things. But then Stewart killed a man and so did Mama. I killed a man too. Have you done that?"

"No. I don't think killing is a good thing."

"You have to be strong."

"How many people have you killed?"

He shrugged, then smiled. "White kills people too. He's strong."

She had to keep him talking.

"Who is White?"

"White?"

"Yes. Who is he?"

"I think he's going to kill us if we don't kill the girl."

"What girl?"

"Susan."

"There's a girl hiding down here?"

The light went out of Pete's eyes. The expression on his face shifted from boyish innocence to irritation.

"You don't like Susan. Why?" Leslie had slipped into the role of psychoanalyst without thinking.

"She's worse than White."

"Worse than the killer? What does she do?"

His eyes darkened. The flesh below his eyes sagged, and he stared at her as if he might be sick. "You can't trust her," he said.

Pete clenched his eyes and screamed. Leslie caught her breath and stepped back. But as quickly as he gave vent to the terrible emotions, he stopped.

Opened his eyes. Stared at her, lost.

Did anyone hear his scream? Please, Jack. Please tell me you heard that.

"Why does White want you to kill her?" she asked.

No answer. Just that blank stare.

"I have to know things if I'm going to be your wife."

Pete refused to respond.

"Why can't you find her? This is your basement, your house."

"I don't want to talk anymore."

Leslie knew she was losing him, but she pressed anyway. "You have to tell me everything. I have to know more about the girl. I have—"

"No!" His face reddened.

She'd pushed him too far.

"I'm sorry. I won't talk about her."

They faced each other in a long silence. Pete still held the bag of dog food. He reached into it and withdrew a jar filled with the stuff, then dropped the bag.

"You like my pudding," he said. "It's vanilla. I'll mix more with water and smash it for you."

He hurried to the closet, picked up a bowlful of water from the floor, and returned, dumping the jar's contents into the bowl.

"It'll make you strong! Like me."

Leslie blinked at the concoction he mixed. She glanced at the bowl of pudding she'd eaten from a few minutes earlier. The same stuff. But its appeal was now gone. Completely.

"Eat it." He shoved the bowl in her face.

Leslie turned her face from a foul smell. It wasn't just dog food, it was rotten dog food. She thought about dipping her fingers in so eagerly and blanched.

"I already ate some," she said.

"But you have to finish. Mama said. It'll make you strong like me," he repeated. "Eat it."

"No . . . No, really, I can't."

"I know you like it! See?" He scooped some out with his fingers and pushed the mush into his mouth. "Sweet. See?" He picked up the bag and showed her the picture of the large juicy steak that evidently tantalized the dogs who ate this particular brand.

"I'm not going to eat dog food," she said. "I don't like dog food."

His face fell and his jaw slackened. She'd crushed him. But she drew the line here. She would throw up all over him if she even smelled that mush again.

"Eat it," he pleaded. "My mama made me eat it. I'm strong."

She just stared at him.

Pete dug his fingers into the mush and approached her with a scoop. "Here, please . . . please." He came right for her, shoved the stuff in her face.

Leslie turned away and pushed his hand. "Stop it! I—"

He grabbed her hair and tried to force the mush into her mouth. "You were eating; I saw you! Eat it!"

Panicked, she flailed. "Stop it!"

The bowl flew free and clattered on concrete, upside down.

Pete stared at the mess in shock. His face darkened. He slowly lifted enraged eyes. It didn't take the psychologist in Leslie to know she had made a terrible mistake.

He lifted his fist like a hammer and slammed it down on her head. She staggered under the blow, dropped to her knees.

Pete screamed long and loud. Then he scraped the mush off the floor and back into the bowl. He set it in front of her. "You are my wife! Eat it!"

13

At first Jack wasn't sure he was still alive.

He had to be. His heart was still hammering, his lungs were sucking and pushing—his breath echoed in the dark chamber into which he'd been sucked.

Maybe he was unconscious. He'd hit the wall hard enough to knock him senseless. But his hands and feet were moving under him, groping on the cool, damp concrete surface.

Were his eyes open? They were. It was just too dark to see.

Jack pushed himself to his knees, then turned and sat on his rear end, trying to clear his head. Where was Randy?

Slowly he reconstructed the events that had deposited him here. Betty and Stewart, the killer, the house, the basement. The black closet, assuming he was inside a closet.

No humming. Nothing but his own breathing.

He stood to his feet shakily and felt around. A wall to his back. Concrete. No door that he could feel.

He inched around, arms extended. Nothing. He walked farther, but he could no longer tell which direction he was walking. Not without light.

The lighter. He dug into his pocket, distinguished it from the spare shotgun shells, and withdrew it. That was some bright idea, putting those two in the same pocket. He made a mental note not to do it again and flicked the lighter. It ignited on the second spark.

A long passageway with a rough concrete floor and an arched brick ceiling ran in both directions. The door . . . there.

He turned back and tried the door in the wall, but it was locked tight.

No draft now. Then what had sucked him in? Could an underground draft be strong enough to do that?

Don't say we didn't warn you.

Jack felt a new kind of fear run through his bones. *Welcome to my house.* What if White knew something about this house that none of them had guessed? What if this game was all about the house. Not White, not the hosts, but the house?

He tried to dismiss the thought. Made no sense. A house was a house. White, on the other hand, was a demented psychopath driven by his thirst for killing. The house might be part of his sick plot, but they had to understand the real threat—flesh and blood, not concrete and brick.

They. He had to get back to the others.

Jack breathed deep, focused on calming the tremble in his hands. The silence, the stillness, the not knowing why or what was getting to him. He should be running down this tunnel, desperate to find a way out. Instead, he stood here frozen, contemplating.

Contemplating and suddenly dizzy. It occurred to him that he was breathing too hard. He closed his mouth and breathed through his nose.

The lighter grew hot and he released the butane trigger. The tunnel went black. He waited a few seconds, then reignited it.

Both directions looked the same to him, so he headed right. The draft had come from somewhere, maybe from an opening beyond the house. If he could find the exit, he could slip past White, head for the high-way, and come back with the authorities.

But he knew that Leslie wouldn't survive long enough for that, even though she was a strong woman. Maybe it was why he had decided to come after her.

Randy, he didn't care about. Unfortunate but true. He'd concluded that the man was a self-absorbed pig.

Stephanie . . . also in the self-absorbed category. He wasn't sure how he felt about Stephanie, but right now he honestly didn't care if she stayed in that closet or not. She could make her choice and let it lead to its natural conclusion for once. How much longer could he protect her from herself? He'd stick to her as he always had, but it was getting harder and harder—

Jack stopped. He wasn't a bitter person

by nature. Was he? No. Steph could take the heat for bringing that on. He grunted. The sound echoed down the chamber. His light reached out twenty feet or so before blackness overtook it. Why wasn't he running? He had no business taking a Sunday stroll down this tunnel.

He let go of the lighter again. In that moment, in the pitch blackness, the terror he'd felt earlier came roaring back to the surface, now without any distraction from contemplation.

There was something evil in this house.

He had to find a way out before the lighter decided to give out. How long had he been down here? Jack put flame to the lighter and began to jog.

A long scream reached him from somewhere beyond the brick walls. He pulled up and whirled. The scream ran on, a throaty wail that sounded more male than female.

It ended abruptly.

He ran thirty feet and slid to a stop when the tunnel came to a sudden end at a large wooden door. He tried the handle. Locked. Like every other miserable door in this miserable basement.

Jack raced back in the direction he'd

come. It took him less time, much less time, to reach the other end of the tunnel.

Same dead end. Same kind of door. Locked.

How was that possible!? Where had the draft come from? He'd gotten in; there had to be a way out!

The lighter wasn't going to hold out forever. How long did these things last, anyway? The idea of being trapped forever in a dark concrete tunnel filled him with a new urgency. Something close to panic.

He searched for the door he'd come through. Maybe he'd get back out to the study.

He traveled the length of the tunnel. Nothing. The door had vanished.

Impossible. He made a return trip to the other end, sprinting, with one hand holding out the lighter and the other shielding it from being blown out.

But nothing had changed. The wooden door was locked. He kicked it and found it solid. He cranked on the knob to no avail.

One final sprint to the far side sealed his understanding of his predicament.

There was no way out.

The faint sound of singing reached his

ears. The same voice he'd heard a half dozen times since entering the house. A sweet song trapped in his head.

The flame was beginning to wane. He had to save the fuel, for what he didn't know, but the thought of running out terrified him.

Jack slid to his seat along the wall, let the tunnel go dark, and tried to slow his racing pulse.

———

There were times when being a trained psychologist came in handy, such as the times when deft mental manipulation justified her choices and her past. And there were times when it was as useful as a degree in stone rolling, such as now. Leslie contemplated this fact in the back of her mind where the subconscious did its thing.

Her head hurt. She wanted to satisfy Pete's childish expectations, but she couldn't bring herself to eat the mush. Unlike him, she wasn't a child who had been forced into a pattern of behavior before the mind was fully formed. Her brain had long ago learned that it was not healthy to ingest food that smelled like something sewers washed away. Her mouth and throat were already reacting—she couldn't will the stuff down if her life depended on it.

And it did, she thought.

She knelt on the floor in front of the mush and began to cry.

That seemed to soften Pete. He backed up and watched her for a few seconds. Minutes.

"Please," he said. "I don't want to hurt you, but you have to be a good wife and eat your pudding. It will make you strong. Do you want to die?"

She was crying too hard to respond.

"Don't cry; please don't cry." He sounded frantic.

"I can't eat it," she managed.

"But you're guilty," he said. "If you don't eat your sin, it will eat you; that's what Mama says. You ate the pudding already. I saw you. Everyone likes the pudding when they try it."

What was it with these people and sin? "I'm not guilty!" she cried, angry now. "I don't care what that witch who calls herself your mother has stuffed into your head. It's sickening!"

Even as she yelled, she knew that she had eaten the pudding. Quite eagerly. And she had eaten something like this pudding before, many times. Like a pig wallowing in its sty.

The thought enraged her. "If your mother forced you to eat this crap, she's a pig," she said.

He put his hands over his ears and paced. "No, no, no, no. Guilty, guilty. You have to eat, you have to eat."

"I'll throw up. I can't—"

He crouched in front of her, desperation etched in his face. "Please, please." He bent to one knee and scooped up some mush. "Please, see?" He eagerly shoved it into his mouth. His eyes begged her. Sweat beaded his forehead.

Okay now. Mind over matter. Eating this garbage was a pivotal part of Pete's psyche. It was part of his religion. As real as heaven and hell to him. An extension of society's obsession with faith in the nonexistent powers of God and Satan.

Leslie had never hated religion as much as she did at that moment.

She had to try; she had to show him that she at least wanted to please him.

"Are you innocent?" he asked.

"Yes," she said.

He stood, shocked. Apparently her claim offended him to the core. "You're better than me?"

She didn't know where he was headed. If she continued to defy him, he might find the need to correct her.

"No."

"Then why won't you eat like me?"

"Okay. Okay, I'll try."

His face relaxed.

Leslie looked at the bowl. She put three fingers into the pasty mush and scooped a portion the size of a candy out. She'd just eaten no less and relished it. And she knew it was no different. Yet now, at the sight, the odor forced bile up her throat. Her hand began to tremble.

She tried, she did. She closed her eyes and held her breath, lifted the stuff to her face, opened her mouth, and gagged.

The day without food had left her stomach empty, and she dry-heaved twice. Then she flung the stuff off her fingers, lay on her side, and began to sob.

Pete was pacing, fists gripped tight, muttering, "Bad wife."

With two long strides he crossed the room, stuck one hand into her waistband, clamped the other around her upper arm, and plucked her from the ground as if she were a Barbie doll.

He threw her on the bed and marched toward the round target board. "You have to learn," he said.

He quickly untied straps on the edge of the board.

"What are you doing?"

"You have to learn."

He grabbed her and slammed her against the board. Strapped her wrists tight. Then her ankles, spread-eagle. He was going to whip her?

"Please . . ."

He pulled a fistful of darts from a can on the ground, gave the wheel a turn, and stepped back.

Leslie's world spun.

"Tell me when you've learned," he said. No doubt he was replaying his own mother's treatment of him. But it invoked no sympathy whatsoever.

"Stop! I've learned . . . I'm guilty!"

Pete either wasn't convinced or wanted to play anyway. He threw his first dart.

It struck her thigh.

Leslie screamed.

14

Two sounds reached out to Jack as he sat in the black silence. The first was a distant scream. A woman's this time.

The second was the faint humming again. Closer, much closer than the scream.

He flicked the lighter and stood, listening intently.

Could it be pipes?

He stepped away from the wall and stopped.

Hmm, hmm, hmm. No. Not pipes. The

sound of a child humming, faint but clear. As if it was in the tunnel!

"Hello?"

His voice echoed, and the humming stopped.

He crept down the tunnel, nerves on edge.

Hmm, hmm, hmm. Ahead and on the right. How was that possible? He'd already been up and down this tunnel.

A small door edged into the circle of light cast by the dwindling flame. How could he possibly have missed it?

Or was it the door he'd been pulled through, reappeared?

Jack lifted the light.

The door was smaller than the one he'd come through, no more than four feet high. He stopped in front of it.

Hmm, hmm, hmmm.

Then silence.

"Hello?" he whispered, but his voice still sounded disruptively loud in the hollow chamber.

He put his hand on the knob, heart pounding.

This is ridiculous, Jack. Just open it.

He twisted the doorknob and pulled.

A small storage space. A girl, seated on

the floor, leaning against the back wall. Her face was pale, and her eyes were closed.

Dead.

The flame in Jack's hand went out, throwing him into darkness. He thumbed the lighter, desperate for light, light, any bit of light. *C'mon, c'mon.* Standing in a doorway facing a dead girl wasn't the time for . . .

The flame caught.

The girl's eyes were open, staring at him but not seeing. Dull circles of gray.

He cried out and slammed the door. Stumbled back to the opposite wall.

Hmm, hmm, hmm.

More singing? She was alive? Then why had she appeared dead? And how could she have hummed if she was dead?

You're losing your mind, Jack. Reality is being distorted by your fear. She's alive!

Still, opening the door again seemed like . . .

Like what? She was a victim, trapped and in need of help, and she'd been calling to them since they first entered the house. But why wasn't she yelling?

Hmm, hmm, hmm.

Jack stepped up to the door, forced his

fears down, then flung it open and jumped back.

The storage space was gone. In its place was a small room filled with junk, lit by an oil lamp. The girl stood now, braced with a board in her hands, ready to strike him. Her face was pale and smudged, but not dead, and her eyes were brown and clear, not gray like the grave. Her dark-brown hair was swept up on both sides and tied at the back. Maybe thirteen years old, but she couldn't be an inch over five feet tall.

She blinked, judging him. But she didn't seem frightened. Resolved to hit him if necessary, but not frightened. By the looks of the rumpled blankets and empty soda cans, she'd been hiding in the room for some time.

"Are . . . are you okay?"

The girl mumbled something that he couldn't understand. He wasn't sure she was entirely lucid.

"Are you okay?"

"Do I look okay?" she asked. "What's your name?"

"Jack. I'm . . ." He glanced up the hall. "I'm trapped down here."

She lowered the board. Cautiously walked

out of the room, glanced in either direction, and looked up at him. She seemed to be okay.

"Who are you?" he asked.

Again she said something softly, then she paused and spoke clearly. "Susan," she said. "Are you alone?"

"No. There are four of us."

She walked up to Jack, dropped the board on the ground, and wrapped her arms around his waist. She clung to him.

He put his hand on her head, awkward. She was clearly a victim in the same predicament as they were. He let the lighter die, and took her in both of his arms.

"Thank God," she breathed. "Thank God."

He wanted to say something that would comfort her, but his nerves were so shot that he was at a loss. All he could do was stroke her hair, forcing back the knot in his own throat.

"It'll be okay," she whispered. "It'll be . . ." He didn't catch the rest.

What a strange thing for her to say. The poor girl was delusional. He hated to think of what events had brought her here. Or kept her here.

"I . . . you looked like you were sleeping or

something when I first opened the door," he said. "Then you were standing. Were you singing? Why didn't you yell?"

Susan stepped back. "There's something wrong with this house," she said. "You know that much, don't you?"

"Wrong?"

"It's haunted."

Jack wasn't a big believer in haunted houses. As a matter of simple fact, there was no such thing.

"How long have you been here?" he asked

She looked toward one of the locked wooden doors. "We should hurry. They might find us now."

The poor girl's fear had been replaced by desperation, he thought. Had the killer done this? Brought her here as part of his game? Jack swallowed.

"Do you know how to get out of this tunnel?"

She reached into a pocket sewn on the front of her white cotton dress, withdrew a key, and held it up. "They don't know about this room."

Jack sighed with relief. "Smart girl. Okay. Do you know where the tunnel leads?"

"Yes. But you have to be fast."

"Do you know the whole house?"

"No."

Jack paused for a fraction of a second. Could he trust her? Of course he could trust her; she was in the same predicament as he was. He couldn't possibly look into her eyes and *not* trust her.

"Do you know where Pete is? Or Leslie?"

"Who's Leslie?"

Of course. "One of us four. I'm pretty sure she's down here somewhere." Jack looked up the tunnel. "What kind of basement is this?"

"A freaky one, that's for sure. Follow me."

"Hold on. Do you know how to get *out* of the house?"

"Don't *you* know how to get out of the house?"

She had expected him to take her to safety. "No, not yet," he said.

She nodded, remarkably composed.

"We have to find Leslie first."

"Follow me," she said.

15

Stephanie sat in the closet, trembling. And crying.

Her predicament had become completely . . .

There was no word to describe how bad her situation was. *Death,* maybe. She was actually dying. Or had died and was now in hell. The hell the priests of her childhood had warned her about.

She couldn't think straight. It was dark; she only had to open her eyes to remember that. Except for a distant hiss that sounded

like it might be rain, the house was quiet.
But Betty and Stewart were out there. She'd
heard them thundering around after they
broke free of the meat locker. After a while
she could hear them creeping around, smell
them when they passed. They stopped in
front of the closet once but didn't enter. She
didn't know why. None of it could be real,
but she was having a hard time convincing
herself of that.

The house seemed alive, looking for her.
Eccentrics or inbreds or devils, it didn't matter; they were all the same to her. She
thought they might be in the dining room,
sliding around, waiting for her to make a
sound.

She mumbled a silent prayer. "Oh God oh
God oh God." But she didn't really mean *oh
God.*

She really meant, *I'm going to strangle
you, Jack. I hate you, I hate you, I hate you!
I hate you for meeting me, for screwing up
my life, for dragging me out here, for leaving
me in this closet! For blaming our daughter's
death on me. For your unforgiving bitterness. For the way you look at Leslie.*

But her nerves were too frayed to con-
sciously process that long thought over and

over, so she just compressed it all into a habitual pseudo-prayer. *Oh God.*

She'd whispered a thousand such prayers since stepping foot into this black space. She even tried to dredge up something from the Book of Common Prayer, which contained a few sentiments she'd memorized, oh, so long ago, but those words eluded her. In any case, she didn't have any illusions that some great being would actually swoop down from the sky, reach his long hand through the roof, and pluck her safely from the closet.

She needed something to hold on to, and it wasn't Jack. And it wasn't a song. Within minutes of Jack's abandoning her in this pit, she'd realized that such a childish, foolish means of escape was no match for this particular reality. In fact, reduced to her shriveling self, she found the idea of singing repulsive.

And she found her raw surging emotion at least somewhat comforting. So she held on to this hatred she felt for Jack.

She hated him for his bitterness.

She hated him for not leaving her, knowing good and well she deserved nothing less.

She hated him for going after Leslie. The tramp might actually seduce him.

She hated him for leaving her to rot in this black closet.

She hated him for making her so angry, because anger meant she still cared for that stubborn, pigheaded mule.

Her mind had snapped again; she knew that much. It snapped first a year ago, when she stood staring at cracked ice over the pond where just a moment earlier her daughter had been standing.

It wasn't really her fault, they all said. There was snow on the ice, and she was from the South—no way to know that the ice was too thin.

No way she could be blamed for posing Melissa on what she thought was snow so that she could take a picture of the toddler in her darling little yellow coat.

No way she could know that the camera would run out of juice at that moment, forcing her to remove her attention from Melissa for those thirty seconds as she replaced the batteries.

She'd spent every waking moment since the tragedy breathing denial; she did know that much. Everything was going to be all right. She just had to move on in the flow of life. Slap on a smile and sing. But here, in this suffocating space, all of that nonsense had been jerked from her.

Give me one dead body, and I might let rule two slide. She'd given her dead body—Melissa—but that wouldn't impress this killer.

While that inbred Stewart had been busy calling them all atheists, Stephanie thought more than once that he might be right. She thought she believed in God. At least she used to, when she was a kid. But someone had once said something to her about being a Christian and still being a "practical athe-ist," that is, someone who believed in God but didn't follow his ways. Heck, even the demons believed in God and shook, didn't the Bible say that?

She was shaking now. Not because she was a demon, but because she was pretty sure something similar to demons was out-side the closet.

Her problem was that she wasn't com-pletely sure she did believe in God. The only demon she knew was herself.

And Jack.

"Oh God oh God oh God . . ."

16

When Randy hit the concrete wall he was running at a full clip in pitch darkness, away from the thumping boots.

Fifteen or twenty seconds at a fast run, then *smack!* He bounced back a few feet and dropped to his butt, dazed and barely conscious. The shotgun clattered to the ground, and he ran his hands about quickly, searching for it.

He needed that gun, needed it like he needed air. He had the knife, but with any luck he wouldn't ever be close enough to

Stewart for the blade to do any good. And if the gun didn't work, he'd use it like a bat. Old Stew had a thing or two to learn about baseball.

More than a few times he'd been tempted to stop in his tracks, turn around, and wait for the running feet to catch up before blasting away. Or whaling away.

Either/or, the fact that he was thinking again was encouraging. In some ways he felt more alive running down this tunnel than he had for years playing tough guy. Why?

Terror. Cold-blooded fear was pumping him full of life. Not panic. Just plain, unrelenting fear. The kind that propelled him pell-mell down a pitch-black tunnel.

Straight into a wall.

Randy found the gun. He staggered to his feet, aware that something cool was running over his lips. Sweat or snot or blood.

He faced the coming boots, which he'd decided must belong to Stewart. *We got us one, Betty!* Somehow Randy didn't figure White as the kind who would chase his prey down a tunnel. He'd more likely just show up at the other end.

Randy was fumbling for the trigger, bringing the gun up, when he felt the door handle dig into the small of his back.

Randy grabbed at it, twisted, pulled a door open, and stepped through the opening.

Rather, tripped through the opening. The threshold consisted of a foot-high retainer. He splashed headlong into some water.

Gray light filtered into the puddle from a shaft a hundred feet or so to his left. Must be a sewer, or a drain. Water ran from right to left, maybe six inches deep. Soaked his good shoes.

The pounding feet slowed. Randy lunged to his left just as a shotgun blast crashed through the tunnel, spraying the water on his right.

A snarl of frustration chased the sound.

Not a cry, not a shout, not a *take that, you rat.*

A guttural snarl. It was Stewart, had to be Stewart, and the sound reminded Randy why he'd had no desire to face the man earlier. Maybe the shotgun-as-baseball-bat idea needed refinement.

Randy splashed down the passageway toward the shaft of light. There was a room beyond it, and another light source, both of which he had to reach before Stewart rounded the corner and got off a second . . .

Bam!

Several pellets smacked his left shoulder, and he yelled with pain. But he made the room and pulled up behind the wall on his right before a third shot could be fired. Stewart was sloshing through the water behind him. Walking now.

Taking his time.

Another single bulb in the ceiling. Water streamed down the walls. It was at least a foot deep in here and rippled around old oil drums, pickaxes, large-bit drills, a jackhammer. A hard hat with a cracked lamp floated by.

A two-foot-wide round pipe ran into the concrete wall on one side. But there was a door on the opposite wall. A tall wooden hatch with a curved top, the kind that belonged in dungeons.

Randy glanced back around the corner. No mistaking Stewart's oxlike form striding down the passage, pump-action shotgun in both hands. Fifty feet off.

He had two choices: he could take his chances with this ancient, untried shotgun, or he could see what lay behind the door.

The only thing that gave him pause was Stewart's slow pace.

What did he know?

Who cared? Randy ran to the door and jerked it open, grateful that it wasn't locked.

But that's where his gratefulness ended. Stewart, walking straight for him over there, walked toward him in this passage too, now only forty feet away. How—? Stewart shifted the gun to one hand and used the other to unbuckle his belt and slide it out of his waistband, which was crazy 'cause the man had a shotgun, why would he need a belt?

Randy was so horrified by the optical illusion that he fired the shotgun without aiming.

Click. The antique would not fire.

Randy slammed the door shut and jumped back. How was that possible? Two Stewarts? Or was that White? He'd imagined it all. No. Stewart was still coming from the other side.

Now Randy began to panic. This was the end. The only other way out was . . .

He jerked his head to the large pipe that ran into the wall. He could fit into that. Without another thought Randy leaped across the room, threw his shotgun through the opening, climbed onto one of the drums, and shoved his head and arms into the hole.

It was a tight fit with his broad shoulders, but he squirmed through like a snake and dropped out five feet later into a concrete room with two feet of standing water. Above and below the open pipe, metal rods em-bedded in the wall formed steps, possibly for servicing. Two sources of light here: the hole through which he'd just come, and a grate directly overhead, facing the stormy night sky.

Bolted into a concrete ceiling.

Water poured into the room through two six-inch pipes. Rainwater? All the walls were concrete. There were no other open-ings. What was this place? A septic tank of some kind?

Something eclipsed the light from the pipe.

Stewart was coming after him? He spun, searching again for any way out. Nothing. He was in a sealed coffin. With water pour-ing in, fast.

And Stewart coming through the only exit.

Randy felt for the shotgun. He'd thrown it through, heard it splash. Good for nothing more than a club now, but he could use a club.

The water was rising quickly.

His fingers bumped the shotgun, and he jerked it out of the water before realizing that he held a spade. Just as good.

Randy screamed and jabbed the sharp end into the hole. The thought of striking his father with a shovel made him tremble, but he had no choice, right? This bigger man was going to kill him!

And Stewart wasn't his father. He was losing his marbles.

A blast of hot lead tore at his side. He jumped back and to one side, slapping at his shirt. Small flesh wound. He was lucky. The next one would cut him in half.

Still the man was coming in, gun first, trigger-happy, and all Randy had was a spade. He'd smack the gun from Stewart's hands when it came out.

It occurred to Randy that the water was now at his waist. And that it was aiming to flow *out* the hole that Stewart was now blocking.

The ingrate grunted. He wasn't coming through so fast. Randy waited for the gun barrel to emerge.

Water was still rising.

Still no gun barrel.

Waiting there in waist-high water, Randy began to anticipate a scenario that frightened him more than the shotgun. Not that he was any expert on death, but of all the ways he'd ever imagined going out, drowning struck him as one of the least favorable.

Stewart snarled with frustration again.

The barrel poked through the hole, and Randy's vision of drowning disappeared. He raised the spade, waited until the bulk of Stewart's weapon was out, and swung down.

Metal clashed against metal. A flash lit the chamber, harmlessly drilling the concrete with lead. Judging by the amount of trouble Stewart was having getting through the pipe, Randy doubted he'd have room to pump the action for a fresh shell.

He grabbed the barrel with both hands and tugged with all his weight. The shotgun came free, and Randy flew back into the rear wall.

He had his gun. A gun that he knew worked. Salvation was in his hands. He pumped the action, chambering a shell.

Stewart's hands were out and clawing at

the mouth of the pipe, pulling himself forward. Randy could see his big beady eyes a
couple of feet inside, filled with fear.

He lined the barrel up with the man's triple
scar and was about to pull the trigger when
his good business sense managed to over-
power his passion. The last thing he needed
was a dead body wedged in that pipe.

"Help me!" Stewart roared.

Help you?

"I'm stuck!"

Randy knew there wasn't an ounce of fat
on Stewart's massive torso. It wasn't lack of
power that had momentarily stalled his
progress. It was lack of leverage. He did indeed need help.

Randy was too stunned to respond. A moment ago he was ready to blast the man's
head from his shoulders given the opportunity. Now that same man wanted his help.

"That room's gonna flood! Push me back!"

"Are you nuts?"

"Please . . ." Stewart jerked, trying to
move. "You're gonna drown. Push me!"

Randy looked up at the grate. Rain
streamed between the bars. There was no
way past the bolts. He looked down at the
pipe with that bald head bobbing frantically.

Stewart suddenly let out a terrifying roar, an unnatural roar. His head began to tremble, then shake. And then it was over, and he just stared up at Randy.

"Please," he said. "I swear, if you don't get me out of this pipe, you'll drown. Push me."

"You were trying to kill me!" Randy said, as if this were helpful information.

"I'll get you out; I swear I'll show you how to get out. You got no clue how to get outta this basement, you know. None. You're stuck down here till you die. But I know how. Push me. Please, you gotta get me out!"

Maybe Randy could shoot the man once he pushed him through. One thing was certain: Stewart's body would block the water. Unless he backed out, they would both drown.

Randy pushed the barrel into the hole. "Grab this and push yourself. And remember, my finger's on this trigger."

The man grabbed the barrel and pushed. But it was Randy, not Stewart, who moved.

"You have to push me!" the man said.

"How?"

"My head. Put your hands on my head and push."

The idea of pushing his bald head seemed obscene.

Water was at his chest, about to spill into the pipe.

Not wanting to get the shotgun wet, Randy balanced it on one of the bars protruding from the wall over the hole. He braced himself on a lower step, reached into the pipe, and placed both hands on the bald head of the man who'd been bent on his killing.

"Remember, I have the gun."

"Push!" Stewart yelled.

Randy pushed. He could bench 400 and was putting about that much pressure on Stewart's head now. Any ordinary neck might have buckled.

The man moved about six inches then stopped with a cry of pain.

"What?"

"My shoulder. I think you dislocated my shoulder!"

"You're stuck," Randy said.

"I know I'm stuck, you sinner!"

"Settle down. I'm trying to get us out of here!"

They were yelling. Water lapped at the pipe.

"What if I pull you?"

"I'll never get out . . ." The man was whimpering now. "Please, you have to help me. Push me."

"I did!"

"Try again."

Randy tried again, but it became immediately apparent that there was no pushing Stewart out as long as his broad shoulders were wedged tight.

Randy considered the knife tucked in his belt, the one he'd snagged from the kitchen. Maybe he could cut Stewart out. Shoot him dead and cut him out.

He pondered this. Randy had never killed a man. Not in defense, not in war, not in rage. And certainly not one stuck in a pipe crying for help, never mind that he was the devil himself.

He suddenly wasn't sure he could do it. The idea of sticking that barrel into that pipe and blowing Stewart away was horrifying. Absolutely out of the question. He began to panic.

Easy, boy. Just take a deep breath. *Give me one dead body.* This would be the one. Self-defense. You do it or you die, as simple as that.

"Please . . ."

"Shut up!" Randy screamed.

"Please . . ."

Stewart's own words from earlier in the evening came back to Randy. *You like water, don't you?*

Water. He might not have the strength to kill the man outright, but he could let him drown.

Dead or alive, the man was stuck. But Randy had a knife. And a spade.

"Please!" The man's voice was garbled now, with water splashing around his mouth. "Get me out of here!"

Randy began to shake.

17

"I swear! I'm guilty! Stop it, stop it!"

Leslie was sobbing, not so much from the pain of the two darts protruding from her body, but from the dread of any further damage.

He was a demented boy, and she was the puppy he'd chosen to extract allegiance from. If there were such things as demons, Pete was undoubtedly a demon trapped in a person who had the body of a man and the mind of a child.

Pete stopped the rotating wheel when she was upright.

"You promise?" he asked.

"I promise!"

"Say it again."

"I'm guilty."

"As sin."

"As sin."

"Will you show me how bad you are?"

Meaning what? She sniffed and took a deep breath. *What did he mean by that?*

"Will you eat the cereal?"

His mother had made him eat the rotten dog food to remind him that he was no better than it was. By forcing him to embrace the notion that he was evil, he became evil. Or more accurately, he believed he was evil, and therefore was predisposed to exhibit antisocial behavior—the real definition of *evil* to her way of thinking—in a sane world stripped of religion.

Leslie was now absolutely certain that he could not be saved from those false beliefs anytime soon.

"Yes," she said, sniffing. Saying it brought relief. "I will. And I'm sorry for being such a disobedient wife."

He stared at her. A dumb grin formed on his face.

"Okay."

He untied her wrists and legs and set her on the floor. Then he walked toward the bowl of dog food.

"Can you take these darts out first?" Leslie asked, sitting on the bed. Adrenaline had eased the pain in her thigh, but now the dart in her biceps was throbbing. She could have pulled them out, but she wanted him to do it. Anything to stall him.

Pete returned to the bed, leaving the bowl for the moment. She lay down, unsure if she could avoid breaking down again.

He sat beside her and reached for her arm. But he didn't pull the dart out. He touched her bare skin lightly. Traced it gently.

Instead of recoiling at his touch, she welcomed it. Maybe . . . maybe if she endeared him. Disarmed him with a show of tenderness. When was the last time he'd felt any tenderness toward a human being? From a woman, never.

Leslie reached across her body and rested her hand on his hand. "I'll be a good wife. Would you like that?"

His breathing thickened.

"Take it out."

He carefully pulled the dart from her muscle. She was only dimly aware of her ability to ignore the pain. She was beyond caring about anything so trivial as pain. He'd tried to make her eat rotten dog food and he'd thrown darts at her—by themselves not as terrible as the things she'd imagined White had planned for them. But she felt violated. Worse.

Shredded. Now she contemplated loosing the cords that held her psyche intact and relinquishing her resolve to him completely.

Why? So that she didn't have to eat the dog food? No. Because she felt a desperate need to cling to someone. To find herself in anything but her own shattered soul.

The truth made no real sense to her, not yet. Nothing in the textbooks remotely mirrored the emotions running through her now, while lying on his bed.

Pete pulled the dart from her thigh.

It occurred to her that she couldn't smell the odor anymore. She'd grown accustomed to it.

"You are so pretty," he said slowly.

She reached up and ran her fingers over

his head, both repulsed and pleased by her strength to do so anyway.

"And you're so strong." Her head spun.

"The cereal makes me strong," he said.

"Love makes me strong," Leslie said.

That stopped him. His eyes searched hers. "Do . . . do you love me?"

"I'm your wife, aren't I?"

Pete lowered his face into her neck. "You are my wife."

He just sat there bent over her, unmoving, clueless. She was nothing but a favorite toy to him. His cheek was pressed against her cheek, and she could smell the sickly sweet sweat on his neck. What was she doing?

Leslie eased her head away from him and dry-heaved.

Pete straightened, frowned. He rose and went to the little-girl's dresser, opened a drawer, and began rifling around in it.

She began to sob quietly. She was in nothing more or less than the same predicament shared by an endless sea of humans who hid in their own prisons of abuse and alcohol and sex and money and whatever other kind of addiction or vice that both tormented and comforted at once. She was no better or worse than any other person who lived behind whitewashed walls to hide the problems in their basement from the neighbors.

Pete returned, holding a rope.

"More pudding, Leslie?"

—~—

Randy did not move, knowing that Stewart was squirming in the shaft now submerged in water. The man's screams had been swallowed by a throat full of rainwater and then silenced.

Father was dead. Dead, dead, had to be dead. And the water was now around Randy's neck. If he didn't get down there and dig out the cork called Stewart, he would drown as well.

He had a spade. Using a spade underwater might take a few minutes, so he really should get started. But the thought of actually going under and digging at Stewart's torso brought with it a strange brew of fear and eagerness that kept him rooted.

The fact was, he wanted to do it. The fact was, he wasn't sure he could. The fact was, the water was now up to his nose, and in a

few minutes it would fill the concrete holding tank.

Randy took a deep breath and dived,
spade in hand. He opened his eyes, but the
water was muddy brown. He'd have to feel
for the hole. Feel for the head.

The prospect of lining up a jab with the
shovel by touch alone forced Randy back to
the surface.

Water poured in.

He gasped, fighting a fresh burst of panic.
He had to do this. He had to get down there
and hack away Stewart's dead body. He
was dead, for goodness' sake!

Randy went down again, felt for the hole,
and found nothing but solid wall. Was he on
the wrong wall? How—

The water began to swirl around him. He
jerked up and found the surface again. It
took only a moment for him to realize that
the tank was draining, and draining fast.

Water dripped off his head, splashed into
a rushing river of muddy water that was being pulled toward the wall ahead. Toward
the hole.

He stood, immobilized legs spread, spade
firmly in his grasp. The large pipe that Stewart had clogged just a few moments ago

was uncorked. Stewart's body had been pushed out! The buildup of water had freed him?

Randy wasn't taking any chances—no way, not now. He peered cautiously out of the hole and searched for Stewart. For all he knew, the man hadn't really drowned and was waiting outside.

But then he saw the body, lying in the room where it had evidently been washed by the receding water.

Randy watched the body for a full minute before deciding it was most definitely dead. He retrieved the shotgun from overhead and pushed the weapon out with the spade. He climbed the service steps, then squirmed through the pipe.

He'd killed the man, right? *You like water, Stewart, huh? You think that's funny?*

Now what? He had to get out of this place before everything flooded. And what about that other Stewart he'd seen, coming from the other door? His mind was playing tricks, right? Had to be.

Back to square one. Two ways out of the room. He checked the shotgun. One shell left. The fact that no one had appeared to help Stewart from behind or stood waiting for Randy when he spilled through the pipe was a good sign.

Not that he would have minded facing an accomplice right now. He had a gun. Bring a few on.

He stood in the muddy water, thinking things through.

"What are you doing, Randy?" he asked softly. "You're in a lot of hot water down here."

That right?

"Yeah, that's right. You heard the man. There's no way out of here."

That right?

"Listen to yourself. You think you're on to something?"

Whatever. The facts were still unchanged. He had to find the others. He had to find Leslie. Assuming they were still alive, which he doubted. More important, he had to find a way past White. Nothing would be the same after today, that was for sure. Nothing ever.

He walked to the door that he'd first come through, poked his head around the corner. Empty. But he wasn't going back there.

He crossed the room to the other door, which meant he had to pass Stewart. He trained the gun on the body, which lay face-down. Maybe he should put a blast into it just to make sure. Of course, he only had one shot. And the noise might alert whoever else was crawling around down here.

Randy crept forward, trigger finger ready, totally ready. The form did not move. He stuck his foot out and nudged it. Dead for sure. He shoved the body over with his right leg.

The light was dim, but there was no mistaking Stewart's big bald head, gruesome scar, and grungy bib-overalls. A thin tendril of smoke drifted from the corner of Stewart's twisted, parted lips. A dark fog. Black smoke.

Randy took a step back and stared at the odd sight. There was something evil in that fog, but his mind was numb and he couldn't attach any reason to it. Maybe White had sneaked in, shot Stewart at close range. That might be gunpowder smoke.

He looked out the door, up the tunnel. No one there.

Randy wasn't sure if that was good or bad. There was no evidence Stewart had even been shot. He was drowned, not shot!

Randy dug into Stewart's pockets and

pulled out a plastic box of cartridges. Good, definitely good. Now he had the shotgun and about what, fifteen or so shells. Bring 'em on, baby.

He reloaded, then headed up the tunnel.

Shotgun in hand, he wasn't as scared as he thought he should be. Killing that pig back there had felt—

A low whisper cut through the tunnel. "Give me one dead body, Randy."

He spun and discharged the shotgun with his right hand. It nearly jerked his arm off. Nothing there.

In fact . . . In fact, there was no body at all! Stewart's body was gone! Could his accomplice have come back? Was that possible?

"That one didn't count." Again, behind him.

He dropped the spade, whirled, and fired again before the garden tool hit the ground. Nothing but black empty space.

"I'm losing my mind," he whispered.

Interesting. He wasn't so upset about losing his mind. Not even sad.

"God help me, I'm losing my mind."

18

The girl named Susan led Jack through a short hall that opened up into the first room that Jack and Randy had entered upon descending into the basement, the one with all the sofas.

He pulled up, confused by their entry point. He didn't remember the door they now came through. The four bright sofas were the same, as were the paintings that covered the walls. The potbellied stove.

Susan hurried through the room toward the main door, gliding with confidence, yet tentative at once. Jack watched her move, unsure how he should feel about finding such an innocent but knowing girl who on one hand seemed as though she'd been made for this place and on the other hand looked the clear victim.

"Hold on."

She turned around. Now in the full light he saw that her dress had been scuffed and torn. Brown streaks dirtied her cheeks. "Yes?"

"I don't remember seeing this hall." He glanced back at the door they'd passed through. "I could swear that was a closet."

"It's confusing, I know," she said.

Jack walked past her to the main door. "Haunted."

"Haunted," she said.

He pulled the door open and looked at the main hall. The stairs ascended on the left to the main floor.

The girl was saying something, but Jack had his mind on those stairs. He glanced down the hall, saw that the other doors were all closed, then ran up the stairs. The door at the top was closed. He tugged on it, but it was locked. Figured.

"Locked," the girl said. She was at the

base of the stairs. "We can't get caught out here."

Jack pounded on the door. "Stephanie!"

If she was still in the nearby closet, she didn't hear or respond. Knowing her, she'd fled and was lying dead on the flagstone walk.

"We have to go," the girl said. "I might know where your friend is."

He descended the stairs two at a time. "Which door?"

She was already gliding to the last one on the left. Opening it, she ran in, down another hall strung with small bulbs on a wire, like a string of Christmas lights. He followed her around three corners.

Susan passed through a low door and ducked into a crawl space. The low-slung ceiling was strung with pipes. She hurried forward, bent over to keep from hitting her head.

"In there," she whispered, pointing to a small door. "It goes into the closet."

Jack stood by the door, catching his breath. "What closet?"

"It's where he hides."

"Who?"

"The slow one."

Pete? "Where are we, Susan?"

"In the basement," she said.

"I know that. I mean this house. There's a killer stalking us, for heaven's sake. We had our tires slashed and just happened to wander into this house conveniently tucked away with inbreds waiting for the next unfortunate soul to walk into their trap. And then there just happens to be you."

She stared at him with those wide eyes. "Getting out of the basement is a problem."

Okay, then. So he'd deal with the big picture later. "You mean we're stuck down here? How did he get you down here?"

"I mean you shouldn't have come down."

"Trust me, it wasn't exactly my first choice." He looked at the door. "We couldn't just leave Leslie. What's through this door?"

"It goes into a closet."

"And?"

"There's something wrong with this house, Jack. You see things. If you just walk in there, he'll kill you."

"Who? Pete? How do you know he's with her?"

Her eyes suggested she knew a thing or two about Pete.

"How did you get down here?" he asked.

She hesitated. "I've been down here for three days. You're not the only one who wandered into their trap."

"So you got away?"

She stared at him without answering. *Dumb question, Jack. Of course she hadn't gotten away.* Her clear eyes searched his. He detected the weight of her ordeal and now felt as responsible for her rescue as for Leslie's, even though he really had no clue what to do.

Jack looked at the small door that led to the back of Pete's closet. *And a child shall lead them.* He'd heard that lyric before somewhere. Maybe it was in one of Stephanie's songs. In many ways Susan reminded him of a child, grown now, but innocent. Like Melissa . . .

He cut the thought short.

"Okay, I'm going to see what I can see. You're sure I'll be in a closet?"

"It could be open."

He nodded and reached for the wooden latch that held the door closed.

"Maybe I should go with you," she said.

"No. Is there really no way out of this basement?"

"One dead body," she said.

So, she was part of this insane game as well. *Give me one dead body, and I might let rule two slide.*

Susan motioned to the shadows on their left. "There's a shaft over there. The house is wrong, remember that."

"You mean—"

"I mean evil."

Evil. Haunted. He didn't know what to think about that. Sure, *evil*, but what was evil, really? Right now he was more con-cerned with surviving people who had meat cleavers and shotguns.

"Okay, I'm just going to take a look. I'll be right back." He lifted the latch.

"Jack?"

"What?" he whispered.

Her hand touched his. "Promise you won't leave me."

Jack turned and saw that her eyes were misted with tears.

He drew her head close and kissed her hair. Another image of his own daughter crossed his mind. "I won't leave you. I prom-ise. Just like I won't leave Leslie. Okay?"

"Okay."

"Don't go anywhere."

Jack pulled the door open and stuck his

head into the closet. Junk was piled up on both sides. Some stale-smelling jackets and overalls hung directly in front of him.

Jack withdrew his head. "I'm going in so I can see past the clothes."

Susan didn't say anything.

He eased into the closet, parted two old jackets. He could see light from a dozen thin cracks in the door paneling now. Could hear the sound of a man's muffled voice. Pete's.

Which meant Leslie was probably in there.

Jack glanced around again for a weapon— anything that would come in handy. Saw a board with a handle. A cricket bat. He didn't know why a cricket bat would be here, and he didn't care; he only knew it was here if he needed it.

He stepped gingerly past the coats, will-fully stifled his breathing, and pressed one eye up to a thin crack.

At first he saw only Pete, sitting on the side of the bed with his back to the closet, mumbling. But then Pete stood and crossed out of Jack's sight, leaving him a direct view of the bed.

Leslie was strapped to the bedposts by her wrists and ankles. Still in her white slacks and the red blouse. She was shaking with sobs.

Jack stared, momentarily overwhelmed.

"You have to be a good wife and eat," Pete said, passing the door with a bowl in his hands. He scooped some paste out. He'd tied her down and was trying to force her to eat something!

Jack didn't know what had reduced Leslie to the quivering form on the bed, but it occurred to him that he was shaking too. With revulsion.

Not just revulsion. With rage.

19

Stephanie had fought back the temptation to leave the closet in search of Jack a hundred times when the loud *thump* sounded in the dining room. She jumped. Had she dozed off? A muffled call reached her.

"Stephanie!"

Who was that? She peeled her eyes wide in the blackness, fully alert. Who was that? That was Jack!

Something creaked. She held her breath. That was where the wall was, right? The closet door was on her left, and the wall was on her right.

There was a long creaking that ran on like a fingernail being slowly drawn down a chalkboard. It stopped.

She could hear feet running down the stairs. Jack was leaving?

"Jack!" she screamed. Her voice rang loud in the closet. "Jack!"

Now Stephanie was faced with a decision. She could get out of the closet and find the others, or she could sit here like she had for the last—how long had she been here? Minutes or hours? Her cell phone was still in her purse in the living room somewhere.

"Jack, don't you dare leave me again!" She swore.

He was gone.

She set her jaw and rage began to over-take her body, one limb at a time. First her hands and face, then her whole body. The anger didn't feel natural, but it brought her a sliver of warmth and courage, the empow-ering kind that came from taking charge of a bad situation. Her breathing was heavy, but for the moment she didn't care who heard her. She reoriented herself to the space. Coats. Boots. Back of closet. Sides.

She brushed something cold and metallic, and it fell over, scraping the wall and landing with a thud. She picked it up. Examined it with her fingers. A crowbar, maybe.

An image of the ax hammer crossed her mind. Only it was in her hands, not Stewart's. She was swinging it. Maybe at Jack's gut. Maybe at his head. Maybe—

She stopped herself. Someone was whispering. Outside the door. Jack?

But she knew it couldn't be Jack because it was more than one voice, and it was coming from more than one direction.

Something tickled her ankle. Slid up her leg. A long, thin reptilian slither.

Oh God oh God oh God! It was a snake, and it was working its way up her leg!

Stephanie couldn't move to yank it out. The closet filled with a terrible, raw scream. Hers.

The floor under her hands moved. Slithered. The closet floor was crawling with snakes; skinny snakes, cold and slippery snakes.

A place deep in Stephanie's psyche rose from the dead. The place where horror and rage collide with the drive to survive. The place were there are no rules, no absolutes, no God, no devil. Only Stephanie. The place where even great risk of death can be braved if it means the chance to save one's self.

Her scream became a snarl. She dropped the crowbar and she moved.

She slammed into the door. She cranked the handle and leaped out of the closet. Then spun back and looked at the floor, ready to stomp the snakes. But the closet was empty. They'd fled. She yelled at the floor for good measure.

Stephanie became aware that she was in the hall by the dining room, where the whispers had come from. She turned slowly. They too had fled. Or never had been.

The house creaked, the long creaking sound that she'd heard in the closet, only now it came from all four walls.

Stephanie made her decision then by a reasoning too complex for her to understand. But having made her decision, she moved quickly. She walked to the basement door, twisted the knob, and jerked. It was locked. A dead bolt. She disengaged the bolt. Then she threw open the door and marched down the stairs.

Jack was down here, and she was going

to tell Jack a thing or two about what was happening. About how she'd had enough. About how it was time to go home, killer or no killer. About how he could take his self-righteous bull—

The door behind her slammed shut. The sound of the dead bolt snapping into place was what it was. She couldn't pretend it was anything different.

She stopped on the steps and blinked. Her courage fled.

"Oh God oh God oh God . . ."

20

He wasn't sure that he really intended to rush out of the closet wielding a cricket bat, but he needed a weapon in his hands to satisfy his rage, so Jack reached back and grabbed the cricket bat.

But in his exuberance to get the thing in his hands, he pulled too quickly. And when the bat pulled free it dislodged something else.

That thing clunked.

For a moment everything came to a standstill. Pete stopped his mumbling. Leslie stopped her struggling. Jack stopped his breathing.

He could hear his watch ticking faster than it ought.

His plan of action became clear in that moment. He had to go, and he had to go now.

Jack dived at the door, shoulder leading, cricket bat already back, ready to swing. Whatever mechanism held the door closed snapped under his weight. He leaped across the room and swung the bat before reaching his target.

Pete didn't have time to throw up a guard. The thick board swooshed through the air and smashed against his skull with a loud *crack!*

He grunted and staggered. Fell to his hands and knees.

Jack reached the bed and ripped the frayed rope that bound both of Leslie's ankles to one bedpost. But her wrists were each tied to either post by her head, and Pete was already pushing himself to his feet.

Jack took another swing at the thug. *Smack!*

The stalk hit Pete in his gut, hardly the kind of blow that would send him reeling. But it surprised him.

Jack cocked the bat. "Get back!"

"Hit him again!" Leslie screamed. "Kill him!"

Jack flinched. Kill? He'd never lined a bat up on someone's head with that intent. Not that he didn't have every justification.

Leslie was trying to free her wrists.

Pete took a heavy step forward, like an ox.

Jack swung. The bat bounced off the man's arm and swung low into his right knee. Something cracked, and it wasn't the bat.

Pete blinked. He looked down at his knee.

"Move!" Jack snapped. "By the wall."

"Kill him, Jack!"

"Stop shouting!"

He had to think. He couldn't just beat the man to death. But maybe he could disable Pete and leave him strapped to the bed.

"Kill him!" Leslie was still frantic. One of her wrists started to bleed.

"Hold on!" he snapped. Then to Pete again: "Move!"

Pete limped to the large dart board. "She's . . . she's my wife," he said.

"Shut up!" Jack crossed to the bed. "Don't move."

He worked Leslie's tethers with one hand.

"You have to kill him, Jack," Leslie whispered. "You can't just leave him!"

"Shh, shh, it's okay!" One wrist free.

"No, it's not."

He ran to the other side of the bed and worked the rope with his free hand, eyes on Pete. The man was edging closer to the door.

"Don't move!"

From the corner of his eye, he saw movement at the door. Two dead bolts were engaged on this side. Both had flat brass knobs.

Both knobs were silently turning at the same time. Opening. Seemingly on their own.

He froze. How—

Pete grunted and staggered toward the door.

"Jack!" Leslie screamed.

The door swung in. Betty faced the room with a shotgun leveled hip-high. There was something about her face that looked different. Something wicked in her eyes. The look of a woman who was done playing hostess.

"Back," she said softly.

Jack dropped the bat and lifted his hands. "Okay."

It was all happening too quickly. She was going to pull the trigger.

"Stewart's right. You're all sinners," she said.

Pete dived at his mother. He struck the barrel with both hands as it discharged a load of lead that blasted the bedpost on Jack's right to smithereens.

Leslie tugged at her remaining tether. "Jack!"

"Don't kill my wife!" Pete roared.

Betty lifted the shotgun and brought its butt down on Pete's head. *Thunk!* He dropped to his knees just as Jack ripped the rope free from Leslie's wrist.

"They both have to die!" Betty said.

A soft voice from the closet stopped them all. "No, they don't."

Jack swiveled his head. Susan stood in the open door, staring at Betty, whose face had blanched with shock.

"White's the one who should die," Susan said, stepping into the room. She spoke calmly, but her eyes were wide.

Jack held out his hand. "Susan . . ."

Susan addressed Betty. "You know that if you kill me, White won't have any reason to let you live," Susan said. "As soon as I'm dead, he'll kill the rest of them. Isn't that his deal? And once the rest are dead, he's going to kill you too."

Betty stood like ice.

Susan looked at Jack. "But she can't kill me yet, because White still needs me for his game."

Slowly Betty relaxed. Began to scowl.

Susan threw herself forward.

"Susan! Don't!"

She collided with Betty, who staggered back into the hall.

Leslie rolled off the bed toward Jack, landed squarely on the floor, and broke toward the closet.

Jack stood frozen by the odd sight, this frail girl dressed in a tattered summer dress, throwing herself at the much larger woman. Three days in the basement had clearly redefined her need for self-preservation.

The bedroom door slammed shut behind Susan and Betty.

The shotgun discharged in the hall beyond.

"Jack!" Leslie warned.

Pete had pushed himself up and was plodding toward Leslie.

Jack leaped over the corner of the bed,

slammed into Pete. The man crashed into the wall.

"Through the closet!" Jack shouted.

Leslie was already in. Through the back. Into the crawl space.

"On the right!" Jack whispered, racing past. "Follow me!"

He grabbed Leslie's hand and ran crouched, fleeing the roars of Pete, who was ignoring his wounds and smashing his way into the closet.

They found a grate that covered a three-foot-wide shaft. Right where Susan had indicated it would be. An air duct or something similar. Jack pulled the grate free.

"Go!" he whispered.

She scrambled past him, stuck her head in the hole, then looked back at him, eyes wide. "Don't leave me." She was breathing heavily, still frenzied.

"I'm right behind you."

She ducked in.

Jack glanced back just as Pete barged into the crawl space. The oaf looked around, failed to see them, then headed in the opposite direction.

Jack entered the shaft, pulling the grate closed after him.

21

3:02 AM

Stephanie walked through the basement so utterly terrified that her fear rekindled her rage.

Room to room, hall to hall, not caring about the paintings or the improbable decor or the pentagrams. In fact, she had to ignore it all so that she could stay focused, because she knew that she was only one snake away from racing back upstairs, and upstairs was locked.

She realized that she might run into Stewart before she found the guys, but she accepted the risk. Or Randy or Jack, though at the moment she thought she would prefer finding Randy.

Or was she just wrong about that? Jack was as stubborn as any man who lived on the planet. He wouldn't back down, never did. In all truth, she needed him now, if for no reason other than to survive.

Randy, on the other hand, was the kind of man who would do anything to get ahead, which meant that if Jack failed her, Randy might be her ticket.

Leslie could rot in the grave as far as Stephanie was concerned. And judging by the look in Pete's eyes at the dinner table, she was probably already doing that.

Listen to her!

She decided in the last few minutes that she liked the new Stephanie, freed of her denial, of her always-all-right philosophy. Never again. She'd quenched her denial with a deep well of rage that now made her feel as alive as she could remember feeling in years. She could write songs about this for eons. She felt enough spunk at this moment to hit any man or woman who got in her way, and she wasn't sure she'd ever felt that way. Good-bye, sunshine.

She entered a long concrete hall and noticed the water leaking down the wall for the first time.

Water. She stopped. The water was pooling along the floor. The house groaned. Her resolve slipped a little. Maybe she shouldn't have come down. But it was a little too late now. She spied a door near the puddle. Open.

She walked to the door, looked into what looked like a root cellar, and stepped in.

The door slammed. She whirled. A draft must have pulled it shut. She wasn't about to consider anything else. The door to her right gaped wide. Someone had passed this way recently.

Stephanie hesitated, then walked though the door into another much narrower hall. The door at the end was open.

She'd taken three steps when a *bang* from behind startled her.

The door had blown shut. Two in a row.

She spun and ran toward the open door.

Jack dropped to the floor of the medium-sized boiler room and examined it in silence. Leslie stood to his right, taking in a dozen iron pipes that rose out of two large boilers on either side and disappeared into chases at the ceiling. A single clear bulb burned above, as in most rooms down here. Two doors stood opposite the boilers.

He saw it all without taking note. His mind was on Susan. It had taken every ounce of resolve on his part not to rush back through Pete's room to find out if she'd survived. He couldn't wrap his mind around what she'd done. He held tenaciously to a whisper of hope that her claims might be true. Maybe the inbreds would keep her alive as leverage. Maybe they knew something that he didn't.

Either way, he'd lost her. He'd promised never to leave her, and although he hadn't exactly, she was gone, maybe dead, maybe just locked up.

Maybe escaped again.

For a moment neither he nor Leslie seemed capable of moving. Not on account of the room, but because of what had just happened.

Beside him, Leslie put one hand on her hip, buried her face in her other hand, and silently wept. He lifted a hand to comfort her but thought it might be inappropriate. She turned from him, started to walk away, then returned.

Leslie didn't look at him; she only leaned against him and lowered her forehead into his neck. He swallowed a knot in his throat and held her with one arm.

"I'm sorry," he said. "I'm so sorry."

She put her arms around him and pulled him close, then seemed to cry harder.

"Leslie . . ." His arms were trembling, but she couldn't have noticed because her whole body was shaking.

He was suddenly eager to comfort her. His need came from more than desire, maybe not desire at all. It came from hours of raw nerves. It came from the dark halls and sickness of the basement. It came from the memory of her lying on Pete's bed.

It came from being trapped in the killer's game.

Jack squeezed her tighter. "I'm sorry . . ."

She caught her sob in her throat and kissed his neck. "No, no, don't be." She kissed his neck again, then his cheek, clinging. "Don't be sorry. Thank you, thank you." Her hands grabbed his shirt, and she kissed him on the cheek again.

She lowered her face into his neck and started to cry again.

They were two lost souls who had escaped death together only to believe that they would still probably die before the night was over. Leslie, the intelligent professor of psychology, and Jack, the bitter writer who'd saved her.

Now both lost again. And alone in this boiler room while the house creaked around them.

For the moment, he held on to her as if she were life itself. For the first time in many long months, Jack recalled what it was like to love someone besides his daughter. They were both victims—his daughter of Stephanie's carelessness, and Leslie of a sadistic maniac.

Leslie took his face in both hands and kissed him on the lips. She pressed her lips to his until they hurt. Then she kissed him frantically on the cheek and neck again.

"I love you, Jack. I love you."

Jack blinked. He pushed her gently away. "Shh, shh, shh."

"I love you . . ."

She resisted him, and he gently pried her

arms from his neck. "No, it's okay; it's okay. You can't mean that."

That settled her.

She dropped her arms, turned away, and lowered her face into her hands.

"I understand," he said. "I know how you feel—"

"You have no clue how I feel!" she said, spinning back. She thrust her arm up at the vent they'd crawled through. "Do you have any idea what I've been through?"

"Which is why you are so distressed right now. I can't use you like that!"

She stared at him hard, searching his eyes. Then her face softened, and she looked away. "I'm sorry."

In that moment the complete failure of his own marriage came into such sharp focus that Jack lost sight of anything he and Stephanie might have once had together. How long had it been since Stephanie had shown such passion, such a backbone? His bitterness toward her was fueled by her own retreat into denial. He wasn't sure why he'd stuck beside her all this time.

"No, it's okay." He put his hand on her back. "I don't—"

"What on earth do you think you're do-ing?"

They spun. A man, wet from head to foot, holding a shotgun over one shoulder and a spade over the other, glared at them from an open doorway.

"Randy?" Leslie said.

He walked in and kicked the steel door shut with the back of his heel. "Answer me! For crying out loud!"

"You're alive," Jack said. Randy looked like he'd walked through a sewer. His hair was wet and matted, his color-coordinated green shirts were brown, and the rivets on his crisp new jeans had been torn off, leav-ing jagged holes near the pockets.

"Disappointed?" Randy said. "I knew it." He slogged toward them and stopped in the middle of the room. Threw the spade down. "I'm gone for an hour, scraping for my life, and I come home to this?"

"Randy . . ." Leslie stepped away from Jack.

"It's not what you think," Jack snapped, feeding on his building resentment toward this man.

"You don't say." His eyes were glazed. "I oughta show you what I do think."

"I was violated, Randy," Leslie said.

"Raped?"

She balked at his offhand tone. "Just as bad."

"I've got news for you. The whole world thinks their uncle violated them. It gives us all an excuse to live like victims."

"Randy!" For a moment Jack thought she might fly at the man and slap his face. When she spoke her lips were trembling. "You're sick."

"You never did take down Uncle Robby, now did you, Leslie? No. But guess what? I have. Only it wasn't Uncle Robby, it was Uncle Stewart, and I can guaran-freaken-tee you he's deader than any man deserves to be." Randy grinned.

"Stewart's dead?" Jack asked.

Jack hadn't taken much notice of the doors opposite each boiler. The second swung in abruptly, and Stephanie ran through and pulled up, panting.

The door slammed shut behind her on its own. She looked back with wide eyes, then turned back to face them.

"Did you see that?"

Jack's mind scrambled. Stephanie, here. Stewart, dead. Randy, soaked.

Sweat made Stephanie's lacy blue top cling to her, and her long blond hair was a stringy mess, but she'd looked the same an hour ago.

"A draft," Leslie said, eyes fixed on the door.

"Not unless a draft has been following me all the way here," Stephanie said. She strode forward, glaring at Jack. "I've been in that closet forever!"

"Settle down—"

"Don't you dare tell me to settle down!" Her face was red and her arms were rigid. "You said you'd be right back! You swore you'd be back. That was an hour ago!"

He blinked, surprised by her forcefulness. Then irritated. "I've been just a tad busy."

Stephanie glanced at Leslie. "I'm sure you have."

"I caught them red-handed," Randy said.

"What do you mean?"

"I mean it seems Jack and Leslie here evidently have more than the big bad wolf on their minds."

"Shut up!" Jack snapped. "Look, Stephanie, things down here are a little complicated, okay? I've only been gone for—" He checked his watch. That couldn't be. He shook it. Still ticked. Must have busted when he got sucked into the black tunnel. "Does anyone know what time it is?"

Leslie looked. "Almost 3:15."

The four let this sink in.

"That's impossible," said Randy. "We've been here thirty, forty minutes tops."

"My watch says 3:15 too."

Stephanie put a palm on her forehead, started pacing. "I was in the closet for *four hours*? I can't believe you'd do that to me, Jack. I can't believe—"

"'I can't believe,'" Randy mimicked, voice pitched high and free palm on his forehead. Then he got in her face. "Listen to you, Barbie. You think you've had it worse than any of us? Huh? Well, believe this: we've got less than three hours to get ourselves out of this pit or we *die*. Have you completely forgotten that?"

Stephanie sagged against the door, scowling.

Jack glared at her, picked up his explanation for Randy. "Pete . . ." He stopped, reticent to justify himself at Leslie's expense.

"Pete what?" Randy asked.

"I'm okay," Leslie said, glancing at Jack.

"Sure you are," Stephanie said. "Who

wouldn't be okay with dear Jack to the rescue?"

"Will you please shut your mouth?" Jack
said. Both Randy and Stephanie knew what
had been on Pete's mind when he eyed
Leslie in the dining room. Maybe the truth
was slowly seeping past Randy's thick skull.
Stephanie, on the other hand, knew and
didn't seem to care.

Jack walked over to the door that Stephanie had come through and locked it.
"We're all alive," he said, heading for the
second door. As far as he could see, this
was the only way in or out besides the shaft.

"For the record, Leslie and I were just ex-
pressing common human emotions of survival. If either of you have a problem with
that, save it for tomorrow."

He locked the second door and turned
back to them.

"Right now we have to figure out how to
survive the next three hours."

22

3:43 AM

It took them half an hour of argument and speculation to figure out what *might* have happened in the last several hours. At least they nailed the critical details—or so Jack hoped, although he doubted Randy was as forthcoming as he made himself out to be.

Even after grasping what had supposedly happened to each of them, they still really didn't know *what* was happening.

What had sucked Jack into the black hall?

What had crawled up Stephanie's leg?

What had happened to Stewart's body?

Who was Susan, and what had happened to her?

The whys were even worse. Why were doors opening and closing on their own? Why couldn't any of them see their reflections in the mirrors? Why hadn't the killer come after them in the basement?

"I can tell you that," Randy said. "He has. You just don't know it."

Leslie frowned. "Okay, so he has some psychological grip—"

"I'm not talking psychological. I'm talking physical. I saw him come in."

"You what?" Jack said.

Randy sat on a fifty-five-gallon drum with the shotgun across his lap, staring at Jack, who'd stopped his pacing to face him. Leslie and Stephanie each sat on a plate of steel that stuck out from the boilers.

"The back door," Randy said. "I saw him step in out of the rain."

"What back door? Why didn't you tell us about this?"

"He padlocked the door. And it's not as if I could tell you where it is. But he's in here."

"And you just happened to forget this little detail?" Leslie demanded.

Randy sneered at her. "It's not important.
We have other problems."

"Like what?"

"Like getting out."

"You mean getting out alive, don't you?"
Leslie asked. "Which means we have to know
who our enemies are and where they are."

"Then like I said, we have a lot more to
worry about than White," Randy said. He
grabbed the shotgun by the pump action and
chambered a shell with one hand. "White's
one guy. We can take one guy. But you have
to ask yourself why Stewart disappeared."

"Because you were hallucinating," Leslie
said.

He grabbed his wet shirt. "You call this a
hallucination?"

"You let Stewart drown," Leslie said.
"Have you ever drowned someone before,
Randy? I don't think so. Do you know why
they put infantry through hell week at boot
camp? So that when they get in a bloody
battle they don't start seeing things. The
mind is a fragile instrument. It snaps easily.
If there's anything you have to ask yourself,
it's why you've become a completely different person since you entered this house."

Randy stared at her without responding. It

was a good question. Even he had to see what the stress had done to him.

"She has a point, Randy," Jack said. "Think about it. You talk about Stewart dying in the most graphic terms without batting an eye, and none of us care. You get to a point where everything starts to shut down, right? The problem is, we can't shut down yet."

"Excuse me," Stephanie said, "but do we really care about all this psychobabble? Didn't you hear Randy? The killer's down here *with* us! People are going to die! What do you think this is all about? Sucking up some dog food?"

Jack wanted to reach across the room and smack her. She wasn't lucid.

Then again, it had been a long time since he'd seen her so full of emotion. The mix of old and new gave him pause.

To her credit, Leslie ignored the cruel jab. "I'm just saying that we really need to get a grip and not let the circumstances get into our heads."

"And I suppose the snakes were in my head too," Stephanie said.

"For starters, yes."

Stephanie just stared at her. Maybe she really didn't know.

Jack paced. "Okay, let's take this method-ically."

"I think the question of whether what seems to be happening is really happening is impor-tant," Leslie said. "The answer lays out the entire framework for how we deal with it."

"How's that?"

"Take Stephanie's snakes. If they're real snakes, you kill them with a knife or some-thing. If they're in the mind, you shut your eyes and put them out of your mind."

Made sense. Stephanie huffed.

"Okay," Jack said. "I'll go with that. What else has happened that could fall into that category?"

"I can't believe we're sitting here—"

"Please, Stephanie, try to use more than your mouth. Just go with us here."

She clamped her mouth shut and glared at him. He had to hand it to her, though— she'd found some spunk in that closet. At least she wasn't in denial, running away. He had to respect her for that much.

"Randy, is there anything you've seen that could have been a trick of your mind?"

"I'm with Stephanie. I don't see how this helps us."

"What if you think you see a lock on a door

and walk away?" Leslie said. "You walk away when you could have walked out."

"I *heard* him lock the back door. I *saw* the padlock before he locked it—"

"What about the shotgun?" Jack said, gesturing to Randy's lap. "We could blow the locks off."

They all looked at him with dawning awareness. Randy slid off the drum, eyes bright. "I knew the gun would be our ticket out of here. We blow the doors. Lock and load."

"Hold up," Jack said, raising a hand. "Let's think this through."

"What's there to think through?" Stephanie said. "Randy's right!"

"For starters, Stephanie, you just came down the main stairs, right? Do you know how to get back? Don't you find it a little strange that you just *happened* to end up here, with us? The halls down here don't make any sense, but you just waltz on in."

She didn't respond.

"I agree, going for the door with the gun may be a good plan," Jack said. "If we can find it. But let's not blow our chances by going off half-cocked. So let's have it: what have we seen that could be in our minds?"

The house creaked above them, and they all looked up.

After a moment Leslie lowered her eyes. "There. The wind's moving the house. We hear a groan, but our minds are already stretched to the breaking point so we all expect more and look up. Stress-induced deception, pure and simple."

"What about the mirrors?" Jack asked.

"They have to be trick mirrors of some kind," she said. "Pete told me they used to travel with a circus. Did anyone specifically notice a reflection from anything as close to the mirror as you were? Randy?"

"You mean in the foreground? Actually, now that you mention it, no. Jack and I couldn't see either of our reflections, but we could see the room behind us."

"Jack?"

"That's right. I never thought of it that way."

"I know for a fact that a mirror can be manufactured in such a way as to reflect no light within a certain distance."

Jack could feel strength entering the room as if it were a force field. They had a gun, they had answers—two things that might have prevented everything that happened tonight. He resolved in that moment never to travel without a weapon again.

"Okay, what about Stewart's body disappearing?"

Randy looked around at them. *He was returning to sanity by the minute,* Jack thought.

"Okay, I was a bit on edge." He closed his eyes, lifted his chin, and took a deep breath. Silence settled. His vulnerability was palpable.

A long, awkward moment passed.

Randy took another deep breath and looked at them. "When Jack got sucked into that door and I ended up in that rising water, something snapped. I was a dead man. You have no idea what it's like, watching someone drown while you think about carving them up."

"I'm sure it was very difficult," Leslie said. She walked over to him and took his hand in a show of support. "You'll be okay."

Seeing her go to him bothered Jack, but not because he cared for Leslie in that way. He simply didn't trust Randy. The thought of anyone extending him trust was unnerving.

"Okay," Jack said, "so some of what we've seen was probably the product of stressed imagination. For all I know, I could have jumped into the tunnel. A strong draft . . ." He frowned. "I suppose it's possible I thought I was being sucked."

Leslie looked at Randy. "Maybe you saw a dead body because you needed Stewart dead—not unheard of."

He frowned. "Maybe."

Jack raised an eyebrow at Leslie. "And the odor—"

"We've grown accustomed to it due to the stress, so we don't smell it anymore. It's a start anyway."

Jack took a deep breath and paced, rubbing his face to clear the cobwebs. "So let me get this straight. We were all taken off the road by a serial killer named White who has a thing for elaborate games. He's killed who knows how many people over the years and ends up in the backwoods of Alabama where no one goes but the stray traveler. Good so far?"

Leslie picked up, walking across the room. "We're not the first victims in this house. The last was Susan, who managed to escape. Our hosts are working with White, but this latest miss—with Susan, that is—has changed their relationship, putting pressure on Stewart and Betty. But that fits into White's game, because he wants others to do his killing. He intends to force his victims to extract the penalty for sin themselves. How am I doing?"

"Give me one dead body," Randy said.

"Rule number three," Jack said.

"It's also what I thought I heard White say in the tunnels."

Leslie turned on him. "You heard his voice? Another little detail you forgot to mention?"

"I *thought* I did. Either way, you're right. He wants us to kill each other. That's the whole point, isn't it?"

It was. They all had to know that by now, Jack thought. "So his plan all along was to get us into the house and lure us into this basement, which apparently isn't just a basement at all. How do you explain the basement? I can't get a handle on the layout of this place."

"Tunnels, shafts, holding tanks . . . ," Leslie mused. "Maybe it was part of a mining operation."

"What kind of mining operation in the middle of Alabama would resemble anything like this?" Randy asked.

"Catacombs," Stephanie said. "Maybe it was more than a mining operation. Something built for slaves after the war. For all we know, this house is built on a mass grave."

Randy snickered.

"Please, let's try to stay focused," Leslie said. "This isn't *Poltergeist*."

Stephanie shrugged. "I'm just saying."

"The point is, White's been manipulating us from the beginning," Leslie said. "He's got us locked in this place with four other people. Eight people to pit against each other. The last one alive gets to live . . . or something like that. Betty and Stewart and Pete are as much victims as we are at this point."

"But they don't count," Randy said.

"What?"

"Something else the voice said."

They stared at him.

"Why wouldn't they count?" Jack asked.

"They are like him?" Randy said. "On his team?"

"But Susan said White's going to kill them for letting her go. One way or another, he intends to kill everyone tonight. Or having us kill each other."

"One down," Randy said.

"Then we have to kill Betty and Pete," Stephanie said.

"No, we have to get out," Jack said.

"But if they get in our way, we kill them," Randy said. "I guarantee, if either one of those two perverts comes into my sights, they're dead meat."

Leslie looked at him.

"What? You disagree?"

"No. If you come across Pete, put a round in his groin for me."

Given the circumstances, Jack couldn't fault her sentiment.

"So we're going to get out, right?" Stephanie asked.

"With Stewart out of the way, we might have a shot," Leslie said.

"And when we get out, what then?" Randy asked.

"Unless we manage to disable White, he'll come after us."

"We could use that truck."

"It's trashed. We'll have to make a run for the main road on foot."

"You think there's any chance that someone could have seen the cars and called it in?" Stephanie asked. "I mean, it's possible, right? That highway patrol officer knew we were taking this road. It's only a matter of time before he comes. The only question is, can he get here before dawn?"

"We have to find Susan," Jack said.

None of them responded.

"I'm dead serious; we can't leave here without Susan."

"Well, that's a bit of a problem, isn't it?" Randy said. "We don't know where this Susan is. And if you're right, they will expect us to look for her. We'd be playing right into White's hands. He's no idiot. He knows someone's going to want to save the sweet little girl."

"What's your problem?" Leslie snapped. "She's as much a victim here as we are. You can't just *leave* her!"

"According to you, Betty's a victim too. You want to go save *her*?"

"She's also a cold-blooded killer!"

Randy shook his head, exasperated.

"There's no way you can find this girl down here," Stephanie said. "You said she's been hiding out for days?"

"You do what you want," Randy said. "You find her, fine, we take her out with us. But we can't all stay down here looking for one girl. We have to get *out*!"

It sounded right. But to Jack it felt very wrong. He caught Leslie's look. They both knew that Susan had saved their lives.

The sound of a long, drawn-out creaking

filled the boiler room. Jack looked for the source, but there was nothing he could see.

It was as if the walls were made of wood and a strong wind was pushing the planks slowly in one direction.

"You see?" Stephanie cried. "That's what I heard. You're saying that's just in my mind?"

The sound finally abated. Even Leslie was breathing hard.

"Something's wrong with this place," Randy said. "We have to get out. Now." He grabbed the shotgun off the fifty-five-gallon barrel and strode for the same closed door he'd come through.

"Hold on, we haven't agreed on a plan," Jack said.

"We go for the doors, that's the plan."

"Which door? Who goes for which door? And what happens if something goes wrong? Just hold up a second!"

Randy turned around. His expression said clearly enough that he hadn't thought that far ahead. Stephanie had started to follow him. Made sense; they thought alike. Get out and get out now; just go.

Like their marriage.

The creaking returned, not quite as loud, but just as long. It was the most unnatural sound Jack could imagine. He shivered reflexively.

Before Randy could set off again, Jack put a thought in his mind. "You sure your gun's going to do the trick against whatever's making that noise?"

"Stop it!" Leslie said. "We're not dealing with ghosts here, for heaven's sake. Act like adults!"

"Then what are we dealing with?" Stephanie demanded, and Jack was thankful she'd asked. "Mass hysteria?"

"I don't know! Pipes? The house above us is moving in the wind. It has a web of rusted pipes underneath. How should I—"

"The sound's coming from the walls, not the pipes," Stephanie insisted.

"Sound travels," Leslie said.

"And the puncture marks on your face and hands? You still think those are incidental? Or were they something more like darts?"

Leslie's face lightened a shade. "What do you mean?"

Stephanie stared her down. "I don't know. But neither do you, do you? And yet you insist that there's *zero* chance we're dealing with anything supernatural here. Are you willing to bet all of our lives on that?"

Leslie didn't answer.

"Well . . ."

"Fine. So maybe there's something going on here that we can't explain without ripping down the house. Call it supernatural if you want. By definition, the supernatural is only that which extends beyond our understanding of nature anyway." She glared angrily. "I'm not even sure there *aren't* such things as ghosts. Some kind of natural existence beyond death—who knows. But your running around frantic because you think an evil spirit is hard on your heels will only get us all killed! You have to keep your head!"

"I *intend* to keep my head!" Stephanie shot back. "Which means getting out of *here*!"

"You and Randy were both ready to tear out of here before we'd even settled on a plan. That's the kind of idiocy that comes from emotionally driven nonsense."

Jack thought it time to intervene. "So you're saying you think *maybe* there could be something supernaturally wrong with the house?" Jack asked Leslie. "Because Susan—"

"I know what Susan said!"

"Take it easy!" he said, drilling her with a stare.

She averted her eyes.

"If White knows there's something wrong with this house—"

"Just say it, Jack," Leslie said. "You mean haunted, don't you? Just say it."

"Okay, I will. If White knows this house is haunted because it was once used to house slaves who were slaughtered here, or what-ever . . ."

Giving voice to the possibility felt strange.

". . . which you yourself admit is a possibility even though we don't understand it . . ."

"Granted."

". . . then wouldn't it be in our interest to know how to deal with a haunted house?"

They looked at him.

"I know it sounds stupid, but isn't that what we're talking about? We understand something about the killer, as much as serial killers can be understood; we know about Betty and Stewart and Pete. We have a plan to blow the doors off the hinges and go for the main road. But what about the house?"

"You're saying the house may be trying to stop us from getting out?" Leslie asked.

"I'm just making sure all of our bases are covered before we try anything."

"I don't believe in haunted houses," Randy said.

"Neither do I," Leslie said, looking at him. "But that doesn't mean this house isn't . . . unusual. We just covered that; weren't you listening?"

He ignored her.

"The question, if I understand Jack right, is how we deal with a haunted house. Right?"

"Right."

No one offered any suggestions. They were all too busy trying to imagine such a thing. Clearly, none of them had a clue how to deal with a haunted anything.

"Anyone have any holy water?" Stephanie asked.

"What does haunted mean?" Randy asked. "That means some ghost or something is haunting it. So we appease the ghost. Or kill it."

The creaking sound came again, louder than before. And longer. They listened, looking at one another without offering any consolation.

"Pipes," Jack said when it quit.

No one commented.

"We go for the back door first," Jack said. "Can you get us there, Randy?"

"I think so."

Jack nodded. "If we get separated and can't get out, we meet back here."

"If one of us gets out?" Randy said.

"Go for the main road."

"What if we can't get out the back?" Leslie asked.

"Then we go for the one at the top of the main stairs and get out that way."

"Shoot on sight?" Randy asked.

Jack nodded, taking up the spade Randy had dropped. "If we run into Betty, Pete, or White, shoot on sight. Below the waist if possible."

Randy nodded. "Okay. Okay. Let's do it."

He led them to the door he'd come through, shotgun on his hip.

23

3:53 AM

They walked quickly and quietly in single file, with Randy leading, followed by Stephanie, then Leslie. Jack brought up the rear with Randy's spade.

The moment they entered the tunnel he had last seen Stewart in, Randy felt the surge of confidence that had fueled his escape from Stewart earlier.

The shotgun was freshly loaded from the supply of shells he'd taken off Stewart. Eleven more in the box. Randy weighed whether he had the guts to do what had to

be done if it came right down to it. He'd
learned a few things tonight, and one of
them was that putting a gun against someone's head and pulling the trigger wasn't
an easy thing to do.

Yes, he did have the guts. He wasn't sure
he'd be shouting this down Broadway, but
he thought he could do it. And now he was
the one leading them down the dark tunnels—without too much fear.

By Randy's estimation, it took only about
five minutes to make it back to the room
where Stewart had drowned. They were trying to move slowly enough to keep quiet,
which it was. Very.

The arched wooden door to the room was
still open.

Randy stopped.

"What?" Stephanie whispered behind
him.

"This is where I saw . . ." He blinked at the
concrete floor.

"The body?"

"Yeah."

"What is it?" Leslie whispered, coming up
in a crouch.

"Still gone," Randy said.

They looked at one another then back up

the tunnel. Enough said. So he'd lost his marbles for a bit. Or White had moved the cadaver. Randy stepped quickly over the riser into the room, eager to prove to them all that the drowned man was indeed drowned.

"Slow down," Stephanie whispered.

I'll slow you down if you don't shut up. Inner thought, meant nothing really.

He could see the water now. The large pipe that disappeared into the holding tank. Randy waded out to the center in ankle-deep water. He turned back, aware that he was grinning and not caring.

The others had stopped at the entry and were looking down.

"This is where it happened," he said.

They looked at him without acknowledging or denying. But that was acknowledgment enough.

"Do you want to see—"

"Just get us out of here," Leslie snapped.

Well, fine then. He cut to his left, over another riser, and into the adjoining passage. Fifty feet and to the right. Through the door he'd run smack into, which was now open, allowing light into what had been a dark space.

But the door that led into the utility room where he'd found the old shotgun was locked.

"Locked," he said. "This leads to the passage with the back door."

"So what do we do?" Stephanie asked.

You put your fist in your mouth and keep it there. Inner thought.

"Blast it," he said.

"They might hear," Jack said.

"Maybe. But we're insulated by a lot of dirt beyond these concrete walls. And there's a utility room on the other side of this door. I think it's okay."

Before anyone could object, he lifted the gun, put the barrel about a foot from the handle, and . . .

"Randy . . ."

. . . pulled the trigger. *Boom!*

Man, was that loud in here!

"There," he said and pushed the door open.

They entered the utility room and stopped to listen. Nothing. 'Course, his ears were ringing pretty good.

"This way."

"I'm not going out," Jack said.

Randy faced the man. "What do you mean, you're not going out? The door's right—"

"Show me the way. I have to at least try to find Susan first."

Randy reached for the door. "Suit yourself."

They were in the passageway with the back exit visible fifty feet to their left when they heard the muffled voice.

Stephanie gasped. Randy put his fingers to her mouth. Down the hall, past the door that led into the large study with the desk and the pentagram and the mirror that didn't work. Betty.

"Hurry!" Randy turned to run toward the exit, but a hand snagged his elbow.

"Give me a minute!" Jack whispered. "Susan has to be with her."

"Are you crazy? We're right here!"

"You have to wait for me."

"Not a chance."

"If you shoot the lock, she'll hear for sure this time, and I won't stand a chance. One minute, just to see."

"And if I wait for you to come screaming down the hall with a girl in your arms, she'll be on your tail with a gun in her hands. We all lose."

"Just give me a minute! She saved Leslie's life!"

He said it like it was supposed to decide matters. Maybe it did, but Randy's mind was foggy again. He had a shotgun, they were well protected in the passage—a minute wouldn't hurt, considering.

"One minute and we go. We'll wait by the door."

"I'm going with him," Leslie whispered.

"Suit yourself."

Randy and Stephanie stood in the passageway that led to the exit. "Fools," Randy whispered, watching them. "They're going to get us killed."

"Do you think?"

"Guaranteed."

"Maybe we should just go," Stephanie said.

Her suggestion half surprised him. "Just leave them and run?"

"Well, we'd get the cops, right?"

He considered the plan. It wasn't really a plan, more of an everyone-for-themselves

strategy. Or at least he and Stephanie for themselves.

Jack and Leslie were still creeping up on the door at the other end. If it wasn't for that little waif they'd met, they'd be out of here by now.

"I can't do that," he finally said.

Stephanie hugged herself and looked around nervously. "I don't like it. We should go."

"Just keep quiet. I said we'd give him a minute, no more. Just—"

The door behind them opened. Randy heard Stephanie grunt. He whirled. Pete was there, with one arm wrapped around her neck and the other over her mouth, dragging her back through the door.

Randy jerked the shotgun around, leveled it at them, and came within an inch of putting a full load of buckshot in her gut. That was the first problem—Stephanie was in the way.

The second was that Jack was right; a shot here would alert the whole house to his location.

Pete ducked through the door and was gone.

Randy's pulse drummed through his skull.

He glanced up the hall and saw that Jack was almost at the door to the study, clueless to the turn of events.

He couldn't warn Jack and Leslie without possibly alerting Betty, which wasn't in their favor. He had to either let Pete take off with Stephanie, or he had to go after them before they disappeared.

Randy swore under his breath and tore through the door.

He could hear Stephanie scream through Pete's fingers ahead, on his right. She grunted and was silent.

Pete didn't have a gun and Randy did; that was what made the difference.

The sound of a door slamming rippled past him.

Pete was outgunned, and he had a body in his hands. Or over his shoulder. Either way, Randy should be able to take him easier than he had the oaf's father. Shock and awe. He'd blow the guy away before Pete knew he had any competition.

Randy came to the door that had been slammed, threw it open, and poked his head through. Two directions. He couldn't tell where they'd gone. But if he understood Jack and Leslie correctly, he had a pretty

good idea which direction Pete's hideout was, and he was sure that's where they were headed.

To the right again. He jogged around the corner and down a hall he hadn't seen before. The leather soles of his ruined shoes slapped on the concrete. Now who was hunting whom?

A left ahead, the only way. He took it without slowing.

But he was running away from the exit. And White was in here somewhere.

The two thoughts entered his mind together, like a twin blast from double-barreled shotgun, and drilled something through his chest that he hadn't felt since Stewart's pursuit.

Fear.

He slowed to a walk, heart crashing so hard that he couldn't hear himself think. They had been right there! A single shot through that padlock and out into the rain. With a shotgun in hand! He would have made it.

"You stupid, stupid, stupid . . ." No word that came to mind accurately described how he loathed Stephanie in this moment. But he was committed.

Or was he? He stopped. Looked over his shoulder. Actually, he could go back. Leave them all and make for the road armed with the shotgun. Get to the cell phones he and Leslie had left in their car. Call for help and get to the city.

Somewhere ahead, Stephanie screamed. He'd let go of her mouth. Which probably meant Pete had reached his hideout.

Randy crept forward, resolve all but sapped in the face of the fear and disappointment he felt for the missed opportunity. Each step took him farther in, farther away. Jack and Leslie would probably get the girl, get to the door, and be long gone while he was back here trying to rescue Jack's wench.

He picked up his pace, keeping his heels from making contact with the concrete. How Pete had covered this ground so quickly he had no clue, not with a cracked noggin like Jack said he had.

Randy rounded a corner and came face-to-face with a door, brimming with yellow light. The hall disappeared around another corner ahead, but this had to be it.

He approached the door cautiously. Shock and awe, that was the plan, but he didn't have the energy for shock and awe right now.

"Please . . ." He could hear Stephanie's muffled pleading beyond the door. "Please, I'll do anything."

"You can be my wife," Pete said.

She didn't respond.

Randy leaned forward, listening. He didn't know where in the room they were, and the cracks were too narrow to give him any real view. If Stephanie could distract him . . .

"Can you put that down?" she asked.

Randy pulled back. The man had a gun?

"I want you to eat the cereal," Pete said.

Randy looked back down the hall. He could still take off.

"This cereal?" she asked.

If he took off now, he could still get out. Jack and Leslie had probably already gone. He pictured the door wide open with Betty screaming at the rain.

"It will make you strong like me."

She hesitated. Cried softly.

"Are you sure?" she said.

"Yes, yes! Leslie was a bad girl."

"Leslie wouldn't eat your cereal?"

"Leslie was a bad girl."

"But if I eat your cereal, then I'll be a good girl?" Stephanie said, voice cracking.

"You will be my wife."

"And you'll be good to me?"

"If you want to be strong like me, you have to eat the cereal. Because you're guilty."

"Guilty."

Randy blinked. She was an operator; he'd give her that much.

"Okay. See?"

She was eating it? He put his left hand on the doorknob and twisted a fraction of an inch. It wasn't locked. He nudged it. No dead bolts.

Stephanie was now sobbing softly and continuously.

"You'll be strong," Pete said.

Randy went then, because he knew any red-blooded male into rotten dog food would have his complete attention on Stephanie.

Pete stood with a bowl in one hand, staring at Stephanie, who had three fingers in her mouth. Her face was streaked with tears.

Randy pulled the trigger. *Boom!* Buckshot tore into Pete's side, and he dropped the bowl. But he didn't fall.

Pump the action. Another load. *Boom!*
This one put the man on his knees.

"Come on!" he screamed. "Let's go."

She looked momentarily stunned, then sprang off the bed. But she didn't fall all weeping into his arms with gratitude. She stumbled through the door, face white.

She followed him down the halls at a full run. All Randy could think about now was getting to the padlocked exit.

It occurred to him he hadn't chambered a round after that last blast, so he did it now, aware but uncaring that Stephanie was falling behind.

He turned the corner and cut into the tunnel that led back to the exit.

That's as far as he got. He wasn't alone in the tunnel. The man with the tin mask was there. Facing him. Twenty yards up the passage, with his hands by his sides, trench coat at his ankles, staring through those jagged holes in his faceplate.

Sickness washed through Randy's gut. He wanted to jerk the shotgun up and put a hole in that face, but he couldn't move.

No sign of Stephanie.

"Hello, Randy," White said. "You're like me; that's why you're going to win this contest."

He still couldn't hear Stephanie; where was Stephanie?

"I need a dead body," White said. "I think Jack will try to kill you. You're scum; they all know that."

Randy's vision swam. White's neck twitched.

"One body, Randy. Give me one body before he kills you."

"I . . . I can't just kill—"

"If you don't kill her, then you will die."

Her? He couldn't think straight. "Leslie?"

"Even the innocent are guilty, Randy."

———

Stephanie had lost sight of Randy, but she was too numb to call out for him to slow down. He had come back for her—he wouldn't leave her now.

Her stomach swam in revulsion from eating the paste, but it was a sickly sweet revulsion. Like chewing on the worm at the bottom of a tequila bottle. No. Worse, much worse—more like sucking up a mouthful of someone else's vomit. But that vomit was laced with a hallucinogen that had sent pleasure running along her nerves.

Her revulsion was for herself, really. For her willingness to do whatever Pete asked of her. Anything. And for her need to be accepted by him.

It hit her then that what she did had come naturally. Her sickness, her sin, preserving herself at the cost of all principle. At the cost of her own worth. The realization made her nauseated.

She'd become a shell of a woman to save herself from pain, and she was powerless to redeem herself.

Some of the paste was still lodged in her throat. Suddenly the sickly sweetness of it all was only sickly. She stopped, bent at the waist, and threw up.

Wiping her mouth, she staggered on.

"Randy?"

When she finally caught up, Randy stood with his back toward her, shotgun in one hand pointed at the ground. He turned toward her. For a moment she thought he looked different.

"You coming?"

She hurried. "Yes." She spit bile from her mouth.

Randy jogged on.

When they reached the hall where Pete

had abducted her, the door Jack and Leslie had approached stood gaping open. The exit was still padlocked. No sign of them.

Stephanie could smell her own breath—like sulfur.

"Come on!" Randy said, running to the exit. "When we get outside we run straight for the forest, not for the front of the house," he said. "We get some cover, and then we figure out how to get back to the main road, okay?"

She didn't answer.

Randy lifted the shotgun to his shoulder, aimed at the padlock, and pulled the trigger.

"Let's go!"

He jumped up on the landing and ripped off the twisted lock with a trembling hand. The door swung open easily. They'd made it?

He whirled back, grabbed Stephanie's elbow, and pulled her roughly through the doorway, outside.

Only they weren't quite outside yet.

In fact, they weren't outside at all. Stephanie blinked, but what she saw didn't change. They were in the boiler room! The hot, suffocating boiler room!

The door clicked shut behind her.

"Oh God oh God oh God!"

24

3:59 AM

Jack eased to one knee by the door and felt Leslie bump into him from behind. She drew close to his face, and by the look in her eyes he knew immediately that something had happened.

"They're gone!" He followed her look down the hall. They'd left Randy and Stephanie less than a minute ago with a promise from Randy to wait. But there was now no sign of Randy or Stephanie. The back exit was still closed.

A distant, muffled cry reached him. Stephanie! Someone had taken her? Pete or White.

For a moment he was torn between giving chase and going after Susan, who he was sure waited behind this door. Randy was also gone—as much as he hated to trust the man, Jack chose to believe that he'd gone after Stephanie.

He would go after Susan.

Jack had thought about the matter while bringing up the rear on their walk through the tunnels. The more he thought about Susan, the more he equated her with his own daughter, Melissa. It was their innocence, not their age, that bound them.

He hadn't been able to save his own daughter from death, but he would do everything in his power to save Susan. He'd always been a stubborn, loyal guy, but his resolve to save this girl now, in the midst of such chaos, surprised even him.

He'd stopped Leslie back at a corner in the tunnels and told her, "I can't leave Susan. I'm going to find out where the exit is then go after her."

She looked him in the eye. "I'll go with you."

"No."

"Yes." She would not be moved. "You're a good man, Jack."

Now they were here, going after Susan, with the surprising fortune of locating Betty quickly. Whether that fortune was good or bad, they would soon know.

Leslie crouched and leaned against the opposite wall, watching Jack.

"It makes no sense," Betty was saying beyond the door. "Not a lick of sense. Why would anyone risk their neck for you? They won't come."

"Jack will," Susan's voice said.

"They still don't have a clue what they're in for; you know that, don't you? They'll all be dead in a couple of hours."

"Then so will you."

Jack heard a slap.

He nearly went then. But he still hadn't formed a plan. He very carefully cracked the door.

The study, as they called it, lay as he remembered it with the lone desk and the large mirror. Betty faced the mirror with her back to Jack. She had a brush in her hand and was working through Susan's long, tangled hair.

No gun. Not that he could see.

Betty jerked Susan around to face her. "You don't think I know a thing or two about killing? The guilty die. That means White isn't beyond being killed if it comes down to it. He may have done what he did to bring the house alive, but let's not forget who was here first."

"You'll be dead by morning," Susan said.

This time Betty didn't bother slapping her. She put the brush in her hair and tugged. "That's long past your dead time, honey. You're right; they're coming for you. But it's not what they think."

Jack knew he should be going in now, but their words gripped him.

"They're stronger than you know," Susan said.

"If they're so strong, they wouldn't be fooled by you, now would they? They don't know if they're coming or going. And they don't know what the real game is."

Susan didn't respond. Could any of Betty's words be true? Was it possible that Susan was actually with White?

"I don't see what anyone would see in this pretty soft face, anyway." Betty was squeezing Susan's cheeks, and both were looking at the mirror. Which was odd. "I don't care what White says, we should have killed you the day you set foot in this place."

Betty squeezed. Tighter and tighter.

Susan whimpered.

Jack pulled back, breathing steady.

"Is . . . is she with us?" Leslie asked. She'd heard.

"Who do you trust: Susan, who risked her neck to save you, or Betty?" Jack whispered.

"But Betty didn't kill her."

He thought a moment. "Betty has reasons to keep her alive. And Susan saved you."

"It could be part of the game."

"No! We can't leave her, even if she is part of their game. I'm going in."

She glanced at the door. "Okay. Be careful."

Jack took a deep breath, gently pushed the door, and spun into the room, spade raised high.

But Betty was already whirling, using Susan as a shield. Instead of a brush, she now held a knife, and it was pressed against Susan's thin neck. Susan saw Jack, and the corner of her mouth lifted ever so slightly.

"It's about time," Betty said, smiling so

that her gaping white teeth were bared. "Drop the spade."

"Don't!" Susan cried.

"I said drop it!"

Leslie stepped in past Jack. "Kill her, Jack."

"I'll give you to three to drop that thing, or I'm slicing her neck," Betty said.

"Then what?" Jack demanded, approaching Betty, jaw set. "Huh? Then what, you sick stain of a woman? I'll make sure you never stand up again, that's what."

Betty backed up, dragging Susan.

"You can't let me kill her; you know that," Betty said. But there was a hint of fear in her eyes now. "She's the only thing keeping you alive! She's part of the game. You'll see that; I swear you will."

"Don't listen to her!" Susan said.

Betty flicked her knife, and Susan gasped. Blood seeped from a thin cut on her chin. "What's the matter, you couldn't get out the back door? Shovel won't help you there, sugarplum."

Leslie walked to the far side of the room, on Betty's right.

"I don't know what you think this sick game is about," she said, "but Stewart's dead and White wants us to kill you. Is that what you want? A bloodbath down here? He won't stop till we're all dead. Surely you see that."

Betty smiled. "You think Stewart is dead? Oh, he drowned all right, but he's got strong lungs."

"Drop the knife," Jack said, stepping closer. "You kill her, and I promise you I'll remove your head. Let her go."

"It's White we have to stop!" Leslie said. "We should be working together, not against each other."

Betty's eyes skipped to Leslie. Jack walked closer. The thought of actually taking her out was turning out to be more difficult than he would have guessed. And there was still the chance that Betty would manage to kill Susan.

Leslie kept walking. She was trying to be confident, but she was trembling.

"Leslie?" Jack said.

"What makes you think you can shove your twisted world down a little boy's throat and not pay for it, huh?" she said in a bitter hiss. *On the edge of snapping,* Jack thought. She was talking about Pete.

"Leslie . . ."

"You're guilty, Betty. You're guilty too. And your sins are about to find you out."

Leslie walked behind her, then past her. Betty's face was drawn tight. She watched Leslie like a hawk. It was the first time Jack had seen her stripped of command.

"You believe in hell, Betty? I don't. But looking at you, I sure wish I did, because whatever hell is, it was made for you and your son. You can either join us against White, or we can take you out. How's that for a game?"

Jack was only eight feet from Betty now. But her knife was pressed tight to Susan's neck.

Her eyes swiveled from Leslie to Jack, then back. She suddenly released Susan, dropped the knife, and lifted both hands. Susan ducked to her right.

"Listen to me, Jack," Susan said, spinning back. "He who has ears to hear . . . Can you hear me?"

"Okay, you win," Betty said. "I know . . ."

"Kill her, Jack," Leslie said.

Susan was speaking as well, but Jack couldn't make out her words. The voices spun through his mind.

". . . how to kill White," Betty said. "I can show you . . ."

"Kill her!" Leslie cried.

". . . how to kill him."

Susan finished a long run-on. "And if that doesn't make sense, it's not really supposed to."

What? Jack looked at Susan and Leslie. "What?"

"What?" Leslie repeated, clueless.

"What's she saying? Susan."

Leslie glanced at the girl. "Nothing."

Silence fell. Betty's head jerked spastically for the length of a second, and then her smile returned. Jack's nerves were strung tight. Or had he seen more? Now his mind was really playing tricks.

He tried to summarize the present scenario. Leslie on his right, insisting that he swing away and bludgeon her to kingdom come. Susan on his left, staring at him in shock. Betty in the middle, hands raised by her head, smiling nervously.

"Kill her!" Leslie screamed.

Jack swung. He heard a crack. Betty's skull. The blade hit Betty with enough force to send her reeling into the mirror five feet behind her. The glass shattered.

Betty dropped to the floor and landed on her rear end. A trickle of blood ran from her ear.

They all stared, not quite believing. Black fog seeped from the wound.

"Follow me!" Susan said. "Run!" She ran toward the door that led into the room with four sofas.

Jack spied the shotgun, the one Betty had hauled into Pete's room. Leaning against the desk. He let the spade clatter to the floor, snatched up the better weapon.

"Out the back!" Leslie cried. "Susan—"

"No, Susan's right," Jack said. "We're closer to the stairs. Up the stairs. Come on!" This time he'd shoot the locks off.

He ran after Susan, who was just peeling into the main hall with the stairs when Jack spun into the living room.

Leslie sprinted on his heels.

In that hall was a flight of stairs that ran up to the main floor. If Randy was right and White was in the basement, they'd be safe on the main floor. They could exit from there. And with the gun he would have no trouble dealing with any lock.

Jack's heart pounded. They were going to make it.

What about Stephanie and Randy? Hopefully they'd made it out by now. He had Susan and Leslie.

He spilled into the hall and almost ran over Susan, who'd stopped and was staring in the opposite direction of the stairs.

"Let's go, let's—"

Leslie screamed.

Jack spun back and saw that she too was now staring at the far end of the hall, face white. He whirled.

The killer faced them from the shadows, unmoving. Black trench coat hanging open down the middle. Tin plate covering all but his eyes, and a slit for his mouth. Shotgun pointing casually at the floor.

"One dead body," he said, his voice deadened behind the mask. "The hag doesn't count."

White started to walk toward them.

"Follow me!" Susan cried. She flung open the door directly across the hall and ran through.

White's gun boomed. The load hit the door behind Susan, slamming it shut. If history was any judge, it was probably locked.

"Shoot him!" Leslie screamed.

Jack jerked his shotgun up and fired a wild shot into the wall.

His arms were weak. All Jack could think of now was getting out. Up the stairs, past the door. White's shotgun came up.

"Hurry!"

Jack leaped onto the stairs and took them three at a time with Leslie pounding up behind him. They didn't have Susan, he knew that, but he also knew that they would soon both be dead if he didn't get past this door.

Boom! White's shot tore into the shiplap siding beside him.

He pumped a round into the chamber as he ran, aimed at the door latch, and pulled the trigger before his foot was firmly planted on the landing.

The blast knocked him back into Leslie, who gave him a shove toward the door. It had been released from the shattered locking mechanism and swung free.

"Go, go!"

He dived through the door, tripped on the riser, and sprawled onto the floor.

Leslie was hung up behind him, trapped momentarily by the door, which had bounced off the adjacent wall hard enough to swing shut.

"Leslie!"

A beat passed.

Then she plowed in and pulled up. She took in the room in wonder, ignoring him entirely.

"What . . . what is this?"

A door to Jack's right suddenly flew open. Randy and Stephanie ran through, winded, eyes disbelieving.

Then the rest of the room came into clear view. And it wasn't the hallway he expected to see.

They were back in the boiler room.

"Oh God oh God oh God!" Stephanie mumbled.

25

4:25 AM

The boiler room had changed, Leslie saw. Large red letters had been scrawled on the walls.

The Wages of Sin Is One Dead Body

Randy's nostrils flared with rage. Stephanie's eyes flittered with fear. Whatever had happened to them had changed them, she thought. Her own mind was in a meltdown; she knew it well, but that didn't preclude her from judging others. Of the four of them, only Jack seemed to be himself.

She was somewhat surprised by how little

she felt for Randy now. And Jack hadn't re-acted to her advances, not that she had an-ticipated much more. Still, if there was one person who could lead them out of this, it was probably Jack.

"Give me the shotgun," Randy snapped, glaring at Jack.

"This is wrong, so wrong," Leslie said.

"Give me the gun," Randy repeated, hold-ing out a hand.

Leslie walked in a wide circle on numb legs, staring at that writing in red. "How's this possible? I don't understand. Some-thing spiritual is happening, isn't it?"

"I thought you were too intelligent to be-lieve in the supernatural," Stephanie said.

"I am." And she was. But how could she deny the physical impossibility of what had just happened? "I am. But the house seems to know what we're going to do before we do it! And it knows us!"

"Knows us?"

She looked at Stephanie. "Our weak-nesses. Our fears. The sin we—"

"I said, give me the gun!" Randy shouted, lifting his shotgun.

Leslie became enraged. "Stop it!"

"I don't trust him," came the snarl.

"Don't you see what's happening here, you idiot? We're back in the boiler room. And we're turning on each other. We're wearing down!" She knew she was babbling, but she pressed on. "It knows what it's doing! Our minds are wearing us down, knowing what haunts us."

"I see that. I still don't trust him."

Stephanie was blinking at Leslie. "You really think that?"

"You have a better explanation? This whole thing is spiritual. Evil. All that, but it's more personal. But spiritual is really mental, right? I mean, we have to deal with this killer on a different level to satisfy his psychosis. Make him think we are responding on some spiritual level or . . ." Or what. She didn't know or what. "This is crap, just plain crap!"

"I'm not going to give you my gun," Jack said, eyeing Randy suspiciously. He checked to see how many rounds remained. Just one. Good thing he checked. He fished the spare shells out of his pants and loaded them.

Leslie walked over and shoved Randy's gun down. "You're losing your mind! You hear me, Randy? Stop this!"

"Are you two nuts?" Stephanie demanded.

"We're trapped in this basement and you're squabbling over guns?"

Randy glanced at her, then slowly lowered his weapon, reloaded it.

"So you still think this is just in our minds?" Stephanie snapped. "If there's anyone who should be shot here, it's you."

Leslie ignored the woman. Nothing any of them said now would surprise her. And Stephanie was right about one thing—they were trapped.

Jack drilled Randy with a stare. "What happened back there? How did you get back in here?"

"Through the back exit," Randy said.

"You're sure it was an exit?"

"I saw White step in through that door earlier. Of course I'm sure."

"How did *you* get in?" Stephanie asked.

"Up the stairs. This was supposed to be the main level."

"We're trapped," Leslie said.

"All in our minds?" Jack said.

She ignored him.

The house groaned.

"And that's *not* the pipes," Stephanie said. "This house is alive."

It was such a clear, obvious truth that none of them dared suggest differently.

Leslie walked over to one of the boilers and put her hand on it. She rapped on it with her knuckles as if testing to see that it was real, then faced them, face flushed.

"There's no way out, is there?"

Her eyes settled on Randy, who was staring at the wall.

The Wages of Sin Is One Dead Body

House rule number three: *Give me one dead body, and I might let rule two slide.*

The killer was demanding one dead body as a payment for their sin. Fanatical, religious nonsense, but Leslie couldn't shake the feeling that if they didn't play the game this way, they would die.

So what was she supposed to do? Kill her sin? Blow Pete's head off? Or kiss his face and do whatever he wanted as a form of penitence?

The inbreds didn't count; they all knew that. They also knew that White could have killed them by now if he wanted to.

This was why religion should be banned in civilized countries. She glared at the wall and stifled a scream of fury.

Jack gripped the shotgun a little tighter. Of the four of them, Randy was the most likely to satisfy White's demand.

And what about him? If it came right down to it, would he kill one of them to save the other three? In spite of the house rules, Jack suspected White probably wouldn't be satisfied with just one dead body. He recalled the newspaper accounts. Whole families, murdered.

On the other hand, Jack wasn't sure he wouldn't comply, particularly if it was in self-defense. What confused him was the "wages of sin" bit on the wall. Maybe Leslie was right, and the killer was religiously motivated. Whatever was happening to them was as much spiritual or psychosomatic as physical.

The problem was, he didn't have a clue what that meant. How do you defeat a killer—or a house, for that matter—that's rubbing your own sin in your face?

Comply? *One dead body.* Randy's dead body.

"There's only one way out," Stephanie said.

The sound of metal scraping against metal squealed through the room. Jack swiveled his head up just in time to see something drop through the shadows between two large pipes twenty feet above them.

His pulse spiked. It was a body. On a thick rope.

The body fell for ten feet then bounced at the end of the rope, hung by a noose drawn tight around its neck.

Leslie jumped out of the way with a startled cry.

The rope creaked over the swaying weight. Slowly the body turned until they could all see who it was.

At the end of the rope, as dead as a sack of rocks, hung Randy Messarue.

Randy?

They were all too stunned to react immediately. A voice was screaming through Jack's mind, telling him that this body on the end of this rope had serious implications, but he was too shocked to isolate them.

Randy's dead eyes were closed and his

mouth was cracked. From the crack seeped a thin tendril of black smoke that streamed down toward the floor. It hit the ground and spread out on the concrete.

The meaning of this dead body hit Jack then, like an eighteen-wheeler barreling out of the black night. If Randy was dead, who was the Randy next to him?

White?

He reacted on impulse, swinging his shotgun up and around toward Randy, who stared at his dead twin in shock.

"Drop the gun!" Jack shouted.

"What?"

"Drop it!" His arms trembled. Had he chambered another round? He did so now—*ca-chink!* "Now!"

Randy held the shotgun in one hand, barrel pointed at the floor. His eyes turned to Jack, lit by fear. "What's—"

"What are you doing, Jack?" Stephanie asked.

I'm allowing myself to be manipulated by the killer. I'm being pushed slowly to killing for the killer. Putting myself on the same plane as the killer. Forcing myself to show my true colors. I am evil. We are all evil.

The wages of sin . . . is death. One dead body.

The thoughts flashed through his mind and were gone. They weren't of any use to him now.

"That's not Randy," Jack said, nodding at the living Randy. "Randy's dead."

"You . . . you think that's me?" Randy asked, still dazed.

Jack didn't answer. They were all following the same thread of logic that he'd found.

"Drop . . . the . . . gun."

Stephanie took a step back, eyes on Randy.

"*This* is me!" Randy said, jabbing his chest with his free hand. "It's a trick. He's trying to get you to kill me! One dead body. He told me you'd do this! He told me—"

"When did he tell you, Randy? You bring that gun up even an inch, and I'll take your head off. And for the record, I've done it before. I killed Betty a few minutes ago. I'll do it again in a heartbeat."

The man stared, angrily now. "If that's me, who am I? An apparition?" His eyes darted to the others, looking for support. "You think I'm not real? I just rescued Stephanie . . ."

But not even Stephanie jumped to his defense.

"He could be White," Leslie said.

"Yes, he could," Jack said.

"I'm *not* White!"

"And I'm not willing to take that chance," Jack said.

Randy regarded Leslie bitterly. "So now not only the house is haunted, but the killer can magically appear in any form he wants to? This from a staunch atheist?"

"I don't know what I believe anymore. But there's two of you, and one of you isn't real," Leslie said.

"What if that one's the apparition?" Stephanie asked, pointing to the swinging body.

"Check it, Leslie," Jack said.

She looked momentarily unsure, then slowly stepped up to the body. Jack watched from his peripheral vision as she cautiously lifted a hand and nudged it. The body swung and turned in place, rope creaking softly.

"Real," Jack said.

"And so was the body of Stewart that I saw," Randy said. "And it was leaking smoke too. That's the sign. I'm telling you, I'm not White!"

A thought occurred to Jack. He had reason enough to pull the trigger now, didn't he? If Randy was White, Jack would be acting in self-defense. If Randy really was *Randy*, Jack would be acting in *presumed* self-defense. And they would have their one dead body.

The sudden urge to do it brought a tremor to his index finger, despite the weakness of his reasoning.

"Why would I rescue Stephanie after Pete took her?" Randy asked. "Tell me that."

Jack glanced at Stephanie. "What about it? What happened back there?"

"He . . . he rescued me."

"Was he ever out of your sight? Any time when White might have killed him?"

She looked at Randy, eyes wider.

"Actually, yes."

Randy's brow furrowed. "What?"

"When you disappeared around the corner. He could have killed you then and switched places. You were acting a bit strange."

"Good grief! He threatened to kill me."

"Threatened you how?" Jack demanded. "What did he say?"

"That he'd kill me if I didn't kill you. That

you'd try to kill me. Which you are. That time is running out. Dawn is coming."

Leslie gasped. "It's gone!"

Jack looked. The body was gone. Rope and all. They'd imagined it? Impossible!

Behind him a door opened, feet pounded in, Jack whirled. The door slammed. What he saw made his knees threaten to buckle.

Randy and Stephanie had just stumbled into the room through one of the doors. The Randy and Stephanie already in the room stared at their twins, aghast. Identical in every way, down to the shotguns held by both Randys.

"Randy?" Leslie's voice was taut.

Jack stepped back and glanced toward Leslie. But it wasn't just Leslie that he saw.

He saw another Leslie standing five feet from her.

And another Jack.

26

4:31 AM

Jack's legs began to shake.

There were eight of them in the room now; two Leslies, two Stephanies, two Randys—and two Jacks. All of them were wearing stricken looks of horror, including the other Jack, who gripped his shotgun with white knuckles.

Clearly, four of them weren't real. Right?

The Stephanie who'd just come in whimpered.

As if reacting to an unspoken signal, the two Randys and the new Jack snatched their shotguns to their shoulders and paired off into a stalemate. The Randys' guns on the Jacks, and the Jacks' guns on the Randys.

He'd lost whatever advantage he had, Jack realized. He should have finished this when he had the chance, because he couldn't now—not without knowing who was real and who wasn't, a luxury now clearly out of reach.

The two Randys were breathing hard. At any moment a gun would go off.

"Easy," Jack said.

"No one moves," the other Jack said.

"What's going on?" the new Stephanie asked, trembling.

None of them took a stab at answering. For long seconds they stood in a deadlock, silent. The house groaned again, loud and distant above them.

The other Jack broke their silence. "We have a problem," he said. "No one makes any rash moves. Just take it easy."

"Who are you?" the new Leslie asked, looking at Jack. "How did you get in here?"

"Through the door."

"That couldn't be. Jack and I came through the door a few minutes ago, and the room was empty. We were here first."

Impossible. But she obviously didn't think so.

"Four of you aren't real," the new Jack said. He switched his gun from Randy to Jack. "Beginning with you. Put the gun down."

A bead of perspiration broke down Jack's forehead and snaked around his eye. The new Jack was taking command, as if he were the real Jack. Jack's mind tipped dangerously. His finger was tight on the trigger, and he forced himself to ease off.

First one Randy, then the other, swiveled their guns to train on Jack. Now all three shotguns were on him.

"Just take it easy," he breathed. "Nothing rash."

Isn't that what the other Jack had said?

"We have to figure this out. Leslie?"

She didn't answer. He cast her a quick glance. "Tell them."

"Tell them what?" Her eyes darted around. "I don't know what."

"That we're real, for heaven's sake!"

"I . . . I don't know which one of you is the real Jack."

"Are you crazy? We were just in here with the dead body . . ."

"What dead body?" the new Leslie asked.

"Shut up!" Randy snapped.

White had told Randy that he should kill Jack.

Would an apparition's shotgun actually work?

"He's going to kill us," Jack said, glancing at the other Jack. "You know that, don't you? And since he doesn't know which is real, he has to take both of us out."

The new Jack thought about his statement, then turned his gun back on Randy.

The new Randy jerked his gun on the new Jack. They were paired off again.

"He's doing this!" Leslie said. Which Leslie, Jack no longer knew. He no longer knew who was who in relationship to how it all began. He only knew he was the real Jack.

The other Jack also seemed to know about himself. What if he was right?

"White's manipulating us," one Leslie said. "Forcing us to kill someone we think might not be real without knowing for certain."

"She's right," the other Leslie said. "He's trying to extract payment for wrongdoing, which in his sick little mind is death."

The hopelessness of the situation was driving Jack mad. He couldn't seem to still the trembling in his hands.

If they could all be reasonable . . .

The notion of reasoning with an apparition struck him as pointless. And Randy was out for blood. There was no reasoning with either Randy at this point.

"This is what White told me would happen," Randy said with a wicked smirk. "He said Jack would kill me if I didn't kill him. Not a chance, hero boy."

"Don't do it," the new Jack said.

"Do it," the other Randy said. "He's got his gun on the wrong Randy."

It only took a moment for the first Randy to understand the meaning. "You're saying I'm expendable because you think you're real?"

"I'm saying we got us a standoff. Someone's going to die here, and it isn't going to be me."

Each of them truly believed they were real. If either of the Randys knew they were unreal, they would have started the bloodbath already without fear of dying.

"We can tell which of us is real," the new Jack said. "I doubt an apparition's shotgun will actually fire. We can all fire our weapons at the wall."

Assuming the assumption was correct.

"And then what, kill the ones whose guns misfire?" Randy asked, wearing that smirk of his. "Why don't we just go for it now and see who's alive when the dust settles?"

"Because you may end up dead, that's why," Jack said. He lowered his gun a few inches. "I'll agree to Jack's suggestion."

After a few moments of consideration, the Randys each lowered their shotguns. One turned his gun on the wall and pulled the trigger.

Boom! The room echoed with the blast. Followed almost immediately by another blast.

Boom!

The second Randy had discharged his weapon as well. As one they both trained their guns on Jack. Then one of them switched to the other Jack, who brought his up as well.

Jack followed suit.

"Like I said," one Randy murmured. "I say we just go for it."

"Which probably means you're not the real Randy," Leslie said. "You're egging us all on and into a bloodbath!"

"You think? I think I'm looking at White." His eyes were on Jack. "And the only way to find out is to put some lead in his gut."

"There's another way," the other Randy said.

They waited.

"Stewart's dead body leaked black smoke. I'm thinking that maybe it wasn't real, like the hanged body a few moments ago. And I'm thinking that unreal bodies leak black smoke."

"Betty was real enough, and smoke came out of her," Jack said. "I'm thinking the smoke has to do with being dead."

"Or wounded," Leslie said. "The stuff oozes out the wounds, right?"

"You're saying we should each cut ourselves?"

Randy shrugged. "You afraid of a cut?"

"Okay. We cut ourselves on one condition," Jack said. "We give up our weapons when we get cut. If nothing happens, we get it back. Leslie can hold them, one at a time."

"What's to keep Leslie from taking us out?" Randy demanded.

Would the real Randy say that? Maybe he would.

"Agreed?" Jack pressed.

"Agreed," Jack said.

The Randy who had suggested a standoff

hesitated, but the other agreed, followed by the Leslies and the Stephanies.

Sweat streamed past both of Jack's temples. He was sure that if they didn't do something soon, one of them would go ballistic. And he was no longer sure it wouldn't be him.

He impulsively handed his gun to Leslie. "Anyone have a knife?"

Both Randys did. Naturally. The real Randy had taken one from the kitchen upstairs. One of them slid it toward Jack without lowering his gun, eyes glinting.

Jack picked up the knife and held his hand out. He placed the blade's edge against his palm and looked at the others.

"We all go. Anyone refuses, they prove themselves to be unreal. Assuming this works. If anyone smokes black, they're incapacitated, not shot outright. Agreed?"

They all nodded.

Because he was sure that no black smoke would pour out of any cut on his hand, Jack had no difficulty with the test. But he wasn't so sure that Randy would be as eager to cut himself.

"Keep the gun on Randy, Leslie."

"That wasn't part of—"

"It is now," Jack interrupted. "Just to even things out. Consider her impartial."

Leslie lifted the gun so that both Randys were covered.

Jack nodded. He pressed the blade against his skin and pressed. But the knife wasn't as sharp as he'd hoped, forcing him to draw it back until it sliced past the epidermis.

Blood seeped from the cut. He held it out. The sight of red blood had never looked quite so comforting.

He showed them. "Satisfied?"

He tossed the knife back toward Randy. It clattered to his feet. "You're next."

"Why me?"

"To keep it even. You nervous? Leslie, get his gun."

The door behind Randy opened. Susan stood in the doorway, eyes wide, breathing hard.

Jack glanced at the others to see their reactions. They all looked similarly amazed. "Are you okay?"

"What do you think you're doing?" she demanded. "You're going to kill . . . the one thing . . ." Her voice wasn't connecting with Jack. It seemed to be hitting dead spots. Skipping like a bad CD.

None of them had lowered their weapons.

"Is she real?" Stephanie asked. "Maybe she's not the real Susan."

"There's only one of her," Leslie said.

"We should cut *her*," Randy said.

Susan looked up at the writing on the wall.

The Wages of Sin Is One Dead Body

"Maybe you all deserve to die tonight. That's what he wants. That's . . . all of us dead. I thought . . . but I think you're just going to get us all killed. You . . ." Her next few words were garbled. "You . . . ba . . . the way out . . . hate . . . blood."

Susan looked at them as if she hadn't noticed her own speech skipping.

"Only those with eyes to see the truth can see it," she said. "I think you're all blind as ba . . . the . . . finish . . . ma . . . Jack's going to ki . . . heart . . . to die."

"She's with White!" a Leslie said.

A shiver touched the skin on Jack's back. What if she was actually White's ally? It would explain how she'd managed to live so long.

He reached for his weapon.

The black smoke began to pour out of the cut in his palm while his hand was extended toward Leslie.

He froze, stunned by the surreal sight. Black fog pouring out, falling vertically, hitting the ground and spreading. Like liquid nitrogen.

How was that possible? He was unreal? The *other* Jack was the real Jack?

His eyes met Leslie's, which were stricken with terror.

"I told you, Jack," Susan said. "You're all guilty . . . You . . ."

But the rest of her sentence was smothered by a loud moan that reverberated around them.

A thick column of black smoke poured out of the large round vent near the ceiling through which Jack and Leslie had first entered the room. Fog just like the fog that came from Jack's hand. An inky black streak over two feet in diameter. It shot out several feet then took a turn straight down and flowed to the floor, where it spread toward them.

Two thoughts collided in Jack's mind. The first was that Randy was going to most certainly kill him now. And then the other Jack, whom he'd believed to be the real Jack.

The second was that his only chance at survival was to grab the gun still in Leslie's frozen hand as she stared at the black smoke now filling the room from the bottom up.

The fog rushed around his feet and sent a slicing pain up his legs.

The Leslies screamed. The Randys back-pedaled in a hopeless attempt to avoid the rapidly rising blanket of fog.

The fog touched the door where Susan stood, slamming it shut in her face. If she was with White, she was leaving them to their own demise.

Jack stepped forward and grabbed Randy's shotgun from Leslie's grip. He pivoted, expecting hot lead to fill his body at any moment, though he wasn't sure he'd be able to distinguish it from the pain that now screamed through his body. The fog was like an acid.

The other Randy saw what he'd done and swung his gun back in line.

Jack lunged to his left and fired at Randy.

The fog swirled over his head before he could see what, if any, damage he'd inflicted. The sound of another shot buffeted his ears. He chambered another round and fired blindly in the direction of the sound.

Then the room filled with a series of

booms, like rolling thunder, as shotguns on all sides fired in rapid succession. Screams and grunts.

The sound of bodies falling. Guns clattering on concrete.

Then nothing but the beating of Jack's heart to accompany the ringing in his ears.

A whooshing sound enveloped him. The black fog began rushing back into the ceiling the way it had come. Jack stood still, blinded by the smoke. He hadn't been hit, but he suddenly wasn't sure that was a good thing. What if Leslie had been struck? Or Stephanie?

His body was shaking from head to toe, more from shock than from the pain brought on by the smoke. Randy had gotten his standoff.

The smoke level fell below his head.

Leslie stood on his left, staring. One Leslie.

Randy and Stephanie stood on his right, shocked. One Randy, one Stephanie.

Then the black fog was gone. No Susan, no dead bodies. Jack, Leslie, Randy, and Stephanie stared at one another in silence.

It was Stephanie who broke the quiet. "Oh, God," she mumbled. And by the way she said it, Jack thought it might be a prayer of desperation.

He looked at his palm. No fog, just red blood. But staring up at them all, Jack knew a few other things now.

He knew that Randy intended to kill him.

He knew he had what it took to kill Randy.

He knew he could leak black smoke.

And he knew that he was guilty of a desire to kill Randy, of bitterness toward Stephanie, of a hundred other smudges on his life. And this killer didn't seem the kind to let them slide.

Not without one dead body. House rules.

The object of this game was to survive by killing, but Jack was sure that real survival wasn't simply a matter of killing or being killed. It was really about confronting the wages of sin, whatever that meant. It was about life as much as it was about death. What kind of contest didn't consist of at least two contestants? If this was a contest between good and evil, then where was the good?

Jack didn't know. And this, too, returned the tremor to his knees.

27

4:48 AM

It took them several minutes to settle into the full dread of their predicament. They were truly, hopelessly trapped by a killer who could reach out and tinker with their lives at his whim in a house that seemed to flow at his will.

Something had happened to Stephanie, but she wasn't talking about it. Her breath smelled like sulfur, and she was oddly quiet.

Jack didn't want to appear threatening to Randy, so he gave the shotgun to Leslie and quietly asked her to keep an eye on Randy.

He went out of his way to appear gracious to the man, knowing that he would look for any excuse to force a confrontation.

That left Randy to stew and occasionally glance up at the words on the wall.

The Wages of Sin Is One Dead Body

They tried to make sense of the multiple characters and the fog that had swallowed them. They'd all seen the same thing; that much was a comfort, however slight. And they all agreed that the house was deliberately manipulating them to expose their own base tendencies. Their sins, maybe. Their eventual submission to the killer's demand that they surrender to the murderer in them all.

This they all agreed on, with Leslie's help. But despite her pinpointing the issues at hand, this shared knowledge didn't offer any solutions. Understanding that you were falling down a cliff didn't provide the proverbial branch to break your fall. Leslie could describe her understanding of the cliff, but she couldn't point to any branches.

"We're screwed," Randy said after a lull in their otherwise-intense discussion. "We're out of options. We're in the sticks in a possessed house that's making us see ghosts or whatever these things that keep popping up are." His voice was resigned. "We're all going to die."

No one argued.

Jack walked over to Leslie and casually took the gun back.

"There's only one way out of this," Randy said.

The gun felt surprisingly comfortable in Jack's hands. Knowing what he did about Randy gave him half a mind to end it right here with a little standoff of his own. He was justified. He knew the man fully intended to kill him at some point.

"What's that, Randy?" he asked, pumping the action. Only two shots left—he would have to be careful.

"You know what I'm talking about," Randy said. He looked at the words on the wall.

"Tell me." Jack faced him, suddenly itching for the same confrontation on Randy's mind.

"He wants one of us dead," Randy said, withdrawing the knife from his belt.

"You want to kill me, Randy? Hmm? Is that it?"

"I didn't say that. Do you want me dead?"

"Did I say that?"

They stared off in silence.

"I'm just saying that he's got us trapped down here for as long as it takes for one of us to kill another. Someone has to die. Either one of us, or the girl."

"The girl? Who said anything about the girl?"

"White told me. The others don't count. Betty, Stewart, Pete—they don't mean anything. But Susan does."

"Unless she's working with him," Leslie said. "She's gone again. Why? There's something wrong with her."

"Maybe," Jack said. "I'm not willing to concede that—"

"Well, what are you willing to concede?" Randy demanded. "He wants a dead body, we give—"

"You *really* believe he'll be satisfied with just one of us blowing someone else's head off?" Jack said.

"I think he'll follow his own rules," Leslie said. "He may not let us all live, but as long as we don't give in to his demands, he won't kill us, either. We start killing each other, and the game is over."

"What's our time?" Randy said.

Jack checked his watch. The crystal was cracked. "Four fifty-two."

Randy chuckled ruefully. Sweat beaded his face. "An hour and change. If one of us doesn't kill someone else pretty soon, he's going to kill us—"

The door rattled. Fists beat on it. "You in there? Let us in!"

A man's voice. Not the familiar sound of White's deep voice behind a tin mask.

Stephanie backed away from the door. "Is . . . is that him?"

"Could be him without the mask," Randy said, standing and raising the knife.

He started forward.

Jack grabbed his arm. "Hold on!"

Pounding again. "This is Officer Lawdale. Open this door immediately!"

Leslie looked a question at Jack. *Who?*

"Lawdale! The highway patrolman Steph and I ran into."

Leslie's face brightened. She ran forward, unlocked the door, and pulled it open.

Highway Patrolman Morton Lawdale stood in the doorway dressed in the same tight gray uniform they'd seen him in yesterday.

He had a revolver out, cocked by his ear.

He glanced behind him and then entered the room, locking the door behind him.

"Well, well, well," Lawdale said, scanning the room. "What kind of mess have we gotten ourselves into now?"

28

4:53 AM

The game hadn't changed, but there was a new feeling in the air. For the first time Jack felt a genuine sense of hope. Lawdale was undoubtedly quirky, but he carried himself with authority and confidence, something they all desperately needed.

Sweat darkened his gray shirt, which was otherwise dry. Apparently the rain had let up. His black leather boots were muddy, but Lawdale was unscathed. His now hatless head was covered in close-cropped blond hair. He'd armed himself to the teeth before

coming in. A gun on each hip, two more behind the belt at his back, blades on each ankle. Lawdale was nothing short of a gunslinger born into the wrong century.

To his knowledge no one had seen him
enter the building, which he'd done without
waiting for the backup he'd called in.

After grilling Leslie and Randy as to their
identities and then assuring himself that
each of the four was not mortally hurt, Lawdale demanded they tell him what had happened, all of it, and they fed it to him in long
run-on sentences interrupted by his con-
stant insistence for clarification. As the story
quickly unfolded, Lawdale began to pace.

The house was still moaning and screech-
ing above them, attracting his periodic
glances to the ceiling. He offered no judg-
ment one way or the other.

He told them how he'd come across
Jack's car. His headlights had caught the
red taillights of a car in the bush as he
passed. Ordinarily he would have called it in
without stopping, but he recognized Jack's
blue Mustang.

"So we can get out of here, right?"
Stephanie said. "You got in, so we can get
out."

"Hold on to your high notes, honey. Give me a moment." He holstered his gun and slapped his palm with that black baton of his as he paced.

"Backup's on the way, but it might take them an hour or more."

"You can't just take us out?" Stephanie cried.

He glanced at the ceiling in response to a groan. "You're saying a killer is out there. You're saying you've been hunted by three inbreds armed with shotguns. You're saying the house is haunted. You're saying there's no way out." He leveled his eyes at Stephanie. "I'd say rushing out into the halls with guns blazing is a tad impulsive, wouldn't you? Give me a moment!"

Jack liked the man, quirks and all. Not even Randy in his rabid state would easily run over Lawdale.

"I've heard about the man," Lawdale continued. "A serial killer who's been on the wires for a few months now. Known as Tin Man, which corresponds with this mask you described. His trail has been leading southeast. No surprise he's finally here, then."

Lawdale slapped his palm with the stick. "Betty and Stewart are dead, you say?"

"We think so," Randy said.

"But badly wounded at least," Lawdale said.

"Right."

"And this girl named Susan keeps going missing, which you think means she could be with him. I doubt that a young girl would be much use to a killer. I'd buy the argument that if she's more than a figment—"

"We didn't imagine her," Jack said.

"Fine. Then I would give her the benefit of the doubt. The house, on the other hand . . ." His eyes settled on the wall.

The Wages of Sin Is One Dead Body

". . . The house is what concerns me most."

"But you believe us," Leslie said.

"If I didn't believe you, I wouldn't be concerned, now would I?" He cracked his neck.

"A haunted house," Stephanie said.

"Could be. You can deal with a man like White by putting him back with some lead in his gut. But the supernatural is a whole different thing."

"You're a religious man?" Jack asked.

"Can't say that I am; can't say that I'm not. But I know that if what you're telling me about this house is accurate, it won't matter if we have a whole SWAT team outside."

"But you got in," Stephanie said.

"And I've been thinking about that," Lawdale said. "Something you should do a little more of."

He walked to his right without looking at her. "When you try to leave the basement, you end up back in. Doors lock behind you, open in front of you. As if the house knows you, inside and out. Am I right?"

"Something like that," Jack said.

"The house won't let you out. But that doesn't mean it won't let someone in. Like a flytrap."

"White couldn't get in at first," Randy said.

"Based on what you've told me, doesn't sound like he wanted in, not until he came into the basement. Sounds to me like he was trying to drive you into the basement on your own."

The man's reasoning mirrored Jack's, although Lawdale was coming at it from a different angle.

A few seconds of silence slipped by.

"It's possible, just possible, that I may be able to get out," Lawdale said.

"How?" Randy asked. He stood, seeming renewed. "I'm going with you."

"Back up, boy. What I'm saying is that I

know Tin Man didn't see me come in. I saw the truck at the front door and avoided the top floor. Same for the basement entrance in the back. I came in through a grate and up a dried-out tunnel. Place used to be a mining operation but was abandoned when they discovered a mass grave on the grounds."

"A grave?" Stephanie said, shooting an I-told-you-so look at Randy. "That would explain some things."

"Tin Man may have turned this house bad somehow—invited in whatever powers to haunt it—but if there's rules, there's rules. House rules. The house will prevent anyone from leaving it, assuming it knows they're inside."

"You're suggesting the house doesn't know you're inside," Jack said.

"Still the dense one, aren't you, Jack? But you're on the right track."

Leslie grunted. She closed her eyes and took a long, deep breath. Shook her head. "I can't believe we're talking like this. What a crock. A house doesn't know stuff! Listen to you!"

Her old training was awakening, Jack thought. "I thought you changed your—"

She held up her hand and stopped him.

"I know, I know. Yes, I said it might be haunted." She waved a hand as she continued. "Spirits, demons, supernatural stuff and all that. I know! That doesn't make it real. It's one thing to talk in general supernatural terms." She looked at the words on the wall. "It's another thing to start talking rules and specifics and . . . whatever. Like there's a whole order or something. Like the house is actually thinking, for heaven's sake! Knows things! Don't tell me that doesn't sound just a little bit crazy to you."

Jack nodded. "But we don't have time to sort out the whys of what's happening yet. We've got barely more than an hour."

"And then what, the house starts beating us to death?" Leslie asked.

"Somehow I think it'll be a little more personal."

"Let's not get our undies in a bunch," Lawdale said to Leslie. "I doubt the house knows anything. But the power, the spirits, the demons, the whatever you want to call it that inhabits this house, do. And they can change the house at will. Yet it let me walk in unchallenged?" He smacked his palm. "The only explanation is that these powers are limited to time and space and they were preoccupied with you. I made it past unnoticed."

"Which would mean if you can get back to an exit unseen, the house won't know to stop you," Leslie said. "That's your point, right? Assuming these things work like you suggest."

"I'm not saying I know how they work. I'm simply dealing with the facts in front of me and drawing as few conclusions as possible. Something you should be very familiar with in your line of work."

"If you go, I'm going with you," Randy said.

"And you"—Lawdale turned to him—"as a businessman, you should be familiar with basic logic, right?"

Randy blinked, insulted.

"Put it together, city boy. They know you—they'll be all over you."

"And why aren't they all over us now?" Randy demanded.

"Maybe they are," Jack said. "The rules are pretty simple. Tin Man's giving us time to kill each other."

"Even if you get out, how do *we* get out?" Stephanie asked.

"We get out when the officer opens a door

for us," Leslie said, staring at Lawdale. "Am I right?"

"Assuming I'm right," he said. "Maybe the doors can be opened from the outside. They let you in, but not out."

He looked at the door by the boiler. He'd given them the first real plan of the night, but he no longer possessed the same confidence he'd come in with, Jack thought.

"If I can get out without being detected, I'll find a way into the house and will open the basement door, the one you say is between the kitchen and the dining room. If you can make it to the top of the stairs quickly, while I have the door open, maybe we can get you out."

They stared at him ambivalently.

"Once out of the basement, we should be able to escape. The basement seems to be the problem."

He paced, concern on his face now even more obvious.

"I don't mind pointing out that I may not make it," Lawdale said, glancing at the door again. He pulled out one of his revolvers and checked the clip. "These things respond to bullets?"

"Yes."

He cracked his neck again. "Okay, tell me the best way to get into the house upstairs. Back door, window, ceiling? Tell me."

"Back door to the kitchen," Randy said. "White bolted it from the outside. If that doesn't work . . ." He shrugged.

"I'll find a way in."

"White didn't," Stephanie said.

"White didn't *want* to," Jack said. "Aren't you listening?"

Lawdale looked at his watch. "Five oh-nine. Give me ten minutes. At exactly—"

"That long?" Stephanie demanded.

"With time for unforeseen difficulties, yes. If I make it, I'll open the main door into the basement at exactly 5:19. Be on the stairs. Can you do that?"

Jack and Leslie synced their watches. Jack glanced at the others, avoiding Randy's stare, and nodded.

Lawdale walked to the door, put his ear against it, and listened for several long seconds. He took a very deep breath and dropped to a crouch.

Unlocked the door. Cracked it. One quick glance outside and closed it again.

"Okay."

"You sure you know the way back?" Leslie asked.

He tapped his head. "I left a few markers. Ten minutes."

Morton Lawdale cocked his gun, extended it out with one hand, opened the door, and disappeared into the hall in a silent, crouched run.

29

5:14 AM

They spent the first five minutes of the wait trying to convince one another that Lawdale's plan would work, but there were too many questions voiced by all of them to bring any true comfort.

Lawdale's plan was a hope, nothing more. And a thin hope at that. But Jack knew that short of hope, Randy would have tried something rash. Like killing him. If the highway patrolman hadn't shown up when he did, at least one of them would likely be dead now.

"You're sure you know the way?" Randy asked Jack. "How long will it take us?"

"The stairs are through three halls—been down them twice now. Unless they've changed."

"Great," Stephanie said.

"You come up with a better idea. Otherwise, stick to the plan."

Both she and Randy fidgeted nervously. Leslie had her eyes glued to her watch and had grown quiet.

The house continued to groan and creak.

And what about Susan? The more Jack thought about her, the more he was convinced that she was nothing more or less than another innocent victim. With every passing minute, he became more convinced that she couldn't be tied in with the killer.

"Down to one minute," Leslie said.

Jack walked toward the door. "Follow me."

They exited the room on edge, in single file. Jack, Leslie, Stephanie, and Randy, bringing up the rear with his shotgun locked and loaded, one spastic forefinger away from alerting the whole house of their location.

"I don't think this is going to work," Stephanie said. She spoke quietly, but her voice sounded shockingly loud in the hall. Jack turned back and drew his fingers across his neck forcefully.

It took them thirty seconds to reach a large wooden door that led into the second hall. So far so good. But it was the hall ahead that concerned Jack the most.

Jack turned back and mouthed instructions to them. "Through this door; stairs are on the right."

"What's that?" Stephanie asked. She was pointing at the floor.

Jack saw it immediately, the black fog they'd encountered in the boiler room was seeping past the crack below the door.

"That stuff's in the hall?" Stephanie said. "We can't—"

"Quiet!" Jack whispered. "We go. Ignore the pain; just get on the steps as fast as you can and run."

Jack grabbed the handle. "Ready?"

He jerked the door open.

Stephanie was the first to scream. They were back in the boiler room, flooded with two feet of black fog. A fist seemed to lodge itself in Jack's throat. Four others stood in the black fog.

One Jack, one Randy, one Leslie, and one Stephanie, facing off with shotguns as they had before. The Jack's hand was bleeding black fog, which also poured from the round vent up high, exactly as before.

They were staring at themselves, as if *they*, not the people in the room, were the unreal among them.

The quartet inside the boiler room spun to the sound of Stephanie's scream. For a moment all eight of them froze, four outside the room, four in the knee-high fog.

"Jack!" Susan stood panting in an abutting hallway. "Hurry! Follow me!"

Without waiting, she ran down the hall, away from them.

Jack decided that he would follow. Whoever she was, he would follow.

He slammed the door shut and sprinted after the girl.

"What if—"

"Shut up! We don't have time!"

They followed him, hard on his heels, as he gained on the girl. Down one hall and to a large door. He recognized it as the same door they'd just assumed was the way into the main hall.

Susan threw the door open. Fog filled the hall to a height of three feet. She hesitated a moment then ran into it. "Hurry!"

The moment Jack entered the fog, he knew that they were in trouble. The acid, for one, but this he could tolerate. What lay ahead was a different matter.

The house had changed again. And this change brought all five of them to an abrupt halt.

They were still in the hall at the bottom of the stairs. Jack knew that because he saw stairs rising to the main floor to their right. But the stairs now ran the full length of the hall, not the mere ten feet he'd expected.

The passage extended just as far to their left. It had doubled in length.

And width.

But not even the matter of an extra hundred feet of hallway had stopped them. The man standing between them and the stairs did.

Stewart. A shotgun readied. Their sudden arrival had startled him, but he recovered quickly, swinging his gun toward them.

Boom! Randy fired. His shot picked the

man up off his feet and dropped him into
the fog that filled the hall to their knees.

"Run!" Susan yelled. She ran toward the
stairs, leaving swirling fog in her wake.

They took off after her.

"Watch for others!" she cried.

Others?

Jack saw the backs of their claw-scarred
bald heads first, just breaking the top of the
fog. Rising slowly, as if the fog was giving
them birth.

The fog's familiar pain pushed Jack faster,
and he crowded the others. "Hurry!"

"The door's not open!" Leslie cried.

"Run!"

The new inbreds were positioned abreast,
forcing Jack to brush past as he sprinted.
Their rising continued, like a choreographed
dance. Their heads showed to the tops of
their ears now. All of them faced away, toward
the stairs. They were all bald, but that's where
their similarity to Stewart ended.

Six of them.

So the basement was infested with more
than just Stewart, Betty, and Pete. Why they
were rising so slowly, Jack didn't know, but
he was sure they were part of White's game.

Susan leaped onto the steps, stumbled on

the first one, but scrambled up using her hands. Out of the fog. Randy was right behind her. The others followed, equally frantic, motivated by a desire to get away from the inbreds as much as from the fog.

The door was still closed. Randy fired at the latch. The buckshot bounced off the door. Didn't even chip the paint. Jack was the last to mount the steps. He clambered to the top, where Susan was pounding on the door with both hands. The others piled up on the landing and looked back, faces drawn and pale.

Jack whirled back and felt his heart skip a beat. The bald heads had risen from the fog so that the tops of their heads and their eyes cleared the black sea. Still rising.

Their bald heads and scars were similar to Stewart's. Their eyes were not. They glowed a fluorescent green.

Stephanie had joined Susan on the door, pounding. "Let us out! Let us out!"

Thud, thud, thud. Boots walked the hall's concrete floor. Jack jerked his head around and looked at the hall's far end.

White was walking down the passage, through the rising clones, trench coat dipping into the black fog. The tin mask hid his expression. But his stride said he had been expecting them.

The moment the killer passed the inbreds, they rose to their full height.

Jack whipped his gun up. *Boom!* White jerked once as if hit, then walked on, unabated.

Stephanie was screaming bloody murder now. All five of them pressed back against the door.

Jack was aiming to fire again when the pressure at his back caved. He stumbled back.

The door was open?

The group surged back through the doorway. But Jack's view was of the hall, not the space they were entering.

The moment the man behind the tin mask saw that the door had been opened, he stopped. But instead of raising his shotgun and firing into his escaping prey, he stood still.

Jack was the last through. He scrambled for the door, eyes glued to the Tin Man.

"Lock it!" Randy screamed. He was seeing what Jack saw. A scene from the darkest of horror stories.

At the last moment, just as they were

shoving the door closed, White grabbed his tin mask and tilted it up, exposing his full face.

It was a face from the grave, half of it bared to the bone. White's jaws snapped wide, as wide as the mask itself, and he roared at them.

Black fog streamed from his mouth. Blasted toward the door.

The door slammed shut. Randy threw the bolt.

A shock wave hit the other side of the door with enough force to bend the wood and send both of them flying against the opposite wall. A thin wisp of black smoke drifted past the cracks.

But it held.

They managed to stand, panting, watching the door. But it didn't move.

"Guys?" Stephanie's voice from the dining room was stretched thin, laced with confusion.

Jack turned around. The first thing he noticed was that some of the lights were back on, blazing bright enough for him to see what Stephanie was looking at.

The once-cheerful dining room now looked as if it had been sitting vacant for a hundred years. Dust covered the paintings and walls. Paper peeled from the walls in long swaths. Most of the furniture remained, but it was covered in dust. The cushions on the good chairs were shredded, chewed by rats.

The table was strewn with rotten food, the same food they'd eaten earlier, crawling with worms and maggots. The stench was similar to the sick sulfuric odor from the basement.

With one glance through the arched entry, Jack saw that the dining room wasn't the only part of the house that had changed.

"It's . . . how's this possible?" Stephanie said.

No one answered as they took it all in, stunned. The house was dead. All of it.

Dead, very dead. But a death that was clearly alive.

30

5:20 AM

It took them a full minute to step beyond shock and find reason.

"Are we imagining this?" Jack asked. "Or were we imagining earlier?"

"Is that possible?" Stephanie said. "I mean, we ate at this table, right?"

No one was quick with speculation, much less answers.

"This can't be real," Lawdale said. "I've been in this house a hundred times."

"It's real," Susan said angrily. "I told you there's more going on here than you realize.

I told you they're wrong." She said some-thing else. Or did she? Her lips kept moving for a few seconds, but no sound came out. Or was that Jack's imagination?

Jack stared at Susan, meeting her eyes. "They? You mean Stewart?"

She eyed him.

"You're saying they were demons or something?"

"Would explain why they don't count," Randy said.

"Don't be ridiculous," Leslie said. "Demons, please. This is about the imagination, not—"

"Shut up, Leslie!" Randy snapped. "Make up your mind! We don't have time for your psychobabble anymore. Call it what you want, we're in a world of hurt here. And we're running out of time."

". . . and he's going to kill you all," Susan said, finishing her point.

Jack headed toward the kitchen then turned back to Lawdale. "How did you get in?"

"Back door."

It was the first good look at the lawman Jack had taken since Lawdale opened the door. He'd removed his outer shirt and used a strip of it as a makeshift bandage on a wound to his upper arm. A bloody bandanna circled his head. His T-shirt was a well-worn Budweiser variety, untucked and hitched over both guns.

"What happened?"

"I had some trouble getting out. Halfway through the grate someone took a potshot at me, and I fell back through. Took me a few minutes to take him out."

"Could explain why they were waiting," Jack said. "But why did they let us go?"

"You call that letting us go?" Randy said.

Stephanie suddenly broke for the kitchen, running. "They let us go because upstairs is no better than the basement," she said.

Jack followed quickly. He burst into the kitchen just as Stephanie took hold of the back door handle. She gave it a twist. Threw her weight into another twist. Fumbled with the dead bolt.

"It's locked!" she cried.

Jack pushed her aside and tried the door. It wouldn't budge.

"It's locked?" Leslie asked behind him.

Jack spun back and faced Lawdale. "You sure this is the way you came in?"

Lawdale didn't bother responding.

"Stand back," Randy snapped. Within

seconds, he'd pulled a plastic box of cartridges out of his pants, loaded the gun, and pumped a round.

Jack and Stephanie stepped back.

The blast tore into wood and shattered the lock. Jack tried again.

No luck. He looked at the seal. It felt like the whole door wasn't a door at all. Solid as a wall. Steel bars ran the length of the broken glass. That was new.

"Surely we can blast a hole," Leslie said, not convincingly.

"How many shells do you have left, Randy?" Jack asked.

The man checked the box. "Eight."

"Okay, save them. Where's that ax?"

Randy set down the shotgun, hurried to the meat locker, stepped over the broken door, and hauled out the ax hammer that Stewart had used to break out.

They watched in silence as he approached the back door, lined up the ax, and took a huge, grunting swing at the window. What glass connected with the ax head shattered. But the bars held firm.

Didn't even bend.

Possible, Jack thought. Some kinds of

steel might resist such a blow. But in this old house, improbable.

Randy took another swing. Again, not even a good dent.

"It's the same as the basement!" Stephanie cried.

"Hold on, just take it easy," Lawdale ordered, stepping forward. He held out his hand for the ax, and Randy gave it to him. "There has to be a way out. If the doors are reinforced, we'll go through a wall."

"Too many cabinets in here." Lawdale returned to the dining room, saw there were no outer walls, then followed Jack to the main entrance. The wall around the front door bulged slightly under the force of the truck White had driven into the house.

They stared at the damage in wonder. Lack of damage, rather. Jack recalled splintering wood, flying plaster, disintegrating doorjambs. More illusions? Or was this the illusion?

"If a truck can't break a board at thirty miles an hour, that ax doesn't stand a chance." Randy loaded another round. *Ca-chink.*

But Lawdale wasn't convinced. He stared at the wall in a kind of stupor, unbelieving.

He suddenly began swinging at the wall in a rage.

Crash . . . crash . . . crash . . . crash!

Each blow bounced off after removing some paint. The wood itself, however, didn't so much as splinter.

Lawdale paused, breathing hard, then raced into the living room, yanked the sofa roughly out of his way, and smashed the window behind it with a cry of anger.

But the bars beyond didn't bend.

He went again, and a third time, before swiveling and taking a huge swipe at the brick on the fireplace.

Mortar sprayed as the ax hammer smashed through the brick. "Ha!"

"That's inside," Randy said, dropping his shotgun and grabbing the ax from the man. "Try the back wall." He swung the hammer through the opening, against the back of the fireplace.

Jack knew by the solid sound that it was hopeless. Randy stood back and stared into the ashes. The tin can still sat on one side where Jack had tossed it earlier.

Tin Man's tin can.

They could all see the writing curving over the bleached label.

Welcome to my house
House rules:
3. Give me one dead body, and I might let rule two slide.

Randy grunted, tossed the ax on the floor, and retrieved his shotgun.

"What's this?" Lawdale reached for the can.

"The can we told you about."

Stephanie was pacing with both hands in her hair, brow wrinkled with stress. She whirled to Jack, eyes blazing with fury.

"How's this possible?! How can this be happening to me?"

"Keep your voice down, miss!" Lawdale snapped.

"And what good are you?" she yelled at him. "You could have gotten us out through that grate you found. Instead you come up with this"—she flung her hand out at him—"cockamamy plan that gets us trapped up here!"

"You got any better ideas?" Randy screamed at her.

Officer Lawdale had one of his pistols out of its holster and cocked by his ear almost too fast for Jack to see. He threw the can into the fireplace.

"The next time one of you yells at me, I put a bullet over your head to show you I mean business; the next time it'll be in your leg to bring you under control. If you hadn't noticed, there's five of us now. And over my dead body, all five of us live through the next hour. You got that?"

"Six," a soft voice said.

Susan stood quietly beside Leslie, who flinched.

"There's six of us," she said.

"Then six. My point stands. Now we have about an hour, is that right?"

"Not quite," Leslie said, holding her watch up to the lamp. "Dawn's at 6:17. Least that's what we've been—"

Something began to pound on the wall behind Jack. He jumped and spun. Again, *thump, thump, thump,* and this time he could see the wall vibrate with each hit. The dining room.

Lawdale pulled out his other gun. "Okay, backup will be here any minute. It's time we make whatever's behind this house think twice. We just have to stall till help comes. But that doesn't mean run. Bring your guns." He strode across the foyer.

Thump, thump, thump!

"You sure that's a good idea?" Leslie said.

"You've been running all night. For all we know, this house is just feeding on your fear."

"We're alive, aren't we?"

"I'm not sure you would be alive if I hadn't come in. Wait here."

Jack raised a brow at Leslie's stare and went after Lawdale and Randy.

"What if it's trying to separate us again?" Stephanie demanded.

Thump, thump, thump!

"Wait!" She ran after them.

"You can't leave us alone!" Leslie's objection covered something Susan was trying to say. They both hurried into the hall after Jack and Stephanie.

After a quick jab of his head into the dining room, SWAT-team style, Lawdale stepped into the room and waved them on.

The pounding had stopped.

The room was as they'd left it. Empty.

"You catch my point," Lawdale said. "From this point on—"

"What's that?" Leslie interrupted.

"What's what?"

She lifted a finger to her lips and listened. A sound like a garbled record, backward masked, played far away. Below them. In front of them.

The sound grew louder, unmistakable now, but unintelligible. Soft wailing bubbling behind, ebbing and flowing. Jack stepped into the hall. It was coming from the door to the basement.

They poured into the hall in a rough semi-circle, listening intently to the strange sound, for the words, because it was a voice, most certainly a voice. At least one.

The door suddenly bent slightly inward.

Jack caught his breath.

Thump, thump, thump!

They all jumped as the door shook under the pounding.

A deep moan reverberated through the whole house. Fingers of black fog seeped under the door, drifted over the wood floor, and burned words into the door's surface.

ONE DEAD BODY . . .

OR SIX DEAD BODIES

Then the smoke was sucked back into the cracks, the sound ceased, and absolute stillness returned.

For ten seconds no one moved.

"Okay," Lawdale said, stepping back. The light in his eyes revealed a tinge of panic.

When he'd found them in the boiler room he hadn't yet encountered the horrors of the house. Now he had, and it showed.

But it struck Jack that the look on Lawdale's face might not be panic at all. It could be eager determination. Even desire. What if . . . what if Lawdale was actually a part of the game? Not White's part, but a kind of counterpart? Good come to fight evil.

No. Couldn't be. They'd met him on the highway a hundred miles from here. And all of them could see that he was the same man they'd met.

Lawdale faced them, now clearly unnerved. "We have to get out. We tear this house down if we have to, both floors, all the windows, the attic, everything. Find a way out."

"There is no way out," Randy said.

"We *find* a way out!" Lawdale snapped.

31

5:29 AM

They moved quickly, following the cop's orders to split up, thereby dividing the house's
attention and confusing it, but Randy held
out no hope for that plan. Stephanie had
found a crowbar in the coat closet, and he'd
raced upstairs with her because doing this
last-ditch thing felt like it needed to be
done, but only to buy himself a little thinking
time before doing what really needed to be
done.

   Amazing how dramatically the place had
changed. Aside from the layout, there was

hardly any indication that they were in the same house. And this new house seemed to know that the end was coming. It had settled down, a calm before the storm.

With barely more than thirty minutes to go before this game ended, killing was now the only thing that needed to be done.

The question was, who? Jack, yeah, but Jack had his eyes on him and his barrel pointed in his general direction wherever they went. It was almost like White had visited Jack and warned him.

"The attic!" Stephanie said, panting from the run up the steps. "Find the attic."

Randy ran into one of the rooms, ax hammer in hand, and threw open the closet door. Nothing on the ceilings that showed an entrance to any attic.

"Watch out."

He took a swing at the window, knowing it would be useless. And it was. Crashing glass. Bone-jarring jolt against the bars. He tried another swing, at the wall this time.

The full force of the blow ran up his arms and rattled his teeth. He cursed. Now if that was flesh and blood, like someone's head, the ax would slice clean through, not bounce. They were swinging at the wrong things.

Randy had left his shotgun in the kitchen at Lawdale's insistence—this wasn't the time to go around wasting ammo. Use the ax, the crowbar, and a sledgehammer that Jack had found in the pantry. The guns stayed in the kitchen for now.

And Randy wasn't happy about it. Not the least bit.

"Where's the attic?" Stephanie asked.

"Shut up!"

She was too frantic to show any reaction. She ran for another room. Randy lumbered into the upstairs hall. Time was running out.

Maybe he'd just do Stephanie in and call it good. Slam, bam, thank you, ma'am. One dead body . . .

But the businessman in him was suggesting a few things. If he did Stephanie and the rest of them managed to live as White promised, who would be stuck holding the bag for murder? If he killed Stephanie and the FBI got ahold of it—which they would—he'd fry.

Unless he left no witnesses—killed all of them. But he wasn't sure he could do that.

"In here!" Stephanie screamed out. "I found it!"

Crawling into an attic without light was

about the stupidest thing he could think of right now. She'd actually found it?

Stupid. A wedge of panic forced itself into his mind. Time was running out. What if Jack snuck up here and blew his brains out first?

Feet pounded on the stairs, and Randy spun to see the cop coming up, two steps at a time.

"Anything?"

"She found the attic," Randy said.

The officer rushed past Randy, carrying a lit lamp. What about him? Take down the gunslinging cop and testify that he mistook Lawdale for Tin Man in the bad light. One dead body.

Could he kill a cop? If it came right down to it, he just might have to. But would Tin Man accept Lawdale? He wasn't one of the original four.

Five. Susan. Betty had made it abundantly clear that White wanted Susan dead. Maybe he should kill Susan.

Randy hurried into the room and found Lawdale on steps he'd pulled down from a hatch that opened into a dark attic. He scrambled up, lamp first.

"Get up here."

Randy was headed up ahead of Stephanie, holding on to the ax, when it occurred to him that the ax was almost as good a weapon as a gun. He wasn't sure he *could*, but it *would* work. He felt for the knife at his waist. A knife might almost be easier.

The attic had a wood floor piled high with junk along the sides. The sloping ceiling was made of old gray boards. The single square window in the gable was barred.

The man hurried over to Randy, grabbed the ax, and shoved the lamp at him. "Hold this."

Before Randy could protest the man had traded tools—Randy's ax for a useless light. Of course, with control of the light, he could break the lamp and have control of the situation, so maybe that was a good thing.

He knew he was slipping, really slipping this time, but he let himself go. He needed to slip. It was slip or die.

Lawdale hefted the ax and swung at the sloping ceiling.

Bang/bounce. Naturally.

What was unnatural was the sudden *groan/screech* that split the air after the blow, loud enough for Randy to feel it in his chest, as if the attic was the source of the groans they'd heard all along.

Stephanie screamed, almost as loud, and Randy came within an inch of grabbing something—anything—and slam-bamming her right then and there. Instead, he reached out and slapped her with the light still in his hands. "Shut up!"

She did. The house fell quiet with her. The look in her eyes reminded him of the moment she came out of Pete's lair.

"Gimme your knife." Lawdale tucked the ax under one arm and held out his other hand.

"What for?" Randy pulled the knife out but didn't want to give it up too quickly.

"For heaven's sake, just give it to me!" Lawdale snatched it from him, started digging with it at the seams between rafters and roof. It barely penetrated. The tip broke off with a snap, leaving a notch in the end of the blade. Lawdale swore and hooked the knife into his belt, took up the ax again.

Lawdale began banging at the wall in a rage. *Bang, bang, bang, bang.* Right along the wall, then on the gable with the window. *Crash, crash,* against the glass.

Nothing.

The cop stood facing the clear black sky outside with his back to Randy and Stephanie, breathing hard. He let the ax down slowly till it hung from one of his hands, solid head just above the floor.

The house groaned softly.

Lawdale breathed heavily.

Randy and Stephanie stared, taken aback by this, the second of the cop's furious banging episodes.

"We're all going to die," the cop said, still looking out the window.

He turned around and faced them. "The Tin Man's never left a victim alive, never failed, never left a clue to his identity, even though he's blazed a trail as wide as the Mississippi through the country in house after house. Now we know why, don't we? But there's no way we can tell the rest of the world."

"What do you mean, we know why?" Randy asked.

The cop looked at the ceiling he'd just lambasted and spoke with more urgency. "It starts with knowledge; it always does. You have to know the game before you can beat it. The world has to know what they're dealing with."

"Well, good luck getting the word out."

Lawdale looked him in the eye. "The killer's game is as much spiritual as physical. The FBI—whoever lies in Tin Man's path—has to know that he can be beat only if they understand the power behind him, that's what I mean. They're not looking at this right. They need to shift paradigms, or he'll go right on killing and leaving a path they'll never understand."

Whatever, Randy thought. "Time's running out," he said.

"Are you listening to a thing I'm saying, boy?" The officer paced. "There's no way out! This"—he gestured at the ceiling, studying the boards, searching for the right words—"this thing, this whole killing spree of his, this house . . . it's about good and evil and about what's inside. But the world doesn't know that!"

They did not have time for this philosophical mumbo jumbo. Lawdale should go find Leslie if that's how he wanted to spend their final minutes. He shone the light in Lawdale's eyes. "Well, unless we beat White, they never will. Got any real ideas? Or are you just talk?"

Lawdale hesitated. "Maybe Tin Man's right. Maybe someone has to die."

Randy felt his heart pound harder.

"Someone has to be sacrificed. We need a sacrificial lamb. The Tin Man wants fresh blood. Innocent blood."

"Who?"

The cop blinked, thought a moment, then shook his head. "I don't know. One of us may have to volunteer."

"What?" Stephanie said. "You actually believe someone will volunteer to die for the rest?"

"Not just the rest of us," Lawdale snapped. "The world out there has to know what's going on!"

"It'll never happen," Randy said.

The cop stared at him for a long time, mind spinning behind those sparkling eyes.

"We'll see," he said. "Think about it. We're running out of time. If someone doesn't die, we all do."

Lawdale picked up the ax. "There's no way out," he said.

Randy swallowed. "We *know*."

The cop nodded. He left the attic without another word, taking the ax with him.

32

5:40 AM

Jack and Leslie had run from room to room on the main floor, looking for any structural feature that appeared even remotely weak. A seam in the walls, an unbarred window, a place where plumbing had been ripped free to expose the night outside.

The patrolman's plan wasn't much more than a last gasp, but Jack couldn't think of a better plan, so he attacked the search with frantic urgency. But the wood, the re-bar, the siding, the plaster—the house and all of its materials refused to break.

All the while, the third rule kept drumming through his mind. *Give me a dead body . . .*

They were in the pantry off the kitchen, the last room to search on this floor, as far as Jack could tell. But there was nothing here that looked hopeful. He took a swing at the shelves anyway.

Empty jars and cans crashed. The sledge-hammer bounced off the wall. Nothing. He stopped and stared, mind numb. Now what? They'd wasted how much time? Ten minutes, at least.

Leslie stood behind him in the doorway—he could hear her steady breathing. The house moaned again. Louder this time. He looked up. Now what?

"We're going to die," Leslie said.

It was a simple declaration of fact. Jack knew precisely how she felt, because he felt exactly as she did. There were times when bravery only mocked reality.

"It's coming after me," she said. "It's forcing me to do what I hate the most."

What was she talking about?

"I'm a whore, Jack. That's what this is about. I hate myself, and I'm powerless to stop it. It knows that."

"Who's *it*?"

She looked around, eyes wide and watery. "Me."

He didn't contradict her, but he didn't think she was right.

The house shook violently for a moment, then quieted. More jars toppled from the shelves and shattered at their feet. Cans clattered about them. It felt like the house was being shaken by an earthquake.

"Do you believe in God, Jack?" Leslie whispered.

He'd thought about the question a hundred times already that night, but only in passing. He wasn't sure he believed in God.

"I don't know," he said.

"If he exists, where is he tonight?" She swallowed. "There's evil in this house, there's supernatural entities I never believed in until tonight, there's a serial killer with his sick, demented game, but where is God?"

"In a cathedral somewhere," Jack said. "Taking money from the poor."

"There *is* no God," Leslie said.

"Maybe not," he said. "Not one that can help us."

From somewhere in the house, Susan began to yell. Leslie jerked her head around.

The girl was shouting something, running down a hall or through the dining room.

Where had she been? She'd started out with Jack and Leslie, making suggestions that weren't particularly helpful in their search. Jack hadn't noticed when she left.

Doors slammed somewhere deeper in the house. Wood thudded and crashed. Susan screamed again.

"She's in trouble!" Jack said. He snatched up the sledgehammer and led Leslie through the kitchen, through the hall, past the basement door, into the dining room.

"Susan!"

Her cries were louder now. She was screaming something at them from the front of the house. Jack ran into the main foyer.

All of the furniture in the adjacent living room looked as though it had been tossed by a tornado, half of it toppled and shattered. Several pieces seemed to defy gravity, stuck to the wall, like the unbroken chair that sat against the wall halfway up by the fireplace.

Susan stood in one corner, pressed against both walls. The large armoire that had once stood across the room was now six feet from her, moving slowly closer. Its doors were opening and banging shut, not rapidly, but in response to her moves, as if to cut her off.

"Jack!" she screamed. "You have to listen to me! You have to stop it!"

The chair on the wall flew across the room toward Jack. He jumped back and swung the sledgehammer at the flying chair. The weighted head crashed into wooden spindles and effectively redirected the chair's flight, but one of the legs struck him in the shoulder, sending him reeling back into Leslie.

"Listen to . . ." Susan's cry was covered by the sound of a dozen doors slamming together. Not just once, but repeatedly. *Bam, bam!* Every closet, every room, every cabinet in the house, it seemed, repeatedly opening and slamming shut in perfect unison.

Bam. Bam. Bam. Bam. Bam.

The armoire that trapped Susan stopped five feet from her. Jack jumped forward, drew his sledgehammer back, and had just started to swing at the armoire when the right-hand door swung open and struck him broadside.

He staggered, fell, dropped his weapon.

Bam. Bam. Bam. Bam. The doors thundered.

"The sledge, Jack!" Leslie cried. "Watch out!"

His sledgehammer had flown into the air and was floating across the room, cocked at a forty-five-degree angle.

He scrambled back. It flew unaided toward the armoire.

Toward Susan.

Bam. Bam. Bam. Bam.

"Jack!" Susan was crying out something behind the armoire, but he couldn't see her now.

The hammer was now over the armoire, over Susan, intention unmistakable.

Bam. Bam. Bam.

Boom!

Gunfire exploded around them. The sledgehammer was hit broadside by a full load of buckshot. Its handle splintered just below the head, which slammed into the wall and dropped from sight behind the armoire.

Lawdale leaped over Jack, swept up his fallen sledge by the stubbed handle, and was into a full swing before Jack fully knew it was him.

His first blow shattered the armoire's right-hand door.

The second door began to flop, and the lawman took it off with another swing. Raging like a bull, he threw himself at the heavy piece of furniture and toppled it with a loud grunt.

The slamming doors throughout the house stopped in unison with the crash of the toppled armoire.

Bam!

Dust roiled.

Silence settled.

Susan ran.

Past Lawdale, past Jack, down the hall. "You're going to get us all killed, Jack!" she cried and was gone.

What was she talking about? What was he doing that would get them killed? What were any of them doing that would get them killed?

Or was it something they *weren't* doing?

One dead body.

Lawdale faced them, breathing steadily through his nose. "You okay?"

"I'm alive." Jack pushed himself to his feet.

"I heard her screams, but I had to go back for the shotgun you boys left in the kitchen."

"What caused *that*?" Leslie asked.

"What's causing any of this? Evil. The house has a mind of its own. No luck, right?"

"What do you think? What about Randy?"

"Attic's no help." Lawdale tossed the sledge on the floor. He seemed to have lost his fire. "I think we're all going to die."

"Thanks for the encouragement, Officer, but we've already reached our own conclusions."

"Which are?"

Jack hesitated. "There's no way out."

"The wise man built his house upon a rock," Lawdale said. "Preacher used to say that. Unfortunately, whoever built this house built it on a grave. Unless we expose that grave, we're all going to die."

"Uncover the mass grave this place was built on?"

"Grave. As in death. He obviously thinks we're all deserving of death. One of us has to die. It's the only way."

His statement would have left Jack floored seven, even three hours ago. But he knew that basic logic had brought the lawman to his summary of the matter.

"We can't just kill someone," Leslie said.

"We're running out of time. Someone has to give their life so that the rest can live, not only here, but out there, in the world. Put an end to this lunatic's game."

"Suicide?"

"No, I don't think that will work for him; it doesn't fit his profile. He's not looking for cowardice. Whoever kills has to do it like he would, out of malice."

"That's murder."

"We aren't murderers."

"Evidently not. Not yet. But that may change in the next few minutes."

He paused then said, "And if it comes down to it, I'm willing to be the victim, even though there may be better choices."

They stared at him. The cop was actually offering to die for them all?

"I've already told the others," Lawdale said. He set the shotgun down. "I'm going to try to find Susan. Twenty-five minutes, my friends. Whatever you do, do it quickly."

He handed Jack his gun, walked past them, and turned toward the dining room where Susan had fled.

Jack glanced at Leslie, who was staring after Lawdale. She turned her head to him, eyes wide.

"It makes sense." Then he added so there would be no misunderstanding, "In a textbook way. Logically."

"This isn't a textbook," she said. "It's a classical case of mass hysteria, and he's contributing to it."

He ignored her. "Maybe he's right; there's a better choice than him."

"Who, Randy?"

Jack didn't answer.

Leslie's jaw flexed. "He may be a bit twisted up here"—she pointed to her head—"but not even Randy deserves to die."

"We can't just ignore what's happening," he said. "White told Randy to kill *me*."

She glared at him.

"Come on, Leslie. You know as well as I do that he's capable of killing *both* of us!" Jack leaned the shotgun against the wall. "If Lawdale told them what he just told us, I guarantee you, Randy's already got me in his sights."

Leslie looked back down the hall. "You can't just kill him, for heaven's sake!"

"And if he comes after me, what would you suggest I do?"

Leslie took a shallow breath. "Pete told me that White wanted the girl dead," Leslie said. "I think this whole thing is about her. I think White really let her go so that we would have someone to kill."

Jack just stared at her, daring her to say what she meant.

"I'm not suggesting you kill Susan," she snapped. "But Randy might try. He's too much of a coward to come after you, but he may try the girl."

The house began to groan again. An indistinguishable scream pierced through the walls. Other screams rose, overlapped.

33

5:40 AM

Stephanie didn't agree to the plan, but she didn't stop Randy either. If there was any other way, she would have stopped him, but the only way for them to live through the deadline was for someone else to die, as the cop himself had said.

It didn't sound right; she knew that it couldn't be right. But it was the closest thing to right she could come up with.

Her hands had done their share of shaking through the night, but now she couldn't stop them if she tried. She didn't feel good about killing someone any more than she felt good about eating Pete's dog food. But she wasn't exactly a healthy person. She'd learned that in the last few hours.

The thought of dipping her fingers into his nasty food and placing it into her mouth made her stomach swim with nausea.

Deep down, where she'd managed to run away from herself, she was a very sick, twisted little girl. If anyone deserved to die here, it was probably her. Jack could attest to that. She had abandoned him in his time of deepest need and retreated into her world of denials and self-pity.

A tear slipped down her cheek. She followed Randy out of the room toward the stairs. "Are you sure we should do this?"

Randy stopped and turned back. "You could wait here. I have to get the gun and find the girl, but I'm coming back, like we agreed. There's no way I'm getting hung out to dry on my own. I want Lawdale here when I pull that trigger. He'll back us up."

"And if he doesn't?"

Randy hesitated. "Then we'll have to do them all."

"You never said—"

The house screamed. A dozen overlapping screams.

"What's that?"

Randy ignored her and moved forward in a crouch.

The scream sounded like it had come from a little girl. Susan, maybe. Stephanie shivered. And in that second, she understood.

It was Susan. Tin Man wanted Susan. He wanted *them* to kill Susan.

And according to Randy, that's what Lawdale had meant when he said the killer wanted fresh blood.

She was a sick, sick person, and she should be stopping Randy rather than sneaking down the stairs behind him.

But she was too sick to stop him.

They hurried to the kitchen for the shotgun. But the guns were gone. Randy stared, face red. "What now?" He stormed around for a few seconds, checking behind the table and the counter. "He took them! He took 'em both!"

"Randy, I'm not sure—"

"You left the crowbar upstairs," he said, pushing past Stephanie. "We'll do her with the crowbar."

Five forty-nine. "We have to go," Jack said. "We have to do this now!"

"And what have you decided to do?"

He wavered again. Kill Lawdale? Kill Randy? Kill Susan? Rage flooded his bones. He slammed his fists against the wall. "This is insane!"

"Jack," a soft voice said.

He whirled to the sound of the girl's voice. Susan stood in a doorway at the end of the foyer, near the stairs.

Tin Man's metal mask hung from her right hand.

Jack was too stunned to speak.

She dropped the mask to the floor where it clattered noisily.

"What's . . . ?" He wasn't even sure what to ask.

"Will you listen to me now?" she asked.

Jack took three steps and stood beside Leslie, who gawked at the sight. There was something unnerving about the way Susan appeared, standing there in her tattered white dress with the killer's mask by her feet.

"Of course we'll listen," Leslie said softly.

"You have to listen carefully. I've been try-ing to tell you, but you aren't listening."

"Of course I—"

"I tried to warn you. The house is keeping you from listening."

"What do you mean?"

"It messes with your hearing. Makes it so that you can't see things right. Or hear things right. I've been trying to tell you all night. Will you listen now?"

He stared at her. "I . . . I can hear you."

"We're running out of time. Will you lis-ten?"

"Who . . . who are you?"

"I'm the one he wants you to kill. But if you kill me, you'll die. You have to believe me. The only way to survive the game is to de-stroy him."

"How?"

"I can show you."

If she was right, their hope for survival had been with them most of the night, and they'd ignored her. In that moment Susan was a picture of perfect innocence. His own daughter, Melissa, reaching out to save him. A guiding angel of light sent to save him, even though she was just a girl White had abducted. But in that moment she was more.

"He's trying to kill me, Jack."

He wanted to rush up to her and throw his arms around her and tell her that he'd never leave her again, but he couldn't seem to move.

"I know." Jack went to her. "But that's not going—"

"Lawdale is trying to kill me," Susan said.

He stopped. Blinked. "What? Who . . ."

"Lawdale. The Tin Man, the one who leaks black smoke even up here. I told you before, he wants you to kill me. That's the real game."

His mind spun. A new terror flashed down his spine.

"Did you hear me?" she asked.

"Are you sure? Lawdale?"

"You'll see the smoke, Jack."

A hand reached out from beyond the doorframe and yanked Susan by her hair. She cried out.

Randy stepped through, grinning, eyes wild. "Stay back, Jack. This is our only way out, you know that."

"Randy?" Leslie brushed past Jack.

"Randy, what are you doing? You're crazy, she's innocent!"

"I think that's the point, doctor," Randy said; then to the girl, "Let's go, sweet pea."

He jerked her back the way they'd come.

Jack reeled. His own shotgun was still back by the armoire. He spun, four long strides, grabbed up the shotgun. He ran to the doorway that Susan had been snatched from, checked beyond with a jab of his head. Clear.

It split at the end—one way led back to the kitchen, around the back of the dining room; one way to the rest of the lower house and the stairs. Which way?

"What are you doing?" Leslie breathed at his shoulder.

Jack held still, gripped by indecision. He couldn't just blast his way through the house while Randy had the advantage.

Something was wrong with his elbow. He rolled up his denim shirtsleeve and stared at his elbow where the armoire door had plastered him. A small gash leaked red blood.

"Black smoke," he said. "When I was in the basement I was leaking black smoke. Everyone who was evil leaked black smoke.

We all would have. But up here it's different. This is where evil can hide."

"The smoke is only in the basement? I don't understand how—"

"I don't know," he snapped. "But up here evil doesn't just walk around for us to see it, like it does down in the basement. I'm not leaking black smoke up here."

"I can see that! But what does that have to do with Lawdale?"

"She's saying that he's different, that he'll leak black smoke no matter where he goes."

"How?"

"I don't know! All I know is that we have to believe Susan."

Too much time had passed. He ran toward the kitchen, shouting. "Randy, you can't do this! We need her!"

No sound. Jack threw caution to the wind and ran for the kitchen with Leslie hard behind.

Empty.

"Upstairs, hurry!"

They peeled back through the other hall into the dining room, but it was as far as they got.

Officer Morton Lawdale stood in the archway, holding a large, gleaming knife from the kitchen. Randy's knife? His eyes were wide and his face was white.

"We're out of time," Lawdale said. He thrust the knife into the table and looked into Jack's eyes, eyes pleading and scared.

He didn't look like the Tin Man.

"I want you to kill me," Lawdale said.

34

5:53 AM

"Kill you?"

"We can't put it off any longer." Sweat beaded Lawdale's forehead below the bloody bandanna. "Someone has to die so the rest can live, and I'm willing. Do it now before I change my mind."

Jack had the shotgun; he could easily lift it and put a hole in the man's chest. If Susan was right, he'd be killing White.

If Susan was wrong, he would be killing a cop. And she could easily be wrong, couldn't she? She wasn't exactly a predictable person.

"Are you deaf, boy?" Lawdale snapped. He began to tremble. "Someone has to die here or we all do. Kill me!"

Jack instinctively lifted the gun. But he couldn't pull the trigger. He just couldn't, not without knowing for sure. Lawdale looked like a man who deserved a medal of honor rather than a bullet. How could he possibly be the Tin Man?

"Jaaack!" Susan's voice screamed from the upper level where Randy had evidently taken her.

What if Susan was working with the Tin Man to destroy their only hope of escape, namely, the lawman, who'd managed to rescue them from the basement?

"Jack?" Leslie's voice quavered.

Lawdale marched forward, angry now.

A small, useful bit of information dropped into Jack's mind. He hadn't chambered a round! He moved to his right with Leslie behind, forcing Lawdale around to their left.

"Randy's going to kill Susan," Jack said, voice ragged.

"Not if you kill me first, Jack." Lawdale walked right up to him. "Pull the trigger."

Before Jack could do so, Lawdale grabbed the barrel with both hands, and pulled it toward his forehead. It pressed into his skin just below the bandanna. He clamped his eyes shut.

"Do it before he kills her. Save her. Do it like you despise the ground I walk on, with malice and hate. With the evil sickness raging inside, boy. Do it!"

Jack's hands were shaking badly. He pumped the action to chamber a shell.

"Now!" Lawdale shouted, nostrils flaring with panic.

Jack's mind seemed to be folding in on itself. He gripped the shotgun with white knuckles and began to yell. "Ahhhhhh!"

"Do it!"

But he couldn't do it. Instead he jerked the barrel up, dislodging the blood-soaked bandanna. A two-inch gash over Lawdale's right eye glared at them. Red.

No smoke.

Jack's scream caught in his throat. He stared at the cut in shock.

No black smoke. He'd almost taken Susan's assumption at face value and killed an innocent man?

"Please, Jack," Lawdale pleaded, eyes

now clenched shut. He didn't seem to have a clue what Jack had just attempted to do. "I'm losing my nerve . . ."

No black smoke.

He'd come within a breath of blowing the cop's head from his shoulders because he'd been led to believe that he was Tin Man, but there was *no black smoke*!

Jack froze.

Lawdale's mouth gaped in a soft cry. Eyes still clenched tight, face wrinkled in agony, flesh quivering. The man was breaking, losing his nerve. And so was Jack. He'd come within an inch of blowing the man's head off!

Black smoke oozed from Lawdale's gash and fell past his right eye, smoking all the way to the floor—black, coal black.

How . . . how was that . . . what was happening?

Black smoke was happening.

Jack jerked the gun away and stepped back.

Lawdale's eyes were still clenched and his face was trembling with fear. A man about to die.

The black stuff began to flow freely now. A

thin black fog pooled at Lawdale's feet, swirled around his boots.

"Kill me, Jack," Lawdale pleaded, seemingly oblivious to what Jack now saw.

"Jack?" Leslie said. "He's leaking smoke, Jack."

Clearly. Jack's hands shook.

"Kill him, Jack," Leslie said.

"Kill me, Jack," Lawdale cried.

"I . . . I . . ."

"Pull the trigger," Leslie snapped.

He pulled the trigger.

Click!

Lawdale gasped. Mouth parted, eyes still closed, but no longer clenched. He looked unsure if he'd been shot.

Jack stepped back again. Pumped. Jerked the trigger again.

Click!

For a long moment the air seemed evacuated of oxygen. Someone had emptied his gun of all but one shell before saving Susan from the flying ax just a few minutes ago.

Lawdale. It could only have been Lawdale, so that the gun would be empty after he shot that last round in the foyer.

Empty so that when Jack tried to kill him

he would be rewarded with nothing more than a click.

Empty so that Jack couldn't use it to kill Lawdale.

The man's face was still gripped by false surprise, mouth gaping, eyes closed. Lawdale closed his mouth. He swallowed deliberately, eyes still closed. He cocked his head down.

Then his eyes snapped open, and Jack stared into black, pupil-less eyes that sent a chill to his heels. He knew without a shred of doubt that he was looking into the eyes of the Tin Man.

A terrifying sight, this tall, well-muscled man with cropped blond hair, head tilted down, black fog pouring from a cut in his forehead, eyes black.

Black.

Leslie screamed.

Tin Man's mouth twisted into a thin smile. "Never leave your gun unattended, Jack."

"Run!" Jack shoved the shotgun at the Tin Man and bolted to his right. He grabbed the knife from the table and spun back, swinging the blade as he turned.

From the corner of his eye, he saw the man casually catch the shotgun with only a slight movement. Jack threw the knife, saw it lodge deep in the man's biceps.

Lawdale flinched, but no more. He held fast to the gun he'd caught in his now wounded arm. He was a man of supreme confidence. With good reason. He'd played his game flawlessly.

But he could be wounded, and if he could be wounded, he could be killed, just like Stewart. White reached for the knife with his free hand.

Jack bolted toward the foyer, hard on Leslie's heels.

A low chuckle reached through the wood. "Very good, Jack. Anger is good."

Jack threw himself at the stairs. Susan was right about Lawdale, which meant her claim that White intended to kill all of them also had to be true.

"Randy!" Leslie screamed. "Don't do it! Wait!"

A scream.

It was too late?

Leslie pounded up the stairs as Jack swung around the banister at the top. "Randy!" He tore down the hall and spun into the first room.

He saw it all in a flash. The orange light of

a dim overhead bulb. Stephanie standing to one side of the guest room; Randy beating at a locked closet door with a crowbar.

"Lawdale's the Tin Man," Jack said. "The killer is Lawdale!"

Randy kicked at the door. His mind was on only one thing.

"He's going to kill us all if she dies," Jack shouted.

The door splintered and caved in. Dust roiled. Jack dived at Randy, knocking him off balance. The man slammed into the wall, cursing bitterly.

"How do you know that?" Stephanie asked.

There was no sound of White's pursuit, but in this house that meant nothing. He could be on the stairs already.

Susan ran from the closet and sprinted out of Randy's reach, hid behind Stephanie.

"Jack!" Leslie screamed from the doorway, looking back at the stairs in terror.

She slammed the door shut. Spun and pressed back against the door, eyes like saucers.

"He's coming!"

"I don't believe you," Randy said.

"Shut up, Randy!" Jack snapped.

"He's going to kill us!" Stephanie said.

Knuckles rapped on the door, and Leslie jumped away from it. She ran to Jack and whirled around behind him. They had no guns. No axes in here. No weapons of any kind except the crowbar.

The brass handle turned. The door swung in with a long creak.

Tin Man stood in the opening with his tin mask in place as they'd first seen him, only now dressed in the Budweiser T-shirt and the gray patrolman's pants. Blood soaked a strip of cloth that he'd hastily wrapped tightly around his wounded bicep.

He held Jack's empty shotgun in one hand, Randy's knife in the other.

"Hello," he said.

35

5:59 AM

The game had played out better than Barsidious White ever dared hope.

The girl was still alive, but that would soon change. He relished the thought of ending it all precisely as he'd foreseen.

The Tin Man stripped off the mask Susan had dropped and tossed it by the door. After taking a moment to study their drawn faces, he addressed them calmly.

"Sit along the wall."

They moved obediently and sat.

Now he had them all in a row. Five of

them. The one called Stephanie, the one called Randy, the one called Leslie, the one called Jack. And the one called Susan. Like five pigeons in a cage, staring at their captor.

He looked at Susan. The mysterious girl who'd appeared at the inn without warning three days ago. An apparently easy prey, but then she disappeared into the basement as if that was her intent the whole time. At first he tried to kill her, but then he discovered something quite unnerving about this child.

She was a good person.

Not a person who just *did* good things to show how good they were, but a person who really was good to the bone. Innocent. The rest were always "guilty as sin," as he liked to say.

But he wasn't so sure that Susan was guilty at all. She hadn't once talked maliciously or revealed any character trait less than virtuous. He always killed the guilty, proving to them that they were as guilty as his own murderous self; every single one of them eventually turned to murder to save their necks.

For the first time he'd met a participant

who didn't fit the profile and therefore wreaked significant havoc with his game.

So he'd made her part of the game. Now it wasn't just *kill each other, all ye who are as guilty as sin.* Now it was *kill this innocent one, removing from amongst you the last vestiges of goodness, all ye who are as guilty as sin.*

She stared at him, fearless, then opened her mouth to speak. "I know how—"

Tin Man put a round into the wall next to Leslie, who shrieked.

Susan shut her mouth. She understood. *If you speak, I will kill one of them.*

He withdrew the small roll of tape from his pocket, crossed to her, and placed a long strip over her mouth and around her head. Then he tied her hands. He didn't know how well the house could obscure what she said, but he didn't want them listening, especially now. She knew too much.

He picked up the knife and paced the floor deliberately, enjoying the sound of his boots on the wood.

"It's time for you to know your own fate. We still have a few minutes to play."

They stared at him.

"I have a confession," he said. "Officer

Lawdale won't be coming by to rescue you. Unless by 'rescue,' you think in terms of being delivered unto death."

They still didn't move. Pigeons. Stupid pigeons.

"You must appreciate the considerable care I've taken in planning your deaths."

Jack and Leslie stared at him stoically. Randy's eyes glared. Stephanie looked confused.

"I went down to the highway patrolman's house two miles down the road, cut his throat, and took his cruiser. This to be sure I had enough players for tonight's game."

"You . . . you're going to kill us?" Stephanie asked.

"If you don't kill each other yourselves," White said. "And if you ask any more stupid questions, you'll be first."

"Why don't you just kill us now?" Jack asked.

Of them all, only Jack was still thinking straight. The man was strong. Resolute. He'd faced his daughter's death and come away bitter but more seasoned. His death would be the most satisfying.

"Patience, Jack. I will kill you. I will because my eyes are black. Aren't you going to ask about my eyes, Jack?"

Jack hesitated. "Why are your eyes black?"

"Because I'm not really White in the house, I'm really Black in the box, and this is my showdown. Good versus evil, only in your case it's evil versus evil. No contest."

He could tell by their expressions that none of them understood. Except for the girl. Which bothered him.

He threw the knife with a flip of his wrist. It twirled twice and sank cleanly into the wall between Jack's and Leslie's heads. *Thunk!*

"Do you know anything about evil, Jack? Hmmm? The black stuff."

Jack didn't respond.

White lifted up his bandanna and let the black fog dribble then pour out of his gash. It pooled on the floor and began to work its way toward them.

"Evil, the stuff in your heart. It's in my head too."

He replaced the bandanna.

"I've decided to give you all one last chance to figure this mess out. Most people are quite dense. They like little white houses with big stained-glassed churches and prefer to do their killing with looks and words behind one another's backs."

He paused.

"Welcome to my house. No secrets allowed. Here we all do our killing with guns and axes and knives. It's more bloody than what most people are accustomed to, yes, but it's far less brutal."

Surely they understood some of this.

"The wages of sin is death, and this time we're going to show the blood, what do you say? No more stained glass or white houses. Now it's White's house, and in White's house we follow White's rules. House rules."

White could hear his breathing thicken, but he easily calmed himself.

"One last chance to rethink rule number three. The girl was right. On two counts: you haven't been listening to her. Well, blame that on the house. And, yes, I do want you to kill her. The game would have gone on until she was dead. But she's also wrong. If you do kill her, I will let whoever's still alive, live."

He let that sink in for just a few beats.

"And if you don't kill her, I'm going to slaughter you like lambs. All five of you.

Starting with the girl, just to show you how you should have done it."

Randy's eyes flittered to his left, then back. A good sign.

"Dawn is coming. I never let the game go past dawn."

He withdrew a match, struck it on his belt, and tossed the flame at the pool of black fog that had fallen from his brow. The fog burned with a whoosh as if it were gasoline. Firelight danced on their frozen faces.

"As you can see, the black stuff likes to burn. This place will go up in flames at first light. That's in six minutes. Six minutes to make your choice."

He retreated to the room's entrance and picked the mask up off the floor. Opened the door. Backed out of the room.

"Six minutes."

White slammed the door shut and began to tremble.

36

6:02 AM

The lines began etching themselves in Jack's mind as White talked, dividing competing forces deep at work behind the obvious here in this house empowered by evil.

Evil versus evil. Jack didn't totally buy White's claim. If there was evil, there was also good, and those forces were in some kind of battle here. Up to this point, except for the face-off in the boiler room, their abduction had felt little like a battle with two sides. But maybe that was the point. He'd been looking at it all wrong! He'd only seen one side, the evil. So where was the good?

And what if the standoff in the boiler room was only a foreshadowing of a greater contest to come? Jack against Jack. In some ways this night was nothing more than a stark playing out of the struggle he faced every day of his life. His own limited view of that struggle focused on what he allowed himself to see. But what if there was more?

What was the guilt that White seemed so preoccupied with? What were their sins?

Leslie seemed to be fighting long-hidden demons that had come to life in this impossible house of White's. Randy . . . Randy was showing his own obsession with power and control. Stephanie had come face-to-face with her own denial and was now terrified and weak without its facade.

And he? His was hiding behind bitterness, no better than any of the rest.

These were the thoughts racing, drumming, screaming as Tin Man talked. Then White was leveling his final challenge and that challenge was to kill someone.

"Six minutes." Tin Man backed out of the room. The door slammed shut as a hundred doors had slammed this night, but now with such finality that for a moment none of them moved.

And then, as if in deliberate response, a hundred doors throughout the house, below them, around them, slammed in one mighty crash. *Bam!* The house shook and shifted.

An echo lingered. Something had changed in the house.

Jack twisted to his right and grabbed the knife handle. He saw Randy diving for the crowbar as he tugged. But the knife was stuck.

"Jack?"

Stephanie stared at him, pleading with desperate eyes.

"Help me," he said.

She blinked then ran to his side. Her hand covered his over the knife handle, and together they pulled. In that single moment of desperation, he felt an overpowering sense of gratitude toward her. And he thought she might feel the same toward him. They were doing little more than reacting to the horrors that had pressed them to the breaking point, but in that moment, with their hands together grasping the one weapon that might save them, the bitterness and denial that had kept them from so much as a touch for over a year became nothing more than a petty distraction.

For the first time in a year, they hoped for the same thing, together. The knife.

But it refused to budge. It was so firmly embedded that it might as well be one of the steel bars that covered the windows.

Jack whirled around, still on his knees. Randy already had the crowbar in his hand, crouched like a tiger, grinning wickedly at Jack.

"Hold on!" Jack stuck his arm out and swept Stephanie behind him. "Just hold on!"

Randy's eyes swiveled to Susan, who was still bound and taped to Jack's left. She was trying to yell through the tape.

Jack shifted closer to the girl. "It's okay, Susan," he said softly.

She quieted.

"He's going to kill us, no matter what we do," Jack said. "Think about it! We've seen his face; we know he's Lawdale; why would he let us live?"

"Listen to him, Randy," Stephanie said.

He removed his eyes from Susan and glanced at Stephanie, perhaps struck by her change. "I'll take my chances," Randy said. "I'm not willing to risk my life based on some stupid theory. If you don't let me kill her, so help me, I'm coming for you." He swung the crowbar once.

"What are you going to do, Randy? Beat her over the head?"

The man held his ground, but he didn't answer. At least he was thinking that through. Jack moved while Randy was at least partly preoccupied. He leaned over and grabbed the tape that covered Susan's mouth.

Yanked it free.

He held up his hands, tape dangling. "Just hear her out."

Randy stared, unmoving.

"Five minutes," Leslie whimpered.

"Tell him, Susan."

"Tin Man's lying to you," Susan said. "He won't let all of you live. Even if you kill me, at least some of you will die."

"That's a lie," Randy said. "If we don't kill her, we all die. She's trying to save herself at our expense."

"I know how to get out," the girl said. "That's one of the reasons he wants you to kill me."

"You see, Randy?" Jack said. "Just calm down."

Randy hesitated then spoke with a set jaw. "If she knew how to get out, she'd have told us already."

"I've tried," the girl said. "You aren't listening."

"How do we get out, Susan?" Jack asked, keeping his eyes on Randy and his hand out to keep him away.

"I can show you how," she said. "But you have to trust me."

"She's going to get us all killed!" Randy said.

"If you look and listen, you can still win," Susan said.

"Think of the mirror," Jack said quickly. "We weren't seeing ourselves. The truth was hidden from us. We weren't really looking. She's making sense. For heaven's sake, listen to her!"

"What truth?" Randy demanded. "The only truth I'm aware of at this particular moment is that White will be stepping back into this room and killing her anyway. You may be willing to throw your life away because she says so, but we're not. Leslie?"

She was starting to waver, looking from Randy to Jack and then back. "What if she's trying to trick us?"

"She saved your life!" Jack snapped. "What's the matter with you?"

Her face wrinkled in confusion, and she stifled a cry. He might have expected this from Stephanie, but not Leslie.

Stephanie put her hand on Jack's elbow.

"Time's going to run out," Susan said. "You have to choose who you're going to believe. If you don't follow me, you'll all die. But we have to go now!"

"That's the stupidest—"

"You're not listening!" Susan cried. "I've been here longer than you have! You have to trust me, or you'll die!"

"White will *kill* us!" Randy screamed.

Jack threw himself at Randy then, like a torpedo. The crowbar swung, but Randy was caught off guard and his swing was weak. The iron glanced off his back as his head struck Randy's hips.

They hit the floor hard, with Jack on top. He wasn't a fighter under normal circumstances, but this was anything but normal. Randy began to thrash. A knee crashed into Jack's side, and he felt himself losing the advantage as quickly as he'd gained it.

Jack did the only thing that came to him at that moment. He screamed at the top of his lungs, a raging cry that flooded his veins with adrenaline.

Another voice joined his. Stephanie's, screaming.

He heard Randy cry out in pain as he rolled to his knees. Stephanie had stomped on the hand clinging to the crowbar.

Jack watched her plant her left foot on the floor like a world-class punter and take a swing at him with her right foot.

She was wearing spring sandals, but the toes were hard and pointed and Randy was kneeling, presenting a broad target for her. Her sharp shoe slammed into the side of his head.

He rolled to his side, dazed.

Susan was already beside Stephanie. "Get my hands free! Hurry!"

She spun Susan around and attacked the tape.

"Jack?" Leslie was watching, frozen.

Randy was still a threat, but they didn't have time to secure him.

"Follow me!" Susan said.

Randy was already pushing himself up.

Jack held a hand out to Leslie. "Come on!"

She hesitated then took a step.

Jack hurried after Susan and Stephanie, who'd reached the door.

"Ready?" Susan said, hand on the door handle.

"He's coming around," Jack said.

"Whatever happens, follow me. Open your eyes. Don't let the house turn you back."

"Where are we going?"

"Downstairs," she said and pulled the door open.

A rushing sound swallowed Jack. The door opened to blackness, not the hall.

Then he saw the stairs, the black fog, the dim bulbs, and he knew that this door now led into the basement. The house had shifted under them when White had slammed the door.

Fear pinged along Jack's nerves from the top of his head to the soles of his feet.

"Follow me," Susan cried and plunged down the dark stairwell.

37

6:04 AM

Randy staggered to his feet, dazed. Confusion swirled through his mind like a thick black fog, rushing with the sound of a gale-force wind.

Then he realized that the sound wasn't in his head. It was coming from the open door that the others had just run through. The doorway gaped like a black throat that descended into hell.

Into the basement.

He stood, swaying on his feet, fighting the confusion. Follow Susan? Not a chance in hell. The fools were actually listening to a girl who'd been trapped in the house for three days.

He inched forward on shaking legs and peered down. Leslie had stopped halfway down and was staring at the black fog that covered the basement floor at the bottom of the steps. The rest of them, including Susan, were already out of sight.

Leslie didn't move. She'd lost her nerve. Funny how he'd lost interest in her over the last few hours. Funny how he had to fight back an urge to kick her in the head now, while her back faced him. Funny how he hated her as much as he hated himself.

How much time? He still had time, didn't he? The Tin Man didn't say the time would end if they left the room. No way six minutes had passed. He could still get to them. Maybe this way was better, because they wouldn't expect him from behind. If he killed the girl, the Stewarts would vanish or something. He would shake hands with White, and then he would walk away from this place the one free man who'd used his head to escape certain death.

Randy looked around for a weapon and saw the knife stuck in the wall. He scooped up the crowbar and ran to the wall. Grabbed the knife and pulled.

It came out like it was set in butter.

A small grin nudged his lips. See, now White was helping. Or the house was. Either way, he was doing the right thing.

He ran to the stairs and stopped at the top. The black fog was thick on the basement floor. No Stewarts. No White. Just Leslie, a step or two higher than a moment ago.

There was something moving in the fog below. Swimming just under the surface—he could see its wake, sweeping slowly across the fog.

Randy gripped the knife in his left hand, the crowbar in his right hand, and put one foot on the landing. Then the other.

He stood shaking, momentarily stalled. Then he forced himself down the stairs.

Leslie watched the moving fog, glued to the steps. Jack and Stephanie had followed Susan into the fog, but as they disappeared, she realized that she couldn't make it.

Wouldn't make it. Panic had seized her

feet. And her mind. Susan's words drummed through her skull, but Leslie couldn't accept them. Running into the basement was suicide. And based on the urging of a girl who couldn't possibly know what she was talking about.

At the same time, Leslie couldn't ignore the evidence. The moving house. The shifting fog. She knew now, staring into the pit of hell, what was happening to her. She was facing her own sin. She'd been abused as a child, but as an adult she'd embraced that abuse by becoming an active participant.

What was abuse, except the bending of something that doesn't want to be bent? Any psychologist could attest to the fact that circumstances are subject to the participant caught within the circumstance. Beauty is in the eye of the beholder.

So is evil.

She'd become promiscuous and inviting, and she thrived on the power that she held over men. More important, she allowed that power to shape her identity.

The horrors of this night were highlighted by the one thin voice that had haunted her for the last two hours: she didn't hate Pete.

Or what he'd done to her. In fact, in many ways she *was* Pete.

They shared a terrifying bond. The truth of it made her ill. But she had always been ill.

She briefly wondered if she should go to his room now. See how sick she really was.

Yet she was who she was.

Leslie stood, unmoving, staring at the moving fog.

—— ——

Jack followed at Stephanie's heels, down the stairs, keeping his eyes on the steps in front of him.

Susan dropped into the fog, which hit her at the waist. "Come on!"

Stephanie stopped on the last step before entering the black stuff. "Will it hurt?" she asked.

Susan ran toward the first door that Jack and Randy had entered.

He nudged Stephanie. "Go! Just go."

She stepped into the fog and cried out with pain. But she was committed, and she rushed after Susan.

The moment Jack's foot passed the surface, pain seared his skin through his shoes and socks. He grunted and pushed on.

It was his third time in the fog, and the pain this time was by far the worst. Sharper, deeper.

He staggered out of the fog into the room with four sofas.

Susan threw the door shut. "Do you see it now?"

Jack looked around. "See what?"

"You're not looking!" she snapped angrily.

"What are we looking for?" Stephanie demanded. "Just tell us!"

"I have told you!"

"Told us wh—"

"The paintings!" Jack said.

The paintings on the walls were no longer actually on the walls. They hung in space a foot or two from the walls, moving slowly, facing him. All of them.

And they were all portraits of . . . of him! Odd and distorted, but unmistakably him!

The one directly in front of him showed him without eyes. The image's crooked smile sent a shiver down his back.

Jack dropped to one knee, eyes still on the portraits. Him, all of them—terrifying images that didn't really look like him at all. White's imagination was demented.

"What do you see?" Stephanie asked.

"They're me," he said.

"That's not what I see. They're me. They . . . they're horrible!"

"He's doing this—"

"No," Susan said. "This isn't White."

The door from the study flew open, and Jack barged in, panting.

Jack?

Dressed exactly like him, the same kind of Jack that was in the boiler room, only this time Jack didn't pay them any attention whatsoever. It was as if he didn't see them.

He threw the door closed and quickly scanned the portraits.

"It's . . . that's me!" Stephanie whispered. She was seeing her own version of what Jack saw. They were both seeing themselves.

"Now do you understand?" Susan asked. She sounded urgent, demanding.

But Jack didn't understand. "I . . ." Jack didn't know what to say.

The new Jack focused on something across the room. His face twisted into a furious snarl, and his hands tightened into fists, a terrifying image of raw bitterness and rage.

Then he was moving like a tiger across the room, sweeping up a lamp as he went. Over a couch in a single leap.

Jack saw what he was looking at. Three of the portraits in the far corner were no longer images of him. Two of them were of people he knew from the publishing world—an agent who'd left him out to dry before his first novel was published, and a critic who'd trashed that same novel when it was finally published.

The other portrait was of Stephanie, posing dumbly in a yellow dress.

The new Jack went for the portrait of Stephanie, screaming. He swung the lamp at the canvas, tearing through Stephanie's face. Jack didn't stop there. He proceeded to rip the frame apart, stick from stick, breaking each piece over his knee.

Then he tore down the other two portraits and stomped on them. He finally stood back, assured himself that there were no other offenders in his presence, and strode angrily from the room, slamming the door.

When Jack looked back at the portraits

he'd shredded, they were hanging in the air again, displaying his own distorted face.

"Do you understand?" Susan demanded. "We have to get out, but I can't get us out. If it were my house, I could do it, but it's yours, each of you. White made this *your* house. You have to get us out, and it won't be easy, so you have to—"

"I'm trying to think!" Jack said. He looked around. "*My* house? I don't see . . ."

His eyes settled on an old wooden placard that hung on the wall above the portraits. An old familiar saying was burned into the wood.

Home Is Where the Heart Is. And he knew then what Susan was trying to show them.

"This house is mirroring our hearts." He blinked. "It's drawing its power from the evil in us!"

"That's what I've been saying," Susan said.

"It's a haunted house that reflects the hearts of those who enter?" Stephanie said.

"Possessed by a power to mirror our hearts," Jack said. "You see the portraits of yourself, and I see them of me. Each of our experiences is unique. We're caught in a basement that's been empowered by White to reflect the evil in our hearts!"

"We've been fighting our own hearts?"

"No," Susan said. "The evil in your hearts."

"The ultimate haunted house," Jack said, staring at the portraits again. "We've been facing ourselves this whole time." He turned to Stephanie. "Our own sins are haunting us."

"I'm sorry, Jack." Her eyes were misted with both fear and sorrow, but he dismissed the fear and accepted only the sorrow. He felt it wash over his own heart. "I'm so sorry."

"No." Jack went to her, horrified by the image of himself tearing into the portrait of Stephanie with so much hatred. That was the truth of his heart!

"I'm the one who should be sorry. I've been so stubborn." He took her in his arms and held her tight, hoping desperately that he wasn't reconciling for his own gain.

She clung to him and cried in his neck. "I'm sorry, Jack."

He still loved her. Regardless of what happened tonight, he did love her. The realization made him squeeze her tighter.

"We have to hurry," Susan said.

Jack faced her, his new understanding increasing his sense of urgency. The fact that none of the pictures on the walls had changed wasn't lost on him.

"If we defeat the sin, we take away the house's power?"

Susan eyed him for a few moments. "No. That's not the way it works. It's not about the sins. It's about the heart. It's about you."

Stephanie stepped forward. "That doesn't make sense! We are what we do!"

"Follow me." Susan hurried to the door that led into the study. "I'll show you the way." If Jack was right, she was headed for the back exit.

The notion that all the evil he'd confronted in the last seven hours had been mostly his own doing flogged at Jack's mind. He was evil? Or was the evil so strong in him that he couldn't see the good?

Susan? She was one of White's victims, come into the killer's own world, but she was more. She was the light in this darkness, wasn't she?

A dozen meaningless sayings cried out to him. A house divided cannot stand. Love your neighbor as yourself.

Light came into the darkness, but the darkness did not understand it.

Susan pulled the door open, took a deep breath, then stepped back. Jack saw what she saw over her shoulder. Stewart, Betty, and Pete stood abreast, bearing shotguns, standing in black fog, glaring at them with glowing eyes. Behind them, the room was filled with twenty or thirty men wearing Tin Man masks, armed with axes. They were all dressed like Jack.

Were Jacks.

"They're me!" Stephanie whispered.

Not possible, not possible. But real, very real, standing right before him.

For a moment, none of them moved. The house moaned. There was a terrible wail behind the deep, guttural sound.

"Guilty as sin," Betty said. She thrust out her finger. "Kill them!"

The Jacks surged forward.

Susan slammed the door, locked it, and ran past Jack. "Run! After me!"

The room reverberated with the sound of splintering wood.

"Run!"

38

6:05 AM

Time came to a standstill for Randy the moment he put his foot on the first step leading into the basement.

Fear stopped him—terrible waves of fear that felt like real waves crashing into his body. *Whump, whump, whump.* His ears rang in their wake.

Leslie began to move again, down the steps toward the fog.

"Leslie?"

His voice was hoarse and soft, so he said it again.

"Leslie?"

She looked back up at him, and he saw that her cheeks were wet. She jerked her head around and stepped down. Into the fog. Up to her knees. And ran, fog swirling in her wake.

Then she was gone.

Randy forced himself down slowly, every step meeting him with a new wave of fear. Which was confusing to him, because he'd been sure that White wanted him do his business. He'd let him have the knife, hadn't he?

He walked a few steps with more confidence and stopped just above the sea of black fog. Another wave of fear hit him full in the face.

It was Stewart, standing bald and glaring with bulging eyes. Not just Stewart. Six Stewarts, each unique in their own way. All armed with shotguns or axes.

He jumped back up one step and lifted the crowbar.

But they weren't coming at him. Right? They stood still, legs planted in the fog, staring at him without moving.

Maybe they weren't a threat to him anymore. In some ways he was on the same team now, trying like them to kill the girl. He'd killed a Stewart, so they probably had some fear of him. Mutual respect.

"I'm going after Susan," he said. His voice echoed softly in the hall.

They didn't move. Neither did he.

The house began to moan, then wail. For a couple of seconds he thought about running back upstairs.

"Hello, Randy."

He whirled around.

The Tin Man stood at the top of the stairs, framed in a gray light from some supernatural source. He was wearing his mask, and he held a shotgun in both hands.

Randy opened his mouth to tell White what his plans were—that he needed just a few extra minutes to take care of the girl. "I—"

That was as far as he got.

White swung his gun down. "Good-bye, Randy."

Randy waited for the fist of lead to hit him. He felt his bladder go. The knife fell from his hand.

"I'll do anything," he said, dropping the crowbar too. "I swear, I'll do anything."

Still no blast. That was good. That was real good. So he said more of the same.

"Anything, I swear, anything . . . I want to be . . . I'll do anything."

Still no blast. The Tin Man had his shotgun angled down so that the shot from its barrel would strike Randy's chest. But he wasn't pulling the trigger. And Tin Man didn't strike him as the kind to hesitate without good reason.

That was good, right?

"Kill her," Tin Man said.

"I'm going to, I swear. That's what I'm doing."

One of the hall doors busted open behind Randy, and he jerked his head around. Leslie stumbled out, pushed by Stewart and another bald inbred who stepped into the hall behind her. Stewarts. Demons, for all she knew.

"Leslie," Tin Man said. "Use the knife."

"Randy?" Leslie sobbed. "What's happening, Randy?"

Tin Man stared at him past the mask, then stepped back and shut the door on the basement, leaving Randy to carry out his orders. Or be killed, for sure. Kill or be killed. No doubt about that.

"Randy! Answer me!" Leslie was broken to pieces anyway. No way she was going to survive this mess. He'd just be putting her out of her misery.

But Randy's legs wobbled like rubber bands as he crouched, felt for the knife beneath the fog, and lifted the weapon into the clear.

"Randy, you can't possibly be thinking about killing me!" Her face wrinkled with terror. "Randy, sweetie . . . Randy?"

He looked at the knife in his hands. He felt nothing for her. Nothing at all. He was going to do this. That's all there was to it. He was going to kill Leslie because he was really on Team Stewart, and the Stewarts always obeyed White.

Randy walked through the fog, toward the woman who had tried to control him without knowing how much he resented it. This was his house. White's house. Stewart's house. Randy's house. Leslie was no longer welcome.

"Randy, you stop right there!" she screamed, spittle flying. "Stop!"

Randy stopped in front of her. Then he thrust the knife forward, into her chest.

Deep into her chest. And let go. The Stewarts let go of her too.

She staggered back one step, eyes wide, and fell backward into the fog. Randy found the look of shock on her face interesting.

He stared at the fog where she'd fallen until it settled completely, rich and oily thick. When he lifted his eyes to the closest Stewart—the same Stewart who'd first chased him, the same Stewart who'd drowned—the thing returned a long, expressionless look. Then Stewart turned and headed through the door, followed by the others.

Randy looked around at the empty hallway, saw that he was alone. Silent. Empty, like himself. An odd numbness settled over him. Hollow and numb and a little dizzy.

He grunted and jogged into the open doorway after the Stewart. The Stewart who was his father.

I'm home. Really home.

39

6:09 AM

They ran single file from the living room into the hall, Susan leading, always leading, then Stephanie, then Jack.

The hall was wide again with the stairs rising to their immediate left.

Jack ran blindly on numb legs, Susan his only guide. Through the door, down the hall, desperate to stay ahead of the pursuit. Madly trying to make sense of what was happening, but hardly able to string together the conscious thoughts required to do so.

Susan sprinted down two halls. Each time they turned a corner, the pounding of feet thundered from behind. Where was she taking them? White was going to burn the house down at first light, he said. If the fog burned as well as the sample he'd lit upstairs, the house would go up like a can of gasoline with them trapped inside.

The house had become their own hell. But ahead of them ran a young woman who knew far more than she had any business knowing. The notion that he had ever thought she was somehow complicit with White now struck Jack as ludicrous. Susan was their only hope. If she died, they would die.

Follow me, she said, so he followed her, completely at her mercy.

They entered the boiler room, locked the doors, and were halfway up the ladder to the vent when the sound of axes striking at the door echoed through the room.

"Hurry!" Jack said, breathing hard. "Go, go!"

Stephanie grunted and clambered up. "Where are we going?"

"Just hurry," Susan said.

"They will die, right?" Jack asked. "I killed Betty! Why is she still alive?"

"They can die," Susan said. "But demons don't die easily."

"Demons? Real demons? But how—"

"Hurry. Quietly!"

The crawl space outside Pete's room was knee-deep with the black fog and crowded with Jacks, wandering around, peering past their tin masks into the shadows.

Jack climbed from the vent shaft and stared at the Jacks, who clearly couldn't see them in the deep shadow. Stephanie was trembling beside him. He reached for her hand in the darkness, touched her fingers, held her tightly. She stepped closer.

The sound of Jacks climbing up the ladder behind reverberated through the vent. Susan motioned for silence and crept along the crawl-space wall, deep in darkness, to the exit hatch. Jack raised it gently and could see the hall. Crowded with Jacks. They had come the back way and avoided most of the undead, but by all appearances all the main sections of the basement were now flooded with Jacks and Stewarts, prowling, hunting them. No matter where they went, they would face an army of evil.

Jack was about to draw Susan's attention to this fact when she lifted herself out of a second hatch he hadn't noticed. He helped Stephanie out, then they squeezed through a narrow passageway that spilled into another hall.

No fog. No Jacks.

Perhaps the house seemed to know that White planned on burning it down, because with each passing minute its moans took on more urgency, lower and higher tones entwined into one terrifying wail that ebbed and flowed.

"This way!" Susan darted down the hall to a wood door curved at the top. This was one of the doors into the dark hall in which he'd found Susan.

The safe place.

But with one match, White could change that. *Would* change that.

They slipped into the passageway, sealed the door quietly behind them, and stood panting in the dark.

"What now?" Jack asked.

"We just made a circle around the main part of the basement," Susan said, winded. "The door that sucked you in earlier leads into the study."

"That door's locked . . ."

"No, it's not. You just thought it was. But we have a bigger problem."

"What?"

"We have to go *through* the study to get to the exit tunnel."

Their voices echoed gently off the close walls.

"So if we can get to it, we can get out through the back door?" Stephanie asked.

"That one *is* locked," Susan said.

"And the hall?" Jack asked.

"Is where he's probably waiting for us with more of them than you can count."

"That back door's the only way out?" Jack asked, shocked by her frank admissions.

"It's the only way."

"That's impossible! There's no way we can get past him!"

Silence settled in the dark passage.

"He's going to burn the house down," Stephanie whispered.

"Follow me," Susan said, taking their hands.

She led them quickly forward into the darkness. Running was one thing, Jack thought, but heading straight into them?

He pulled up, panting now as much from

fear as from their run. "This is crazy. They'll kill us!"

"They might," Susan said. "And they *will* if you don't start dealing with them on their terms."

"I'm supposed to head into a mob of these with my bare hands?" He knew that's not what she meant, but he felt he should point out the considerable imbalance of power.

"He's right," Stephanie said. "We don't stand a chance."

Susan pulled them forward. "Stop thinking about them. You're giving them more power than they really have."

They were speaking in hushed tones, very quickly moving deeper into the tunnel.

"But they're real," he said. "Their axes are real—"

"Of course they're real. I'm not saying you should walk right into them. But there are greater powers beyond what you can see."

"God? You're saying this is about God? Some huge whatever in the sky set this up?"

"*You* set it up."

"What are you talking about? We were just

driving by when White slashed our tires and lured us to this hellish house."

"It's your house."

"That's crazy."

"It draws most of its power from you. We've been over this! Accept it, Jack. You're at the heart of the battle between good and evil."

"I've prayed to God," Stephanie said. It sounded like a question.

"Prayed? But do you even believe? Really believe? And do you know how to love, really love?"

"Love the Lord your God with all your heart," Jack said quietly. "Love your neighbor as yourself. Isn't that a famous teaching? Jesus?" He hesitated, meaning settling in his mind like a falling snow. "So what's love look like in a house of horrors?"

"The same way it's always looked," Susan said. Then added after a pause, "It's not just what you do, it's who you are. You've got to change who you are. That's how you change the house. You'll have to see it; words don't mean much at times like this."

One of the far doors opened without warning, flooding the passage with light. One of the Jacks stood backlit in the opening. He issued a grunt and ran in, followed by others.

Susan flew toward a door along the wall now illuminated by the light. He looked into shadows beyond them, frantic for anything. The closet that he'd found Susan in—he couldn't see it, but he knew it was there, farther from the door that led into the study, for which Susan was now headed.

"The closet!" he whispered.

The Jack yelled something. They'd been spotted.

"We don't have time to hide," Susan snapped. "He's going to torch the house!"

But Jack sprinted for the closet anyway. He had to get his mind straight. Susan hesitated only a brief moment, then followed his lead. They ran into the shadows, into the large closet, closed the door, and stilled their breathing as best they could. With any luck they had entered unseen, covered by the darkness.

"He's going to burn the house," Susan said. "You should have followed me."

"We're powerless out here!" Jack whispered.

She put her hand on the knob. "Watch me.

When I go, you go, hard and fast. Just try to get a weapon. Anything. Okay?"

He could hear their feet slapping as they approached. With any luck they hadn't been seen entering the closet in the deep shadow. Without that element of surprise, they would be overwhelmed.

"Jack?"

"Shh . . ."

"Jack, I can't do—"

He put his hand on Stephanie's mouth. "Shh . . . shh . . . shh. Yes, you can. We have to trust her."

"I don't know—"

"Shhhhhhhh . . ."

The feet were slapping closer, closer. And then they were there.

Past them. Susan waited a moment longer.

"Now!" she whispered.

She shoved as hard as she could, grunting loudly. The door crunched into a body. A clang of door against tin mask resounded down the passage.

Susan leaped out and sized up the situation. Jack saw it all as if in a dream. Three copies of himself wearing Tin Man masks. Two of them ten feet to the right. One right in front of Susan, surprised by her bold entrance. The ax he'd been carrying fell to the ground.

For a moment they all stood frozen by indecision. And then Susan moved, quickly, soundlessly.

Jack watched as she snatched up the fallen ax before the Jack had time to react. She swung the blade with all her strength as the Jack recovered and tried to jump back.

The blade connected with the man. Sliced into his chest. Through his body. Into thin air, as if the man had been made of all flesh and no bone.

The man roared with pain. The throaty cry immediately rose to a high-pitched scream that hurt Jack's ears. Then the man was sucked into himself, and became a twisting pillar of black fog. The fog, heavier than air, collapsed under the tin mask, which clanged to the concrete floor with the man's ax.

No blood. It occurred to Jack then that these copies of himself must come from the fog. *Were* the fog in this haunted place empowered by his heart. The fog of evil.

Human nature.

The two Jacks who'd passed the closet

door started back, roaring with fury, wielding knives. The sound was enough to stop Jack's heart.

One of the Jacks threw his knife. It was a large blade, maybe a foot long, and Jack watched it turn lazily in the air, glance off his shoulder, and tumble to the floor.

Pain flared down his arm. "Hurry!" Susan ran for the door that Jack had first been sucked through. They didn't needed any encouragement.

That moment came two seconds later when Susan pulled open the door into the study.

As far as he could see, there was only one person in the room. But this wasn't a Jack. This was Stewart. And Stewart was armed with a shotgun.

Jack pulled up abruptly, barely aware of Stephanie's collision with him from behind.

"Go!" Stephanie cried. "They're coming!"

Jack went.

40

6:12 AM

Susan slammed the door behind them the moment they were through, twisting the lock and for the moment protecting their backs.

But their backs were now the least of Jack's worries.

The first and most immediate was Stewart. And his shotgun. He faced them from the middle of the room, amused more than stunned.

Black fog covered the floor to his ankles.

Jack's second concern was a dread that

came from his still-dawning realization that the threat facing him was somehow coming from him. From his own heart.

"I believe," he whispered. "I believe; I swear I believe." But he still wasn't sure what that meant.

Stewart still hadn't brought his gun up. He was clearly as aware as Jack that one ax in the hands of a girl was no match for a shotgun at this distance.

Stephanie's cry of frustration upon seeing Stewart was like a dagger.

Susan stepped forward, ax in both hands. She faced Stewart, putting herself between him and Jack. Stephanie pressed close behind.

Somewhere in the house a dozen doors began to bang in unison. *Bang, bang, bang, bang!*

But Stewart made no move. Susan faced him, eager neither to attack nor retreat. They'd run into a dead end.

Jack wanted to ask what was happening, what he should do, what she was doing, but his mouth wasn't forming the words.

For an extended stretch, they faced off. The floor shook with each bang of the doors beyond. It was as if the house was sending its own signal to all inhabitants.

We have them; we have them; we have them; we have them!

Then Stewart calmly brought the shotgun up and aimed it at Susan. The doors stopped banging in unison. A soft grin nudged the man's lips.

"There's more, isn't there?" Susan said.

The man's smile flattened slightly before he recovered his confidence.

"This is our house now," he said.

"Is it? Do you know who I am?"

"One of them."

"Are you sure?"

Stewart didn't answer.

The door opened and Betty walked in. And behind her, Pete. Betty's head was bandaged with red rags. Jack was quite sure that she was made of more than mere flesh and blood. Either possessed or the stuff of possession.

Still, these monsters could be killed; Susan had made that clear.

Mother and son walked up to Stewart's side and stared at Susan. Pete's eyes locked on Stephanie over Jack's right shoulder, consumed with lust.

"There she is, Mama," he said.

This demented oaf knew only one thing. He had the emotional dimensions of a lump of coal.

Betty ignored him. "Remember, he wants these three alive."

"You're going to die today," Stewart said. "All three of you. They always die."

"That's what you told me three days ago," Susan said. "I'm still alive."

"Drop the ax," Betty said.

Jack fought panic. How was he supposed to get out of this? He thought about taking the ax from her and going straight at them.

Susan hesitated then set the ax on the floor.

Fear flashed down Jack's back. Not a single bone in his body agreed with anything similar to a plan that included him rushing an armed Stewart. It would be like leaping off a cliff.

But in that moment, Jack ignored the shaking in his limbs, leaped around Susan, grabbed up the ax, and rushed Stewart.

He was halfway there before Susan's cry cut through his ears. "No, Jack!"

No, Jack? He was already committed! He had to do something! Jack responded by screaming as he threw himself forward, ax swinging down.

Oddly enough, Stewart wasn't shooting. In fact, he wasn't demonstrating any sign of concern at all, unlike the Jacks they'd just killed. Stewart wasn't a reflection of him.

At the last second, after the ax was about to complete its trajectory, Stewart moved, easily sidestepping the falling blade. Jack was pulled off balance by the heavy weapon. The butt of Stewart's shotgun slammed into his head as the ax bit through empty air.

He released the handle to catch his own fall and knew then, before the bone-jarring crunch of his knees smashing into the concrete, that whatever strength Susan was talking about came from neither boldness nor idiocy.

He hit the floor hard and felt Stewart's boot crash into his side.

"Fools," the man spat.

"Don't!" Susan shouted, rushing forward.

The shotgun boomed. "Stay back!

Jack pushed himself to his knees, blinking to clear his head. They were restraining Susan and Stephanie, who was protesting loudly. She was silenced with a loud *smack*.

Susan screamed something, but Jack's

mind was yanked back to his own predicament as Stewart grabbed him by his arm
and hauled him to his feet. Shoved him to
the center of the room.

They'd forced Susan and Stephanie to
their knees. Blood dripped from Susan's
nose. She stared at Jack with sad eyes.
Stephanie's cheek was bright red. But they
appeared otherwise unharmed.

Stewart forced Jack to his knees beside
them.

"Wait for me," Susan whispered.

"Shut your stinking little pie—"

Susan screamed and shot to her feet
while Stewart was still standing over Jack.
"Now, Jack!"

He didn't know what he was supposed to
do *now*, but he dived at Stewart with as
much strength as he could assemble on
such short notice.

Susan had her hands on his gun when
Jack's head crashed into Stewart's head.
His left ear was all that came between their
skulls, a piece of flesh that had never been
designed to withstand such a hit.

Stewart screamed.

Jack plowed forward, threatening to topple the man. From the corner of his eye he saw Pete rushing to help.

Saw Stephanie throw herself into his path like a woman possessed. She brought her knee up into his groin with enough force to stop an elephant, screaming with Susan to maximize her effort.

Betty was screaming as well, but none of their cries mattered, because now Stewart was falling with Jack, and Susan had the gun.

She flipped it around, crammed the butt against her shoulder, and put a round into the ceiling to make sure there was no mistaking that she knew how to use the thing.

"Against the wall!" she shouted, aiming for Betty's head. Then at Pete. "Against the wall!"

Jack rolled off Stewart and came to his feet, breathing hard.

For several seconds Betty, Pete, and Stewart were too stunned by the reversal to move.

"Move," Susan said.

They moved slowly to the wall, eyes fixed, still unsure they had actually been foiled.

"Make sure the doors are locked," Susan said. "Jack, hurry."

He wasn't sure what she had in mind, but he ran to the main door and secured the dead bolts.

"You'll never make it out," Stewart said, resolve back. "You're outnumbered."

"Shut up," Susan said.

Jack hurried for the door that led to the back exit tunnel, eyes on Pete, who even now was fixated on Stephanie. The dead bolt was already engaged.

"Are you going to kill them?" Stephanie asked. "Maybe we should kill them. They're not real people, right?"

"That won't help us," Susan said. "We need to—"

Rap, rap, rap.

Susan jerked her head to the door behind Jack. Knuckles sounded on the door that led to the exit.

Rap, rap, rap!

"No matter what happens," Susan said. "Remember . . ."

The door shook, then bowed under a tremendous force. Black fog seeped into the study.

". . . that light always pierces the darkness."

The door shook violently and bowed again,

this time several feet, straining against whatever held it in place.

Jack rushed for the ax. Snatched it up.

"Check the chamber," he said again.

She did.

The door behind them—the one that led into the living room—began to rattle. It too bent. As did the third door and the fourth door.

"Light came into the darkness, but the darkness didn't understand it," Susan said. "Look to the light. Only the light can save you from yourself."

"What's there?" Stephanie asked, eyes darting from door to door.

"He's come," Susan said.

But it sounded like more than one *he*. Jack couldn't help thinking that all of the undead, however many hundreds of them crowded this house of his making, had come and were pressing in on all sides, leaving no escape.

"Jack." Stephanie was whispering, scared. Her eyes darted from door to door. "I don't know what's happening . . ."

The knuckles on the door that led to the exit tunnel rapped again.

The door to the exit tunnel blew open.

Wisps of black fog roiled in, but nothing else. The other three doors stilled.

Then they came, like a pack of jackals, a dozen, two dozen Jacks, surging into the room. Half broke to the right, half to the left, forming two fronts like a forward guard.

Jack backpedaled to where Susan and Stephanie stood in the middle of the room.

Still they came, thirty, forty, crowding by the door now, glaring at him, gripping weapons, but otherwise waiting.

All with tin masks.

Except for a handful of inbreds that Jack now recognized from the hall, they were all Jacks. All him. He was facing himself, and it made his knees tremble. Stewart, Betty, and Pete were now content to look on, wearing smirks.

"Susan?"

She had the gun up, but she wasn't shooting. What good would one gun do against so many?

Stephanie held onto Jack's arm tightly. That was one good thing, he thought. Stephanie. She was here, facing no less than he. They would die together. An appropriate end to the misery that had haunted them for so long.

To a man, the Jacks' eyes were on his. Not

a single one averted their stare, and for a moment, not a single one blinked.

Then the Jacks by the door parted, and Jack knew that their waiting was over.

Tin Man stepped into the room.

41

6:14 AM

The room stilled. Tin Man walked toward them and stopped ten feet away at the edge of the lines formed by the Jacks.

He faced them in stoic silence. In his right hand he held the shotgun. The wounds to his arm and his forehead had soaked the bandages, but they hadn't slowed him down.

For a few seconds he just stared at them through the jagged holes in his tin mask. His breathing was hard and steady.

"The wages of sin is death," Tin Man said. "In the end they always pay up."

Susan made no attempt to aim the shotgun at him. The ax in Jack's hands felt small and flimsy. They didn't stand a chance.

"Drop the shotgun."

Susan released the weapon and it clattered to the ground.

Tin Man's eyes shifted to her, and he regarded her for a moment.

"I'm sorry, Jack," Stephanie whispered frantically. "This is all my fault. They're all staring at me . . . I'm so sorry."

She was seeing herself, Stephanies, not Jacks, and their stares were telling her that she was guilty.

Jack eased sideways on trembling legs, putting himself between Stephanie and White. His heart was banging in his chest. Like the banging of so many doors in this house of his heart.

"Welcome to your house," Tin Man said. He grunted with satisfaction. "Do you like it?"

He unceremoniously lifted the shotgun. Silence sucked all but the sound of ragged breathing from the room. The Jacks stared.

"Kill her," Tin Man said.

At first Jack didn't know what he was ordering. With the tin mask, it was hard to tell whom the man was addressing.

"Kill Susan," White said. "Or I will kill all three of you."

"What?"

"If you kill her, I will let you and Stephanie go. Like I let Randy go."

"Randy?" He'd hardly thought of Randy since entering the basement. He'd been released? What about Leslie?

"Free as a bird," Tin Man said. "Kill her."

Jack couldn't speak. He couldn't kill Susan. And he couldn't *not* kill her and thereby kill Stephanie.

Both choices were unforgivable.

Tin Man breathed hard and slow behind the mask. Jack's mind spun through the most glaring elements of this mad moment.

Element: This was their last chance. Dawn was here.

Element: Tin Man was lying. He would kill them both anyway.

Element: Tin Man had always wanted them to kill Susan, so he probably *wasn't* lying.

Element: He owed Stephanie his life. He'd badly mistreated her in this last year of mourning. She didn't deserve to die. He had to save her.

Element: He could save her with one swing of the ax in his hands.

Element: He could never swing the ax in his hands at Susan!

The thoughts overlapped one another, tilting his orientation toward no clear conclusion.

"Would thirty pieces of silver help?"

Thirty pieces of silver?

"You know you can do it," Tin Man said between breaths. "They all want you to do it. All of you."

As if on cue, all four doors began to rattle. Then shake violently. Bent inward. More black fog.

None of the Jacks turned to look. Their eyes were on Jack.

The doors crashed open, pushed by a sea of Jacks who flowed into the room like a swarm of insects. An army of rushing Tin Man protégés who were Jack, every last one fixed upon him.

Stephanie screamed.

Jack saw beyond them, beyond the doors, where hundreds, maybe thousands of them crowded the basement hallways and rooms. The fog had given birth to a thousand Jacks.

The Jacks packed every conceivable corner, leaving a ten-foot circle at the center where Jack, Stephanie, and Susan stood.

Their tin masks and weapons clicked and clanked, and their shoes thudded, but they didn't speak. They only drilled him with their eyes through jagged holes.

"Dear God!" Stephanie whimpered. "Oh, dear God."

Tin Man glared at Jack. Impossible to tell if he was relishing the moment or bitter.

"You know you want to kill her."

He'd addressed Jack, but now all the Jacks answered by shifting eagerly on their feet, some bouncing as if to nod. All still drilling Jack with their stares. Their breathing quickened, and now a few couldn't restrain the odd grunt or whimper. They were desperate for him to kill Susan.

Why Susan? Why such an obsession with this one girl?

"Your heart is dark. You have to look to the light," Susan said.

Her words seemed to agitate the Jacks even more. They swayed and jostled and clicked against one another.

"What light?" Stephanie cried.

Tin Man moved toward Stephanie. "Don't be a complete fool," Tin Man said. "Kill her."

Jack's eyes settled on a Jack standing perfectly still to his left. Only it wasn't a Jack. It wore a tin mask and was roughly the same size as the others, but it was dressed differently.

It was dressed like Randy.

Was Randy.

White saw Jack's shift in attention and glanced over at Randy.

"I killed Leslie," Randy said.

Just that. Just *I killed Leslie,* as if he was at once both proud and ashamed of the fact.

Tin Man swung his shotgun to face the man and pulled the trigger. The lead took Randy in the chest and pushed him into the wall of Jacks behind before dropping him to the ground.

The energy from the sea of Jacks doubled. Their sound grew to a dull roar of banging and bouncing. They were urging Jack. Pleading with him.

He felt compelled. Irresistibly drawn to satisfy the demands of these Jacks.

Tin Man swung his gun back in line with Jack. "Kill her."

Jack hesitated for a long moment. He spoke without fully understanding himself.

"No."

Almost immediately the Jacks stilled, as if stunned. He said it again, to assure himself that he'd really said it.

"No."

Silence. Breathing.

"You're a fool," Tin Man said.

Susan took one step out between him and Stephanie, then turned her back on him and looked at Jack.

Tears wet her cheeks, but there was a softness in her eyes.

"Kill her," Tin Man growled, angry, shaken. It was the first time Jack had seen the man lose any control. "She has to die!"

"You think one dead body will satisfy his lust for death?" Susan asked Jack. "Not unless that person has no guilt. Not unless they are blameless. Only one Son of Man can do that. Look to the light, and you'll understand. I'll show you the way. Look to the Son of Man."

Son of Man?

Tin Man seemed to become unglued behind Susan. It made no sense. He could just pull the trigger and end all of this. Instead, he was shaking.

"Kill her," he roared.

Susan spun to face him. "He said no!"

～～

Barsidious White stared at the girl through the holes in his mask, feeling the hatred boiling in his gut, knowing he couldn't stop himself now.

Until just a few minutes ago the game had proceeded perfectly, as it always did, even with this interesting new twist presented by the girl. He'd lost track of how many houses he'd played this game in. He'd enter the house, invoke the powers of darkness to fill the house to personify the evil of all who entered. The house, like himself, obediently became a crucible of power.

To each house he invited enough demons to make life hell for the victims. Stewarts and Bettys and Petes and other inbreds. But more important, there were these hosts of Jacks and Stephanies who mirrored their own natures.

Jack and Stephanie were guilty, and so in the end they would die.

But what about Susan?

His earlier suspicions that she might not be guilty at all were now screaming to the surface. She was less and more than anything he'd ever confronted.

His urgency to see Jack kill her forced him into betraying his desperation. Jack had said no, and he'd nearly killed the man then. He would have if Susan hadn't stepped in the way.

And why didn't he just kill her? An hour ago he would have said it was because she was for the others to kill.

Now something deep in his psyche suggested her death might not be such a good thing. But he couldn't connect any reasoning to it.

Stephanie's face was distorted, terrified. This much he relished. But the still, small voice of Susan shredded any delight he could milk out of the unfolding scene. She was too confident, too aware of the reality between dark and light.

But who was she? And where had she come from?

Then Susan turned her back on him and

spoke clear, soft words, and the Tin Man knew who she was. Or at the very least, what part she was playing in this contest between light and darkness, life and death.

He began to panic.

"Kill her!" he roared.

The girl spun to face him. "He said no!"

Tin Man pulled the trigger in uncontrollable rage.

——

The shotgun spewed fire with a tremendous boom. Jack couldn't see the impact of the shot because Susan was between him and the Tin Man. But he felt the impact a moment later when her body flew backward and crashed into his chest.

He instinctively grabbed her.

Felt the wetness on her belly.

Saw the room tilt as his mind began to shut down.

Susan groaned once, then slumped forward, dead in his arms.

42

6:16 AM

Jack dropped Susan in horror and let the body fall facedown. Blood snaked out from under her body.

Stephanie began to sob. They'd been in some harrowing situations, but this was the first such innocent death, and Jack was surprised by the sudden pain in his gut. Her frail, dead body there on the ground screamed foul.

He felt his heart begin to break in stages, like a tall building being brought down by demolition charges. But there didn't seem to be any foundation to catch all the rubble. It caved in on itself and fell into a deep void of emptiness.

The Jacks had all broken eye contact with him for the first time and now looked at the girl, mesmerized. The Tin Man chambered another round slowly, as if needing time to contemplate what he'd just done.

Jack heard a faint crackling sound. His eyes went to Susan's blood on the floor. But it wasn't the kind of red blood he expected to see. Red, yes, but laced with a crackling white light, as if it carried a charge.

Look to the light.

The Jacks had seen it too. Several directly in front of Jack stepped back. They began to bob anxiously. A murmur swelled. Clicking and banging gradually filled the room.

White stared at the girl.

In frantic style, the hundreds of Jacks crowded into the room began to bounce in a strange, ritualistic dance.

Like the banging door earlier. *Now, now, now, now . . .*

What now?

Or was it some kind of celebration?

Stephanie rushed past Jack and dropped to her knees beside Susan's prone body.

She reached a hand out and began to whisper urgently past streaming tears.

"She's the light! She's the light!"

She was the light? Of course, he'd seen the light, but was she actually the light?

White shifted his eyes to Stephanie. Then up to Jack.

Resigned to whatever fate now awaited them, Jack lowered himself to his knees. His throat knotted with pain, but he saw no remedy, no way to survive, no reason to live, no reason to die. He only felt pain.

Look to the light.

Had he seen the light?

The Jacks' bouncing cries rose to a loud roar. For the first time, Jack could actually hear words in their chant. "Kill." They gripped their axes and knives, chanting, and with each chant their voices came closer to unison.

"Kill, kill, kill, kill."

They seemed to be waiting for permission before tearing in. White stood flat-footed, head tilted down to show the lower whites of his eyes.

Stephanie's whispering rose to a shout; he barely heard it above the din. "You are the light!"

Jack's heart quickened. He said it silently with her the first time, staring at her mouth as his mind reached back to make sense. "You are the light."

Is that what Susan had meant? That he should look to a source of light outside himself? The light came into the darkness.

Stephanie's cry changed again, sobbing and wailing at once. And now her words cut through the din so that they were clear.

"Son of Man, have mercy on me, a sinner!" She drew a long, loud, gasping breath and wailed again. "Son of Man, have mercy on me, a sinner!"

Son of Man.

The truth struck Jack full in the face. Susan had taken their death as the guiltless one. She was the light in the darkness, but the wages of sin really was death. The guilty really had to die, just as White insisted. That was the game.

But Susan was the Christ, who had died instead. And Tin Man seemed to know his mistake.

Jack screamed the words with Stephanie, "Son of Man, have mercy on me, a sinner!"

He gripped Stephanie's hand as if it were his last lifeline, and together they cried out

at the top of their lungs. Their words stumbled over one another in a jumble.

For long seconds he yelled, until it occurred to him that the hissing had stopped.
And so had Stephanie.

He opened his eyes and lowered his head.
The room had come to an absolute standstill. The crowding Jacks had stopped two
strides back, axes raised but frozen.

Why?

He heard the crackle of electricity again.
The light? He glanced down.

The blood from Susan's body was brimming with light again, arcing with white-hot
fingers of power. The electricity gathered
and blasted into his face. Into his mouth.
Into his eyes.

A thick shaft of mind-numbing energy
rushed into his body.

He trembled under its power. Too much; it
was too much! He jerked his head up and
screamed.

And then the power flowed again, as
strong as before, only this time *from* his
mouth. From his eyes.

Jack could see through the light as it
blasted from him, white-hot. He saw it all at

what had to be one-tenth of the actual speed, a surreal display of searing power.

The Jack closest to him went rigid at the approaching shaft of light, then screamed and evaporated into a black fog before the light even touched him.

The blaze cut through the Jacks behind him, twenty-deep, as if they were nothing more than ash. The light spread out on all sides, joined by as much light from Stephanie, who was screaming beside him.

The terrible shrieks of the undead filled the room, crumbling to ash before the low, crackling hum of power that came from him and Stephanie.

The light came into the darkness, and the darkness did not understand it, but that no longer mattered because the light was now obliterating the darkness.

Still they screamed. Still the light flowed.

White's body jerked with the full impact of light streaming from both Jack and Stephanie. He came off the ground, folded forward, screaming with pain.

For a few moments he hung in the air as if gut-punched, shaking under the raw power that ran through his body. His screaming was swallowed by a roar of light. He was unceremoniously released and dumped to the floor where he lay in a pile, unmoving.

Still they screamed. Still the light flowed.

And then Jack collapsed.

——

From outside the house, no one would know the horrors that had ravaged Jack and Stephanie deep in the basement as the dawn showed its face.

A faraway scream now and then, the faint sound of milling insects . . . all sounds plausibly from the nearby forest rather than from inside the large, long-ago-abandoned house.

All the windows were barred and dark, all the doors sealed tight. Any soul on a casual stroll through the woods might see the old brown pickup truck wedged up on the front porch and think a youthful joyride had gone bad, but otherwise the house looked like many other similarly abandoned homes in the backwoods.

But all of that changed at precisely 6:17 in the morning.

It started with a barely visible flash of light that momentarily lit the house and then was gone, as if a flash grenade had been set off in the basement.

Then the light was back, only now brimming from the space below the doors and through the cracks in closed shutters and in some cases glowing bright from uncovered windows.

The light grew brighter, blinding white. Rays of light broke past thin cracks and streamed into the air.

Windows rattled as if attempting to contain the surge of energy that pressed them to the breaking point. The front door creaked, and for a moment the whole house began to tremble.

The shutters and windows throughout the house loosed from their latches with loud bangs and blew open. Light shot into the sky in thick shafts, riding a hum that lasted seven or eight seconds.

Then, as if someone had pulled the plug, the light disappeared, and the house was once again shrouded in grayness. The windows swung lazily on their hinges for a moment.

Then the house was still.

43

7:00 AM

Jack stood behind the stone wall a hundred feet from the door, holding Stephanie close to him, staring at the silent house.

To their right, two police cruisers sat with lights flashing red and blue. Three officers were approaching the house, one still on the radio.

"It looks that way. We found Officer Lawdale's cruiser a half mile up the road, abandoned with the other two cars. We have reports of two survivors here who believe the killer impersonated him."

The radio crackled. "You're saying three dead, two survivors?"

"That's unconfirmed, but we're going in now."

"Copy that."

The cop shut the door to his cruiser and turned toward Jack. "You sure you're okay?"

He nodded. "Fine."

"Stay put. We're going in. You're sure no one's alive inside?"

"I'm sure."

The cop nodded and headed toward the house.

An old rusted washing machine sat to the left of the flagstone path. Tall grass rose to their calves. The house itself stood stoically before them, an old abandoned house now showing its true colors.

They could see the concrete stairwell that descended to the basement on the right side of the house. The door at the bottom was still open as they'd left it, and one of the cops had just disappeared through it.

Birds chirped. Insects sang.

They'd woken inside and found only three dead bodies in the basement. Randy, Leslie, and White. No Stewarts, no Bettys, no Petes, no Jacks.

No Susan.

The first police cruiser arrived as they crawled out of the basement. They'd found Officer Morton Lawdale dead in his house an hour earlier; he'd failed to report for his midnight shift. The abandoned cruiser had led them here, to the only structure within three miles, an abandoned house set back off the road.

Jack took Stephanie's hand in his.

"They're dead," Stephanie said.

She meant Randy and Leslie, Jack thought. It was hard to believe. Staggering.

"What about Susan?" he asked.

"I don't know."

"Who was she?"

"I . . . I don't know."

"But she was real, right?"

"I think so. We saw her blood."

They didn't know. What they did know was that they'd come face-to-face with themselves and with evil and perhaps with Lucifer himself and survived only because of her.

They were quiet for a few seconds, awash in the effects of the reality that had presented itself to them in a dark corner of the world.

A hundred miles from here, Tuscaloosa was waking up to one more day of traffic, and appointments, and soap operas, and a thousand other mundane trivialities that consumed the world. Here the authorities were about to be confounded by unbelievable events. Unless they believed in haunted houses and killers filled with the power of darkness.

"Are we sure this really happened?" Stephanie asked.

Jack blinked. "It happened. Like the game of life, it happened, all in one night."

"Game of life?"

"You live your life, and in the end you either live or die, depending on what choice you make."

She said nothing.

Movement on their left filtered into Jack's vision. He looked over and caught his breath.

A girl had stepped out of the trees and was walking toward them. Susan . . .

Jack released Stephanie's hand and stepped forward. "Susan?"

"It's her!"

The girl was still dressed in the same tattered white dress, now stained red with blood. Jack glanced back at the house, where three of the officers had just entered. The fourth was making a sweep behind, weapon drawn.

Susan stopped in front of them. A gentle smile softened her face.

"What happened?" Stephanie asked, dumbfounded.

"I knew you could do it," Susan said. She winked.

Jack was unsure of what his eyes were seeing. He asked the same question. "What happened?"

"Light came into the darkness," Susan said. "That's what happened."

Jack caught a glance from Stephanie's wide eyes.

"You . . . who are you?"

"Susan."

"But you're real, aren't you?"

"Of course I'm real. Just as real as the day he locked me in the basement. Although I will admit that I came willingly."

"So . . . so you're an . . ." Stephanie stopped short of the question.

"What?" she asked.

"An angel?" Jack said.

"An angel? You mean a real angel that

walks on the earth and looks like a regular person? Think of me as someone who's shown you the way by shedding a little light on the situation."

Jack looked up at Stephanie. He'd heard of such a thing. Angels walking among humans. But he'd never given them a second thought.

The radio in the closest cruiser hissed to life.

"We only have two bodies in here, Bob. Do you copy? Two bodies. A male dressed in what's left of a green shirt and jeans, and a dark-haired woman. Copy?"

Static. "Can you verify that?" More static. "They said there was a killer in there, dressed in Lawdale's slacks."

"Roger that. No sign of a third body, not in the basement."

"Copy. Proceed with caution."

"How . . . how's that possible?" Stephanie said.

"There's something else you should know," Susan said. "White's not finished."

One of the windows to the attic drifted open.

"I thought we beat him, beat the house!" Stephanie said.

"You beat the evil in your heart." She nodded at the house. "Look closely."

Jack and Stephanie stared.

At first Jack saw nothing. It looked exactly the way it had a moment ago, except now all the windows were sealed shut again.

Then he saw the faint gray shape in the attic window. It was a person, staring down at him without moving.

A bald person. Stewart.

And next to Stewart, Betty. And Pete.

He heard Stephanie gasp; she'd seen it too. The undead stared out the window, faint, so faint but there, really there.

Stewart moved away from the window and disappeared into the house.

"They're still there?" Jack asked.

"For a while," Susan said. "They'll find the place a bit too clean for them now. They'll move on."

"Why let them? We could walk in there and wipe them all out," Jack said. "Couldn't we?"

"Yes, I think we could," Stephanie said.

"They'd probably run out the back the moment they saw us coming," Jack said.

"After what we did? They're afraid just looking at us."

Stephanie took two long steps toward the house and shouted so that her intention was unmistakable.

"Shoo!"

The window emptied.

Amazing.

"What do you think, Susan? Are they gone now?"

She didn't answer.

"Susan?" Jack turned around. "Susan?"

But she was gone. He scanned the clearing. "Susan!"

"She's gone," Stephanie said.

"So she *was* an angel?"

"Maybe."

Stephanie looked around and let the silence stretch.

Jack caught a glimpse of a Stewart in one of the windows. "They're not gone yet."

Stephanie turned around, looked at the Stewart for a few moments, then threw up her hands and lunged forward.

"Shoo!" she cried.

It shooed.